MURDER HIGH

ALSO BY LAUREN MUÑOZ

Suddenly a Murder

MURDER HIGH

LAUREN MUÑOZ

First published in the UK in 2025 by
HOT KEY BOOKS
an imprint of Bonnier Books UK
5th Floor, HYLO, 105 Bunhill Row, London EC1Y 8LZ

Copyright © Lauren Muñoz, 2025
Dedication artwork © InnaPoka/Shutterstock.com, 2025

All rights reserved.
No part of this publication may be reproduced, stored or transmitted in any form or by any means, electronic, mechanical, photocopying or otherwise, without the prior written permission of the publisher.

The right of Lauren Muñoz to be identified as author of this work has been asserted by them in accordance with the Copyright, Designs and Patents Act 1988.

This is a work of fiction. Names, places, events and incidents are either the products of the author's imagination or used fictitiously. Any resemblance to actual persons, living or dead, is purely coincidental.

A CIP catalogue record for this book is available from the British Library.

ISBN: 978-1-4714-1653-8
Also available as an ebook and in audio

1

Typeset by Kathryn Li
Printed and bound in Great Britain by Clays Ltd, Elcograf S.p.A.

The authorised representative in the EEA is
Bonnier Books UK (Ireland) Limited.
Registered office address: Floor 3, Block 3,
Miesian Plaza, Dublin 2, D02 Y754, Ireland
compliance@bonnierbooks.ie

bonnierbooks.co.uk/HotKeyBooks

shakes Magic 8 Ball
Is this book dedicated to Erin?

PROLOGUE
Two Weeks from Now

SIERRA FOX HURRIED DOWN THE MUDDY PATH, TYPING A message on her phone.

> Livestream ran late. Omw.

It autocorrected to On my way! just as she hit send. Fantastic. The cheerful tone would make Xavier even angrier.

Sierra glared down at her heels, which were caked with dirt and crushed pine needles. "Ruined," she muttered. And for what? Why did he need to meet her so far from everyone else? Things were bad between them, but it's not like they were actually over. Her misstep had been a small thing. A forgivable mistake. Without Xavier . . .

She wouldn't think about that.

Sierra breathed in the fresh air made sharp by the evergreens that cast long shadows over the ground. A few birds squawked overhead, but otherwise the path was silent. Her classmates were having lunch inside, away from the mud and the damp.

A loud rustling broke through the quiet. Sierra paused to listen, but the noise didn't come again. *Probably just a forest animal,* she thought. It had sounded big, though, and she continued a little faster. No student had ever been attacked by a bear, but every year, Dean Whitaker reminded them not to go into the woods alone, especially during cub season.

Suddenly, a huge brown blur streaked across the path, almost hitting her.

"Ah!" Sierra shrieked, covering her mouth with a fist. She wanted to run, but she was frozen in place. The creature stopped a few yards into the woods. Trembling, Sierra forced herself to meet its eyes.

It was a baby doe.

"Stupid deer!" she yelled, sending the doe sprinting into the trees. Sierra tried to calm her racing heart. If she was freaking out over a cute little animal, she must be more nervous about meeting Xavier than she thought.

As she moved down the path, the knitting needles in her bag knocked against her arm, and she carefully shifted the tips away from her skin. Everyone else in the Stitch 'n' Bitch Club she'd started used metal needles, but for Sierra, it was wood or nothing. She'd even had her initials burned into the ends.

The greenhouse at the bottom of the path was as lovely as the rest of campus. Tall panes of float glass rose in a Gothic arch, like something out of a storybook. A few special stained-glass pieces were set in casement above the door, which was closed.

Sierra frowned. Xavier had told her he would leave the door propped open, but maybe he hadn't wanted the rain to blow in. She pressed her face against the nearest glass pane, careful not to smudge her makeup. Nothing moved inside.

The heavy scent of compost and violets made her nose wrinkle as she pushed the door open. It was surprisingly chilly in the greenhouse—nothing like its typical balminess. The last time she'd been inside was with . . . No, she wouldn't think his name. He'd shown her the tobacco plants he'd been growing to make vape juice.

"You've got to be careful extracting the nicotine," he'd said, pointing at a plant with broad green leaves. "It's strong enough to take down a horse. Dope, right?"

Sierra had not thought it was dope. The only thing she disliked more than guys who smoked were guys who had a passion for killing things.

"Xavi?" she called into the space.

The only answer was a terrified flapping of wings as several birds escaped out a missing windowpane in the peaked roof, revealing the gray sky. She didn't remember the opening being there when she was with *him*, but they'd been preoccupied with other things.

"Xavi, are you in here?" she asked again, walking between the rows of greenery, most of which had been planted by the forensic science students for their experiments.

The chill in the air entered Sierra's bones. Had Xavier stood her up? Was it possible he was serious about dumping her? Angry tears pricked her eyes like needles. She wouldn't let that happen. They belonged together.

A strange snuffling sound, like an animal crawling among the plants, made her hurry toward the table at the back of the greenhouse, where pothos vines spilled onto the ground, blocking her view of whatever was behind it.

Sierra stopped dead when she reached the table. Something white was sticking out at an odd angle, nearly touching the uprooted remains of the tobacco plants. There were plenty of tools lying around the greenhouse, but this was something else. Something she recognized.

Xavier's shoe.

Sierra rushed around the corner, nearly twisting her ankle in her heels. When she saw what lay beyond the shoe, she screamed an endless agonized scream that traveled out of the greenhouse, up the path, and into the lunchroom.

At a table near the back door, Dulce Castillo's ears perked up. Her best friend, Emi, was still talking about how unfair it was that Xavier Torres got picked for everything.

"Shh," Dulce said. "Can you hear that?"

"Hear what?" Emi asked. "Everyone chomping on their food? Of course I can. It's disgusting."

"No, it sounds like—" Dulce paused, trying to listen over the sound of the noon church bells ringing down the road. "Never mind. It's gone."

Twenty minutes later, Sierra Fox came sprinting into the lunchroom from the hallway, her red curls in a tangle and her sheath dress covered in mud.

"Xavi's in the greenhouse!" she screamed, her voice full of anguish. "He's been murdered!"

Sierra gazed around the cafeteria in wide-eyed horror before crumpling to the ground. The entire student body fell silent.

Then everyone broke into applause.

"That was fast," Emi said over the clapping. "Usually no one finds the body until after Labor Day." She began stuffing chips into her mouth. "We should finish up so we can get to the greenhouse first. Early bird solves the murder."

Dulce smiled. Xavier Torres was dead. The game had begun.

1

WHEN MY DAD DROPS ME OFF AT SCHOOL, IT TAKES ME A minute to figure out what's different about the main building. Nothing obvious has changed. The red bricks look like they always do: old but clean, as if the gardener power washed them over the summer. The mansion still spreads like an L across the grassy lawn, the longer left side resembling a fallen redwood grown fat with ivy and steel windows. Even the brass lion knocker hangs on the door with a comforting familiarity.

My eyes move up to the black eye of the security camera that's watching my dad's car turn out the rocky front drive and onto the highway. He spent so long taking first-day pictures that the parking area near the forest is now silent except for a warm breeze shaking the stop signs on the buses that bring students in from outside Cape Cherry.

"Aha," I say, finally spotting what's new. Someone has draped wreaths of daffodils around the winged gargoyles squatting on top of the gables. They glare down at me like I personally hung the decorations around their skinny gray necks.

"It's an improvement," I call up at them before remembering that I'm already risking a tardy.

The front door is unlocked, but I give the brass lion a friendly tap anyway before hurrying down a long hallway filled with portraits of James Everett's family and the more famous criminologists who have taught at J. Everett High. A few dried flower clusters still cling to the gold tassels of the rug, remnants of the summer weddings that help fund the school's scholarships.

Right before I pass the front office, the door swings open, and I almost collide with a tall blond boy whose eyes are hidden behind tinted glasses. Even though he's wearing a ridiculous sports coat that makes him look like a leftover wedding guest, he's the kind of attractive that's impossible to miss, so I know he can't be a returning student.

Backpack slung over his shoulder. Schedule peeking out of a folder stamped with the J. Everett High crest. School map hanging loosely from his fingers.

Conclusion: He must be a freshman or a transfer.

"Sorry," he says, holding up an apologetic hand. Then his eyes meet mine, and he smiles brightly as if he recognizes me. "I was so anxious to escape all those transfer forms I wasn't watching where I was going."

A transfer, then. "It's fine," I say. "I've been talking to statues, so we're both having bad mornings."

The boy's smile doesn't falter, even though I've just admitted to conversing with inanimate objects. "Can you point me to the ballroom?" he asks. "The dean's assistant gave me this map, but—" He stops, staring down at the hastily drawn lines that are supposed to be J. Everett's hallways.

"It's confusing at first," I say, beckoning him to follow me. He walks with a slouching confidence, his long strides easily keeping up with my pace. "Dr. Everett had to keep converting rooms in the house as he accepted more students because Cape Cherry's town council wouldn't let him build higher than two stories."

The boy glances back down at the map. "Must be weird to take chemistry in someone's old bedroom."

"Wait until you see the blood spatter photographs in the bathroom," I tell him.

The ballroom is packed with students for the first-day assembly, which thankfully hasn't started yet. Emi, usually the late one, is already seated, her tulle skirt puffed out over one of the white wedding chairs still set out in rows. Little stuffed animal bags and bright plastic toys are slung across her ripped T-shirt, which is hand-printed with the words YOU CAN'T HANDLE THE TRUTH. As usual, she looks like she belongs in Tokyo's fashion district, where her dad lives, instead of a seaside town in Virginia.

When she sees me hovering in the doorway, she waves at the empty seat next to her with giant arm motions, making stacks of candy bracelets shake up her forearms. "Dulce!" she calls. "Come sit with us!"

Us is apparently her and Rose Martin, a girl we had gym with last year who spent class meditating instead of jogging in the woods with everyone else. We barely know her, so I can't think of a single reason why she's sitting on our side of the room when the rest of her friends are across the aisle with Sierra.

I consider asking the new boy to join us, but before I can say anything, he ducks his head and moves to an empty corner seat in front of Emi, as if he's embarrassed to be arriving late. I follow him, confused by his sudden attack of self-consciousness.

"Who's the hottie?" Emi says when I sit down.

I glance at the boy, hoping he hasn't heard her, but with

almost two hundred other voices in the room, she probably could have shouted the words.

"Transfer student," I say before quickly adding, "And no, I won't introduce you. He and I exchanged ten words max, so you can introduce yourself."

"A new record!" Emi looks at the Keroppi watch on her bony wrist.

"What are you talking about?"

"I bet Rose it would take you less than two minutes to say something grumpy, but it was only ten seconds. She owes me a root beer float."

I ignore the fact that Emi is making bets about me with a stranger. "Wait until you hear my thoughts on how many barrettes a person can wear at one time," I say, sticking my tongue out at her as I tap one of literally dozens of rainbow clips dotting her silky black braids.

"Happiness is in us, not in things." Rose leans forward in her seat, smiling softly at me. Her name suits her. She's plump, with porcelain skin, pale blue eyes, and rosy cheeks, like a hobbit from *Lord of the Rings* if hobbits had pink hair.

"Says the girl who lives in a gated neighborhood on the beach." Emi snorts.

I expect Rose to look hurt by Emi's criticism, but she just spins one of Emi's candy bracelets around on her wrist and giggles. The casualness of her touch makes it seem like they're friends, which makes no sense because Emi never talked to her in gym. A little sting of unease pricks my belly; did Emi hang out with Rose over break without telling me?

"Why does it look like Dean Whitaker spent the summer

inside an oven?" Emi asks, watching the head of our school walk to the microphone at the front of the room.

When Dean Whitaker reaches the mic, he taps it before flashing us a smile that looks very white against his tanned skin. It's hard to tell his age because he dyes his hair, but he's probably over forty, and richly polished, like he belongs on ski slopes or in a men's magazine. I don't see it, but I know plenty of students—Emi included—who have drawn hearts around his name in their notebooks.

New porcelain veneers. Shoes made of alligator skin. Picture in the school's "Welcome Back" email standing in front of the Trevi Fountain.

Conclusion: Being engaged to Mayor Fox has some real perks.

"Good morning," Dean Whitaker says, his deep baritone booming around the ballroom. "I'd like to take this opportunity to welcome you to the Dr. James Everett School of Criminology!" He smiles at a group of students sitting in the front row. "It's wonderful to see so many familiar faces, and a joy to see all the new ones. Dr. Everett would have been proud that this freshman class is not only the most diverse in the school's thirty-year history, but that they've also achieved the highest ever pass rate on the aptitude exam. It's a testament to each of you and to our incredible teachers that Virginia's best and brightest young minds continue to show interest in making the field of criminology more dynamic and equitable than ever before."

He reaches for the iPad his assistant is holding. "I'm going to take roll call and give out your homeroom assignments," he continues. "But before I do, I want to remind you that after the assembly, Cape Cherry's very own Mayor Fox will be giving us the details of this year's Grand Game, so you'll want to stick around for that." He beams at his fiancée, who's standing in the corner of the ballroom, arms crossed tightly over a pink plaid jacket.

"I think someone spiked her coffee with lemons," Emi says, pointing at Mayor Fox's pursed red lips. "Or cyanide."

"Like mother, like daughter," I whisper, glancing at Sierra. Back when we were friends, she thought her mom running for mayor was embarrassing, but now she's sitting ramrod straight in her seat like she's worried Mayor Fox will lose the November election if she's spotted slouching.

Not sitting next to her boyfriend. Red curls perfect, like he hasn't been running his hands through them in the parking lot before school. Heavy concealer under her eyes.

Conclusion: She and Xavier have been fighting.

While Dean Whitaker runs through the alphabet, Emi relaces her knee-high boots. They're so stilted they add four inches to her height, but she's still shorter than I am, even though I'm not tall.

Average height, average build, average brown hair and skin. Nothing about me stands out, except maybe the birthmark between my eyes, which looks like a bunny.

"Dulce Death Castillo," Dean Whitaker calls when he reaches the *C*s, drawing out the first syllable of dool-say.

"Present," I say. The blond transfer student peeks over his shoulder with raised eyebrows, as if he isn't sure he heard my middle name right. My mom never had the test scores to get into J. Everett, but she named me after her favorite detective (Lord Peter Death Bredon Wimsey) in the hope that I'd have better luck.

"You're in homeroom with Ms. Moss," Dean Whitaker says, nodding in my direction.

The boy shoots me an apologetic grin before turning back

around, like he feels bad he didn't thank me for helping him find the ballroom. I trace the echo of his smile in my mind.

Cocky. Crooked. Confident.

Conclusion: He and Emi match.

"Emi Nakamura?" Dean Whitaker says a few minutes later.

"Here against my will!" she yells, which gets a laugh from several students, including Rose, who playfully tugs on one of Emi's braids. I'm happy when the dean says Emi's in homeroom with me and not with Rose in Dr. Saka's amphitheater full of dead things.

After Dean Whitaker calls the final name, he hands the iPad back to his assistant. "Those of you who don't want to stay for Mayor Fox's presentation may head to the breakfast buffet," he says. "But you should know that this year's prize money is significantly more than last year, so it would be in your best interests to hear her out."

Despite the dollars being dangled in front of their faces, at least a hundred students get noisily to their feet, messing up the perfect rows of wedding chairs as they dash for the exit. That's the thing about private-school kids: Tons of them are rich enough to care more about fresh doughnuts than cash.

Once the others have left, Dean Whitaker smiles at those of us who are still seated. "As most of you know," he says, his voice even louder now that there are fewer bodies in the ballroom, "Dr. Everett began the tradition of hosting an elaborate murder mystery each year to give his students the chance to put their criminology learning into practice. Today, the Fox Family Trust, which generously helps fund our school"—he nods at Mayor Fox, who smiles like stretching her lips is painful—"continues this tradition. While the competition does demand a substantial time commitment, it also comes with rewards, which I'll let Mayor Fox explain to you."

Mayor Fox's Jimmy Choos flash like puddles of blood as she clicks across the floor. Her hair, the same red as her daughter's, is cut into a severe French bob, like a model had a baby with a drill sergeant.

"Thank you, Stan—I mean Dean Whitaker—for that introduction," she says in a voice sharp enough to cut glass. "James Everett and my dad were lifelong best friends, so I spent much of my childhood inside this house. Some of my earliest memories are of him in the library, smoking a pipe while he read to me and Claire in his leather chair."

"Maybe *she* killed Claire Everett," Emi says under her breath.

"Despite the vicious crime that stole his daughter's life," Mayor Fox continues, "James Everett never lost his love of creating murder mysteries for his students. Which is why, when he died ten years ago, I decided to continue the Grand Game in his memory." She sniffs like she hates what she's about to say. "Many of your classmates left before they could hear about the prize money, so I'd like you to spread the word that this year, in order to encourage more students to play, the board has voted to give the winning team thirty thousand dollars."

Emi makes a choking sound. "That's twice what it was last year," she says, her voice rising above the disbelieving whispers spreading across the ballroom. "It'd pay for our whole trip!"

"What trip?" Rose asks, leaning in like she's part of our team, which she very much is not.

"We're going to England after graduation next year," Emi says. "We want to see Dorothy Sayers's house and stay at every place a Lord Wimsey book was set."

"Sounds fun," Rose says, but I can tell she doesn't actually think so. I could explain it's the trip my mom planned and never got to go on, but it's none of Rose's business.

Dean Whitaker comes back to the microphone to settle everyone down. "Game packets will be available in the front office after school," he says. "They'll contain police interviews, witness statements, an autopsy report, and pictures of physical evidence—all the things you'll need to solve the murder of the soon-to-be-deceased Tim Riggs." He smiles. "Everything *except* the crime scene itself, which one of you unlucky students will stumble across very soon."

Scattered giggles echo off the walls. The allure of a corpse, even a fake one, seems to increase every year.

Dean Whitaker grabs an envelope from Mayor Fox. "And now, the moment you've been waiting for. The naming of the body."

The room holds its breath. Emi clutches at my knee like it might bring us good luck. Any previous player is eligible to be the murder victim, and everyone wants to get picked because they get extra clues to help them stage the scene. The team with the body wins over 60 percent of the time.

Dean Whitaker opens the envelope and slides out a piece of folded paper. "This year's victim will be . . ." He unfolds the paper. "Xavier Torres!" he says like he's announcing an Oscar winner.

Cheers erupt from Xavier's friends as he jogs to the front of the room, but a few boos join them, Emi's included. "The lottery is rigged!" she yells, only half joking, but no one pays attention to her except for the transfer student, who turns and peers at Emi through his tinted glasses.

Emi attracts guys like hummingbirds to nectar, so it's no surprise when his gaze lingers on her. It's not until he catches me watching him that he bites his lip and turns back to face Dean Whitaker. They're nice lips, like tulip petals. But all that matters is that Emi and I haven't been chosen.

"Why is it never us?" I say.

"We're the smallest team." Emi shrugs, her protest already forgotten. "The odds aren't in our favor."

Xavier's gelled bronze highlights and picture-perfect smile are on full display when he returns to his seat. In his navy-blue sweater and slacks, he looks like a Puerto Rican pop star about to play a round of golf. When Sierra stands up to give him a quick peck on the cheek, his chiseled jaw flinches.

"I've seen dead flies with more passion," Emi says.

Enzo Torres, Xavier's younger brother, looks just as unimpressed. He's the off-brand version of Xavier, and everything he's wearing, right down to the spike in his eyebrow, is black. The Torres brothers can't stand each other, so I have no idea why Sierra let Enzo onto their team unless it was to rub in my face that he'd quit ours. As if we'd miss his outbursts.

"I hate that Sierra thinks she's better than us," I say, grinding my teeth. "Promise me we won't lose to her again."

Emi grabs the Magic 8 Ball key chain that's always attached to her teddy bear backpack and gives it a hard shake. "Will Dulce and I make Sierra cry with our badass detective skills?"

We watch as the triangle swims lazily around in its ooze until it stops on IT IS DECIDEDLY SO.

"See?" She grabs my hand, her plastic rings digging into my palm. "This year is going to give us nothing but rainbows. We'll find a forensics student a hundred times better than Enzo."

At her words, the new boy spins around again. "Are you a detective?" he asks Emi.

Emi drops her elbows onto her skirt, obviously thrilled he's talking to her. "Dulce and I are the Lord Wimseys," she says, leaning closer to the back of his seat.

"The whats?"

"The teams are named after detectives from books," she explains. "The list was in the 'Welcome Back' email. You didn't see it?" When the boy shakes his head, she says, "The Miss Marples. The Sherlocks. The Lord Wimseys. It lets them give us a literature credit for the game." She bops her head in my direction. "We're the only team with two detectives, though."

"How does that work?" he asks.

"Dulce collects facts, and I read people's emotions."

The boy grins. "You know what I'm feeling?"

"Of course, new kid," Emi says. "You're nervous, but not too nervous, because you're tall and good-looking, so you know you'll be popular anywhere you go, but you're also worried your public-school classes might not have prepared you for the academics here."

The boy raises his eyebrows. "What makes you think I'm not from another private school?"

Emi points to me, and I pick up my cue.

"You're too dressed up," I say. "You picked your clothes based on the idea of a private school, not on the reality."

"Might want to lose the sports coat." Emi smirks.

Unfazed and still smiling, he takes off his coat and stuffs it into his backpack. "I wouldn't want to play against you two."

"You should join a team fast," Emi says. "Otherwise you'll end up with a bunch of freshmen. What capsule are you in?"

Before the boy can answer, the bell rings, and Dean Whitaker yells, "Happy detecting, everyone!" as the people around us grab their bags and get to their feet. The new student gives me and Emi one last grin and then heads for homeroom with . . .

I frown. Why can't I remember what teacher he has homeroom with?

Little alarm bells ring at the back of my mind as I realize: Dean Whitaker never called his name.

2

WHEN MY DAD AND I SHOW UP FOR OUR WEEKLY MONDAY-night dinner at Maldonado's Pizza, we're guided to a red leatherette booth by Beth Calhoun, the sheriff's daughter. She's technically Sierra's stepsister (Sheriff Calhoun was married to Mayor Fox when we were younger), but even though I've spent countless days at Sierra's house, I don't know Beth or her sister at all because they stayed with their mom after the divorce.

In middle school, Sierra became obsessed with the idea of having sisters, so we started a pretend detective agency called Death & Fox Investigations to solve "The Case of How Beth and Avery's Mom Kidnapped Them." It was the only reason we could think of that they would choose not to move into the Fox mansion. We discovered, through the not-very-exciting interrogation of Mayor Fox, that Beth and Avery lived with their mom because the court had awarded her custody.

I'd like to believe a tragic past is the reason Beth thrusts laminated menus at us with undisguised hostility before returning to her hostess stand, but I'm pretty sure it's because she hates J. Everett High as much as her father does.

"*Such* a pleasant girl," my dad says theatrically, bringing his hand to his chest as he watches Beth seat another family. "We're clearly her favorite customers. She'll probably bring us sodas on the house."

"Or maybe a free dessert," I say.

"Or a puppy." He laughs.

Bushy black beard. Round belly. Always cheerful.

Conclusion: My dad is a young Mexican Santa Claus.

"We're finally going to beat Rocco tonight, *conejita*," my dad says, his mustache twitching with excitement, while I cringe at being called *bunny*, the childhood nickname my mom gave me that he still won't let go even though my birthmark has faded a lot since I was little. "I've been thinking about it all week, and there's no way he has the ingredients I've come up with."

A waiter's board shorts appear at my elbow. "Welcome to Maldonado's, home of Cape Cherry's cheesiest pizza," he says from somewhere above me. "What would you like to order tonight?"

"Two Sprites, please," I say. "And we won't be needing these." I go to hand the waiter our menus, but they slide out of my fingers and onto the floor. We bend down for them at the same time, almost knocking heads.

"Sorry—" I groan, but I stop short when I see his face, which looks familiar even though I'm positive he's never been our server before. He's wearing a necklace made of tiny beads, like all the local surfers do, and there's something nice about the lift of his lips. But it's his eyes that capture my attention. One is blue-green, while the other is brown, giving the impression of twins that got entangled in the womb. They were hidden behind tinted glasses this morning.

"Hey," I say. "You were at the assembly."

"And you're the girl who talks to statues," he says, lips curving into a smile. I'm surprised he recognizes me. I thought he'd forget my existence in the whirlwind of meeting Emi. She talked about how hot he was all day, even interrupting our English teacher's lecture to show me that her Magic 8 Ball had promised he'd kiss her at the Poisoner's Festival. "I just transferred from Cape Cherry," he adds. "You know, the *public* high school."

"Must have been last minute," I say. "Otherwise you would have been on the roll-call list."

He scratches the side of his neck, leaving pink streaks. "Uh, yeah, it was."

My dad clears his throat like he doesn't see what any of this has to do with dinner, and the boy draws a notepad from his apron.

"If you don't need menus, I'm guessing you're regulars," he says, poising his pen at the top of the paper. "What'll you have?" He asks the question with a fake accent like he's James Bond, and my initial impression of him crystallizes: He's an extrovert, and he thinks he's charming.

"There's this game we play with the owner," my dad starts, but the boy quickly interrupts.

"Oh, *you're* the ones," he says, as if Rocco has told him all about us. "What two toppings will you challenge us with tonight?"

My dad knows Rocco from high school, and after my mom died, he suggested we all play a dinner game. Every week, we pick two toppings, and if he doesn't have them in the back, we get our pizza for free.

Rocco has three rules: Our choice must be vegetable or animal. It can't be anything extinct or endangered. And it can't be something illegal, rare, or exorbitant, which is why the rosy sea bass and caviar pizza I tried to stop my dad from ordering last year was disqualified.

"Tell Rocco we want a Cornish game hen and fresh yuzu rind pizza," my dad says.

"Gross," I mutter.

"One bird and fruit pizza coming up," the boy says, clicking his pen shut. Then he winks—winks!—at me and walks away. I'm pretty sure no guy has ever winked at me in my entire life. I'm not sure if I like it or hate it.

Beth Calhoun comes over and bangs our Sprites on the table, smirking when they slosh over and puddle on the checkered tablecloth. The smirk changes to a flirty smile when she walks over to the boy from school, who's entering our order into a computer. I distantly register the way her fingers play with the black ties of his apron while he types.

He's a good sport. Likes new things. Flexible.
Conclusion: He's the opposite of me.

Emi and I play the Grand Game together because the two of us make one perfect Wimsey: She has his sparkling personality, and I weave the facts I collect into a kind of mental tapestry I can view whenever I want. Sometimes I wish I didn't notice things—like the bright red letters on the hospital bills my dad's been squirreling away. I haven't told Emi that if we don't win the prize money, our trip to England will be as out of reach as Mars.

As the minutes pass without any pizza, my dad's smile grows wider. I can almost see him preparing the victory speech he'll deliver to Rocco. I look over my shoulder for the boy and notice a middle-aged man in a Stetson scowling at us. I'm glad my dad's too wrapped up in the challenge to notice his nasty glance.

It's been two years since Sheriff Calhoun announced that my

mom had been drunk driving when she got into a car wreck with Deputy Armstrong, but small towns don't forgive fast, even when the story they've been told is a lie. Maybe especially then.

Fifteen minutes later, the boy from school slides a bubbling pizza into the center of our table. Game hen and yuzu rind.

"Nice try, Jorge," Rocco yells from across the restaurant, where he's spinning dough high in the air.

My dad looks at the pizza with naked shock. "But the grocery store doesn't sell fresh yuzu! I checked!"

"Maybe we should give up," I say. "I don't think we're ever going to win."

"I'll never surrender." My dad's belly almost knocks over his Sprite as he slides out of the booth. "I'm going to find out how Rocco pulled this off."

Once my dad's gone, the boy stares at me with a sly smile. "Can *you* figure out how we did it?"

"Oh, um—" I stutter.

The last person to set me a puzzle at the dinner table was my mom, and since her death, I've been going all bunny in the headlights whenever someone does something that reminds me of her.

"I . . ."

The boy is starting to look like he wished he hadn't asked, but luckily, my body chooses that moment to unfreeze.

"Yes," I say. "Armchair solves are easy."

"All right, impress me."

Rocco's pizzas take twelve minutes to bake. The boy delivered the pizza to the table half an hour after we ordered. There's a bus pass sticking out of his pocket, so he didn't drive to work.

Conclusion: He purchased the yuzu somewhere he could walk to in under ten minutes.

It was me who suggested Lord Wimsey's methods to Emi freshman year, and since then I've been hammering them into her head: Ignore the motives and the psychology. Forget the gossip and the whys. Figure out *how* a thing was done, and you'll discover who did it.

The solution to the new kid's puzzle pops into my mind fully formed thanks to a book I read about foods that might be toxic to Penny, the stray cat that stays with us during bad weather: Yuzu is from Japan.

"The sushi place three blocks over," I say, crossing my fingers under the table because I really don't want to fail in front of him. "I bet they use fresh yuzu."

A slow smile blooms on the boy's lips. "Wow," he says.

"I'm right?" I ask.

"They use it in their cocktails." He slides into my dad's abandoned seat like he cares more about our conversation than earning tips.

"I'm sure you could have guessed it too," I say. "They don't let just anyone into J. Everett."

"There's your first mistake," he says, looking at me from under long blond lashes with unnecessary intensity. "I'm not in the detective capsule."

"Journalism?" I ask, then quickly regret my guess. He has the looks of a news anchor, but the superficial charm of TV-star wannabes like Xavier Torres is always covering up an acid vat of insecurity, and this boy's confidence doesn't seem fake.

"Forensic science," he says, playing with his pen. "I want to be a doctor."

My stomach clenches, though that may be from the smell of

the game hen and yuzu. A student in the forensics capsule is exactly what the Lord Wimseys need.

The problem is that the last time we invited a guy Emi liked onto the team, we got Enzo. I wish I'd brought my flip phone so I could text Emi and get her to promise not to let this boy be a giant distraction. If I wait until tomorrow, there's a high chance he'll be taken because every team is now required to play the game with someone from forensics, and it's the smallest capsule at school. I grind my teeth, annoyed that I'm going to have to make the decision myself.

I usually have a good sense for people. I can tell if they're lying or if they suck. Kind of like a golden retriever. But, weirdly, I can't with him. He's giving off two vibes—split, like his eyes. His good nature seems real, but there's something distant about him, like he's hiding part of himself behind his smiles.

Then again, we all have secrets. Pieces of ourselves we bury deep. I look into his blue-green eye and see the unpredictability of the ocean. The way the water draws you out so gently you don't know you're far from shore until it's too late. Then there's his brown eye, which looks like the center of a sunflower. Warm, with a strong stalk. Always reaching for the light.

He points to my soda glass. "Do you want more Sprite? I can put grenadine in it if you like Shirley Temples."

His kindness stirs something in my brain that makes the choice for me.

"Emi and I need a forensics student," I tell him. "The rules say teams can have up to eight players, but Emi and I have agreed to never have more than three, so if we win, you're guaranteed a third of the prize money. Ten thousand dollars."

The boy's thick eyebrows fall into a confused furrow. "You're inviting me to be on your team? Just like that?"

My brain begins to backtrack. I thought the way he smiled at Emi during the assembly meant he'd jump at the chance, but maybe I misread him.

"Aren't you going to test me?" he presses.

"Oh, right, yeah." His presence has made my sense of order slip. "What's the most likely cause of a hyoid fracture?" I ask, posing the first medical question that pops into my mind.

He answers without hesitation. "Manual strangulation."

"Good enough for me," I say. "Do you want to play the game with us?"

He bites his top lip and traces the squares of the tablecloth with a finger. He's going to say no, I suddenly realize, my heart sinking. I should have waited for Emi. She could have glammed up the offer. Talked about the fun parts of the competition. That would have appealed more to a guy like him than my facts.

Then he smiles, and my heart buoys back up to my chest. "Sure, why not?" he says.

"Really?"

He laughs at my surprise. "But only if you tell me why you picked this Duke of Whimsey guy," he says. "I've never even heard of him."

"Lord Wimsey," I correct, a pang of unease making me hesitate over my next words. Explaining why I love Wimsey is always awkward because there's no way to talk about him without bringing up my mom. Which is hard enough, but since the boy is from Cape Cherry High, he might already have heard the bullshit story about how she died.

I plunge forward, hoping he doesn't keep up with local news.

"My mom was a huge murder-mystery fan," I say, watching him process my use of the past tense. The skin around his lips tightens a little, but otherwise he doesn't react. "My dad had to convert our garage into a library because every wall in our house was piled high with paperbacks. He even built her a rolling ladder so she could pretend to be Belle from *Beauty and the Beast*." The boy smiles in an uncomplicated way that suggests he's never heard about the car crash or Sheriff Calhoun's smear campaign against my family. "She used to read me books about Wimsey at bedtime even though my dad told her they would scare me."

"Did they?"

"Oh yeah." A little stab of pain pricks my chest. "But I never told her, because I didn't want her to stop."

Why don't you read him your diary, Dulce?

"Anyway," I say, quickly backpedaling away from the personal, "she read them to me so often that the first fictional character who felt like my friend was a rich British lord whose hobby was solving crimes." I sniff. "Even if everyone else at school would rather name their teams after detectives with their own TV shows."

"C'mon, that last *Sherlock* series was good," he says.

I wrinkle my nose. "Sherlock's brilliant, but he treats people like crap. Wimsey, on the other hand, is kind." *Like you,* I add in my head, thinking of his offer to make me a Shirley Temple. "And fair, and compassionate—"

He interrupts me with a laugh. "Okay, you've convinced me," he says. "I swear my undying fealty to Duke—*Lord* Wimsey, no matter how many flashy Netflix shows my fellow students throw at me."

I giggle-snort like a dork, which makes the boy's eyebrows

arch upward. Talking to gargoyles and snorting like a pig. I'm really on a roll with the good impressions. To cover my embarrassment, I put my head down and search for a pen in my backpack, letting dark waves of hair hide my face. When I find my black Sharpie, I write my number on a napkin.

"I don't use my phone much, but if you text me tomorrow, I'll give you details about our first meeting," I say, my feelings back under control. I stop before I reach the last number. "I know I'm kind of—" I try to think of how to put it. "What I mean is I know Wimsey sounds like a simp, but Emi and I are hardcore. We're playing to win."

His face is unreadable. "I can do hardcore."

"Okay, good." My fingers shake a little as I finish writing my number and hand it over.

The boy stares at it for a few seconds like he thinks there might be a hidden code there. Then he stands up and shoves it into his pocket. "Until tomorrow," he says, giving me a little salute.

As he walks back to the kitchen, I realize I have to stop thinking of him as *the boy*, like he's the only boy in the world. "What's your name?" I call after him.

He turns around, both of his mismatched cat eyes focused on me like I'm the center of the universe. "Zane," he says softly.

My heart jackrabbits against my chest. Lord Wimsey solves cases with a woman he rescued from a murder conviction. Her name is Harriet Vane.

Vane. Zane. It's fate.

3

A FEW DAYS AFTER THE START OF THE SEMESTER, EMI passes me a note during homeroom.

"I almost forgot," she says. "Dean Whitaker gave this to me during zero period."

She returns to flicking a cymbal with her pinkie. Ms. Moss teaches band, so our chairs are surrounded by music stands and drum kits. Emi's not the only student messing around with the instruments, which makes it hard to hear the morning announcements playing over the intercom system that—no joke—Dr. Everett installed to give the spirit of his murdered daughter an object to communicate through. It's thanks to him that rumors of Claire haunting the school have been around for decades. During my last birthday party, Emi told my dad she'd seen Claire's ghost in the library, but I'm pretty sure she was just messing with him because he's the kind of superstitious that burns sage during full moons and makes the sign of the cross every time Penny the black cat comes into our house.

I unfold the note, which is written on stationery embossed with the dean's name and title on top. It looks expensive, and I wouldn't be surprised if it was a gift from Mayor Fox.

Dulce, please see me in my office after school. —DW

I flip it over, hoping there might be more on the other side, but it's blank.

"It has to be about the internship, right?" I say.

"Of course it is." Emi's fingernail on the cymbal sounds like something from a horror movie. "No one ever applies for the coroner's internship. Dead bodies. Sawing open heads. What kind of psycho would want to spend a whole semester in that smelly basement?"

Dulce Dahmer. That's what Emi called me all summer, like I was some kind of serial killer because I'd applied to do my junior internship helping Dr. Bates perform autopsies. She doesn't know I plan to use my access to the coroner to get more information about the night my mom died. I'm positive the sheriff falsified Dr. Bates's report to make it look like my mom was drunk when Deputy Armstrong rear-ended her car, and I want to prove it.

"Why doesn't she do her makeup at home?" Emi frowns at Ms. Moss, who's applying lipstick in the reflection of the television hanging dark on the wall. She'd hurried into the band room after the bell, her guitar case hitting the door jamb in her rush. Students make fun of her for being a mess, but they don't know her history like I do.

The Dead Moms Club. An awful thing to have in common, but at least she'll talk about my mom's car wreck, unlike my dad. He thinks ignoring storm clouds means life will be full of rainbows; really, it means you won't have an umbrella when it pours.

"She told me it takes forever to get her twins ready in the morning," I say.

Emi scrunches her nose. "Remind me never to make that mistake."

I try to imagine Emi chasing after toddlers and laugh. Ms. Moss is all soft curves and sunshine voice and kumbaya on her guitar; Emi is about as maternal as a sword. Not to mention her love life is a revolving door.

"I'm pretty sure you'd have to like a guy for more than two weeks first." I grin. "Maybe even fall in love."

"A fate worse than death," she says. "I'll stick with clothes and cats for company, thanks." She eyes her Magic 8 Ball key chain like she's remembering its latest prediction. "Zane might be cute enough to last three weeks, though."

I've seen Zane in the halls a few times since Monday, and while I definitely understand his appeal (*Hypnotic eyes. Pretty lips. Floppy hair that looks like fields of wheat. Conclusion: Adorable.*), the competition is too important to be derailed by a crush. Something I've been trying to get through Emi's head before the first team meeting this afternoon.

"Zane is off-limits," I say, a portent of doom creeping up the back of my neck. "It'll ruin the group dynamic if you date him, because you'll totally break his heart and then he'll either quit or pine and be completely useless. We don't need another Enzo."

"Emi the Heartbreaker," she says, drawing a heart around the name Zane on her iPad before adding little devil's horns on top. She sees my horrified face and winks. "Relax. I'll leave him in one piece. I promise."

For some reason, that doesn't comfort me.

I enter Dean Whitaker's office after the final bell with an eager fluttering in my throat, but my mood jumps off a cliff as soon as I see his face.

Lips pressed together. Cheeks hollowed out. Puckered eyebrows.

Conclusion: This is not a man about to congratulate me for landing the coroner's internship.

My mind races, trying to figure out what I did wrong. Did I mess up the application? Forget to attach my personal essay? Or worse. Did Dr. Bates see the A- I got in biology freshman year and decide I wasn't qualified?

"Sit down, Dulce," Dean Whitaker says, but I stay frozen by the door like he can't give me bad news if I'm ten feet away. My eyes dart wildly around his office. Old leather books and dark wood line the walls, which are covered in pictures of Dean Whitaker climbing mountains and riding his motorcycle through the desert. Even upset, I can smell the faint hint of smoke, as if he's picked up Dr. Everett's pipe habit.

"Ahem." He points to the chair in front of his desk. I trudge over to it like I'm walking the plank, sit down, and wait for the inevitable.

"I'm sorry, Dulce," he says in the deep voice Emi imitates when she gets too high at parties. "The coroner's internship is no longer available."

"But how?" I whisper, all my plans collapsing. "You said—" I flush. I don't want it to sound like I'm accusing him of something, even though he absolutely, positively told me I didn't have to apply anywhere else because I would get the internship. *You're a shoo-in,* he'd said when I submitted the application to him at the end of last year. I'd appreciated the compliment because I wasn't sure he knew who I was. He's always seemed so intimidating, like one of those chiseled Mount Rushmore faces.

"I promised you the internship," he says, taking responsibility with a nod. "I know." He pushes his laptop aside and raps his fingers on the desk like he's playing Mozart. "Sheriff Calhoun overruled my recommendation and gave it to the coroner's kid at the last minute. I can't wait until Lily gets reelected so I can stop kissing his—" He stops talking like he's just realized he shouldn't finish that sentence in front of a student. "Point is I'm afraid there's nothing I can do."

On any other day, I'd care that the sheriff is trying to get his cousin—a man running on the slogan "Keep Cape Cherry Pure"—elected as mayor. But it takes everything in me not to let the tears burning behind my eyes fall onto the dean's gold paperweights, which are shaped like dice from a board game. First the sheriff stole the truth about my mom's death; now he's stolen the way I was going to uncover it.

"I'm sure something else will come up." I try to make my quivering voice sound enthusiastic, as if internships grow on trees and don't have to be applied for months in advance. "I appreciate your help."

Dean Whitaker snorts. "Stop trying to politely accept your fate, Dulce," he says. "I haven't finished." He picks up one of the paperweights and flips it around in his hand. "Ms. Moss was in my office when the sheriff called this morning, and she convinced me that we couldn't leave a high-performing student like you without a junior elective. So here's what I'm willing to do: I can offer you an independent study class with the same curriculum as the coroner's internship. It won't have a hands-on component, but"—he grimaces—"speaking from my med school experience, that might not be the worst thing." He tips his chin at the books behind him, but the only name I recognize is Freud. "There's a reason I chose to be a psychiatrist instead of a surgeon."

When I don't respond, he raises his eyebrows.

"Is something the matter?" he asks, like he's suddenly wondering why he agreed to offer up his valuable time to an ungrateful student he barely knows.

"It—it's just so nice of you," I stutter. I know Ms. Moss was trying to make things better, but studying one-on-one with the dean sounds like a nightmare, not a fairy tale. "I don't know what to say."

He puts down his paperweight and stands up, which I take as my cue to grab my bag. "Happy to help," he says briskly, with a glance at his watch. "You have a shot of getting into a top-tier college, which will reflect well on our school. So long as you perform to your usual standard in my class, I'm prepared to write you a glowing recommendation." He smiles with all his teeth as if to show me what he means by glowing. "We can talk more about it tomorrow if you'd like, but I'm late for a campaign event with Mayor Fox."

The conversation with Dean Whitaker has made me late, too, so I hurry up the stairs toward the band room, which Ms. Moss has let us use for team meetings since freshman year.

I'm moving fast down the hall, but the clicking heels behind me are moving even faster. Someone that smells like Chanel No. 5 knocks my shoulder without apologizing. As the girl passes me, her red curls swing across her back like coiling snakes.

Sierra.

Emi would have told her not to be such a bitchwitch, but I settle for saying "rude" so far under my breath it's barely audible even to me.

And yet somehow Sierra hears it. She twists around, a hard look on her face, which is all cheekbones and milky white skin. At another school, she'd probably be a cheerleader, parading the halls with a short skirt and an even shorter temper, but here she dresses like Jackie O, statuesque in sleeveless dresses and half gloves. Practice for when she inherits her trust fund.

Her scarlet lips curl, and I immediately feel like I've walked onto the sun. Angry heat rushes across my arms, turning into goose bumps. Even though we see each other in the halls every day, we haven't spoken since my mom died.

"Do you *need* something?" I ask in my bitchiest voice, because I'm not going to stand in the hall and be glared at.

Sierra rolls her eyes like I'm still not worth a single word of her time, but before she can leave, a door clicks open behind me.

I half turn, my eyes registering the briefest outline of a boy stepping out of the janitor's closet, before Sierra's words jar me face forward.

"Nice earrings," she says loudly, stepping close and flipping my hair behind my ear. Her friendly touch, after so long, sends shivers down the backs of my legs. The last time her fingers were on mine, she was clutching my hand in the back of Sheriff Calhoun's police car, trying to hold me together as my life fell apart. At the memory, my heart begins thumping unevenly, like it's forgotten how to beat.

She taps my right earring with her pinkie. "Is this a radish?" she asks, voice dripping with derision.

"Yeah," I say, my face heating up even more. "And?"

Sierra doesn't answer immediately because she's making dramatic motions with her eyes in the direction of the staircase. I begin to turn again, but she grabs onto the radish and pulls it so that I'm facing her. "It's just that your mom had such good taste." She smirks. "Guess some things skip a generation."

My mouth gapes like a carp. How *dare* Sierra bring up my mom like it's nothing. She should be begging forgiveness for abandoning me. Apologizing for taking the sheriff's side instead of mine. Crying about missing my mom's funeral. And instead, she's making fun of my jewelry?

I desperately want to speak, but I can't find any words in my head. *Not now,* I scream at my brain. *You can't freeze in front of her.*

A few cautious footfalls sound behind me. I try to turn and find out who's sneaking down the hall, but the most I can do is clench my fists.

"Go!" Sierra hisses over my shoulder in her why-are-boys-such-idiots? voice.

Heavy footsteps take off running across the wood, then down the stairs, their hollow echo moving to the first floor. After they're gone, Sierra casts me an uneasy glance, like she's freaked out by my stillness. For a second, she looks like she's going to say something else, but then she turns on her heel and clicks down the hall.

As soon as she enters the chem lab, my body unlocks, and I stumble through the nearest door into the empty amphitheater, where tiers of mahogany benches overlook the pit that Dr. Saka uses to conduct necropsies of sharks and pigs. The only illumination in the room is leaking from the skylight.

Tears fly to my eyes as I collapse onto one of the benches, breathing in the mote-filled air like I've run a mile. For two years,

I've imagined Sierra talking to me again. But in all those visions, I'd never guessed that her words would be so casually cruel, or that I'd stand there like one of the school's gargoyles, taking her abuse.

After a few minutes, my heart stops racing. As if they're tied to my brain with a string, my thoughts calm down, too—enough to dissect Sierra's appearance.

Freshly applied lipstick in her signature crimson. Too much perfume, probably to cover up another smell. A twisted bra strap, like she put it on in a hurry.

Conclusion: She was making out with a boy in the janitor's closet and only talked to me so he could escape without being recognized.

I close my eyes and try to remember the outline of the person I saw in the brief glimpse before Sierra stole my attention. A flash of brown hair tipped with gold highlights.

Xavier?

No, that doesn't make sense. She wouldn't need to protect her boyfriend.

I open my eyes. It's no good. I didn't see the person well enough to identify them. But I did learn one thing from her efforts: Sierra has something to hide. What I don't understand is why she'd bother hiding it from me.

Then again, who cares? The game is afoot. Everything else is noise.

4

WHEN I REACH THE BAND ROOM, ZANE AND EMI ARE SIT- ting together on the piano bench near the window. I can only see the back of Zane's head, but Emi's laughing face is in my direct line of sight. She's leaning close to him, her hand dangling next to his knee like she wants to rest it there. Her pupils are dilated and shiny, telltale signs of one of her instacrushes.

The future flashes in front of my eyes: Emi draping herself around my neck after the meeting, saying, "I'm madly in lust, Dulce. If he's not mine by the end of the week, I'm giving myself bangs." Emi and Zane tucked away in the corner of some party, drinks spilling onto the carpet as they grope each other. Emi making increasingly outlandish excuses for why she hasn't interrogated any of our suspects. Then the inevitable: Emi losing interest, declaring that Zane kisses like a dog or has the conversational ability of a piece of chalk. And our team disintegrating like a dandelion in the breeze.

Emi finally spots me in the doorway and waves her arms like she did at the assembly, hot pink bangles falling to her elbows. "About time," she says. "I thought you and Dean Whitaker had run away together, and I was going to be terribly jealous."

Zane scoots off the bench fast, like he's embarrassed at being caught so close to Emi, but not before I catch the remnants of the very familiar way he's smiling at her. My heart deflates. Zane is a flirt. The kind of guy with the same winking dimple and intense stare for everyone. Our conversation at Maldonado's wasn't special at all.

"Why's the window open?" I say, taking my time to walk over to it so I can hide my disappointment. I didn't realize I hoped Zane would see me beyond Emi's bright glow, but it's for the best that any more-than-friendly feelings get stomped out now, before they muddy my focus. "You're letting all the bugs in."

I flick several ladybugs off the sill before closing the window. This side of the building looks east over the forest, smudged like a postcard against the blue sky. Underneath the band room is the ballroom, and to the left of that is the cafeteria, which exits onto a dirt path that winds along the edge of the tree line until it reaches the front driveway, where my dad dropped me off on the first day of school. From the second-floor window, there's a clear view of the greenhouse, which is set about halfway down the path. The sun is shining off the glass panels that make up its peaked roof, and beyond the glare, I see Enzo Torres, all in black, moving like a shadow between tables full of pots and flowers. I guess when you have no friends, you hang out with plants.

"You have to stop making that joke about Dean Whitaker," I tell Emi, turning from the window and sitting down on a plastic chair one row away from Zane. "Some teacher is going to hear you and call the police."

"Fine," she sighs. "But I want him to marry my mom. We need someone to fix up our house."

"Maybe your dad will help when he's here next summer."

"Yeah, right," Emi says. "I doubt he knows the difference between a screwdriver and a hammer."

I dig in my backpack for the folders I've been making notes in all week. Green for **SUSPECTS**. Yellow for **MOTIVES**. Red for **RED HERRINGS**. Emi calls me Grandma for using a flip phone and taking notes by hand, but ever since my mom died, I can barely look at a smartphone without panicking. Since explaining why would mean telling Emi what actually happened that night, I just say that if Lord Wimsey didn't need modern technology to solve murders, neither do I.

"That's why I don't bother studying the game packet," Emi says when she sees Zane gaping at all the highlighter tabs sticking out of my folders. "Dulce *is* the packet."

"And Emi gives compliments whenever she wants to get out of work," I say, while Emi grins because she knows I'm right. I flip to my first page of notes, even though I don't need them. "This year's victim is Tim Riggs. Forty-five-year-old male who worked as a decorative tree pruner at a botanical garden."

"Like Edward Scissorhands." Emi flaps her arms. "Turning bushes into animals."

Zane looks confused, like he's never seen the movie, but I don't stop to explain. "Tim Riggs is killed in the greenhouse when someone jabs a knitting needle full of nicotine into his back."

"That's ridiculous," Zane says.

"Not really," Emi says. "Nicotine is super deadly. Inject it, and five minutes later, voilà, no more Tim Riggs."

"So it's untraceable?"

Emi snorts. "It's very, very traceable. That's why the question is *who* killed Tim Riggs and not *what* killed him."

"But why not use a normal syringe?"

"The Fox Family Trust always makes the murders old-school," Emi says. "Arsenic hidden in chocolates, bullets made of ice, snakes curled up in air vents. That kind of thing."

"Sierra's family must have let her help write the game this year," I mutter, annoyed that I can still feel her hand on my ear.

"No way." Emi shakes her head. "That would be super unfair."

"What makes you think they let her help?" Zane asks.

"She's been obsessed with knitting since freshman year," I say, tapping the WEAPONS folder. "That's why she named her team the Miss Marples." Zane looks confused again, so I add, "Miss Marple is one of Agatha Christie's detectives. She knits all the time to make suspects think she's harmless." I erase the W and rewrite it more neatly. "My mom thought her investigations were like watching paint dry."

"Perfect for Sierra, then." Emi grabs my folders and flips through them. "We can't do much more until someone finds Xavier's body."

"When will that be?" Zane asks.

"Xavier gets to choose, but it should be sometime in the next few weeks," Emi says. "Then we'll have access to clues the packet doesn't include, like the position of the body. That's why there are all those blank pages at the back." She pulls a piece of gum from her pocket and pops it in her mouth. "If you know how to sketch, tell us now, because we both suck at it."

Zane chews the inside of his cheek, looking overwhelmed.

"Don't worry about any of that," I say quickly. "You focus on the pathology."

"I'll do the nicotine research." Emi makes a note on her iPad with a stylus.

"You?" I ask, clutching my chest. "Do research?"

She pulls a hair tie off her wrist and flicks it at me. "Deadly plants are my passion," she tells Zane before sliding along the piano bench until she's right next to his chair. "Speaking of awful ways to die, you have to come to the Poisoner's Festival with us this weekend. There are hayrides and cider and places to get lost in the woods." She says the last bit suggestively, but Zane doesn't seem to notice.

"Um, sure." He looks back and forth between us. "I mean, if that's all right with you, Dulce. I don't want to butt in."

"Don't be silly." Emi's smile is strained, like I'm single-handedly torpedoing her chances of making out with Zane among the evergreens. "Wimseys stick together, right, Dulce?"

She and I have a silent conversation with our eyes.

I said he was off-limits.

But look at him! He's cuter than a basket full of puppies wearing bunny ears.

You're going to ruin everything.

Trust me. It will all be okay.

I sigh. Emi wins arguments even when no words are spoken.

"Yeah, you should come," I say. "The whole school turns out. There's a bunch of games to play and food trucks and—"

"I'll be showing off my archery skills," says a voice from the doorway.

I swing my head around to find a smiling Ms. Moss walking into the band room.

"Hannah!" I jump to my feet and give her a hug that shakes the scent of her perfume into my face. Jasmine and pears, just like my mom's. It's the only time I get to smell it because my dad gave all my mom's things to charity. "How was your summer?"

I've seen Ms. Moss in homeroom all week, but we haven't had a chance to talk, and it's not until now that I figure out why she's felt a little like a stranger.

Long black jacket cinched over a new dress. Curled hair pinned up in a loose bun. Lips that look strangely bee stung.

Conclusion: She's finally started dating again.

"Summer wasn't long enough," Ms. Moss says, walking over to her desk and digging for something in the drawer. "The twins are growing up so fast, I feel like I'm missing it." She touches a picture of two little boys in matching gray suits standing in front of a newly painted church, then glances up at Zane. "I don't think we've met. I'm Hannah Moss, the band teacher."

"Zane Lawrence," he says, standing up. "And that's perfect, because I'd like to audition for first flute."

Emi's mouth falls open, showing the gap between her bottom teeth. "You're a *band dork*?"

Ms. Moss, used to Emi's tactlessness, ignores her. "How about next Thursday?" she asks. "I can only meet during lunch because I pick my kids up right after the bell." Her hands brush aside loose pens and orphan reeds. "In fact, they're waiting in the car. I had to drive back from day care because I forgot my cell." She pulls her iPhone out of the drawer and looks at the time. "I better get them home before they strangle each other."

She's halfway to the door when she turns and says, "I'm sorry about the coroner's internship, Dulce. I know how much you wanted it."

"Wait, what?" Emi's eyes are wide, like she can't believe Hannah found out before her. "Why didn't you say anything?"

"I was going to," I mumble, embarrassed when I catch a glimpse of Zane's knit brows.

Ms. Moss's amber eyes crinkle with pity. "I was talking to Dean Whitaker about the budget for this year's band trip when the call came through. The sheriff didn't even apologize. He's such a jerk." Her phone dings, and she reads the message in silence with a frown. "Come have lunch next week," she says, glancing up at me. "I want to hear about the vacation you took to Disney World with your dad."

"She's a lot nicer than my old band director," Zane says once she's gone, the tiny taps of her keypad trailing down the hall.

Emi sniffs. "She wasn't so nice in Dean Whitaker's office this morning."

The zero-period aides get all sorts of front-office gossip. Most of it is boring, but occasionally Emi overhears something good, like last year when she learned that Dean Whitaker bought Mayor Fox a fifty-thousand-dollar engagement ring.

"What do you mean?" I ask.

"They were fighting. I couldn't hear much because the door was closed, but Ms. Moss said something about taking pills."

"She probably said *bills*," I say. "Pretty normal when you're talking about a budget."

Emi rolls her eyes. "You always think the best of her."

"Because she's like Mary Poppins."

"I hate Mary Poppins," Emi says. "With her spoonful of sugar and bullshit."

Zane laughs but quickly covers his mouth when he sees my expression. "Sorry," he says, looking apologetic. "I didn't know anyone else hated Mary Poppins."

My dream of the three of us working in harmony begins to float out the door. I can already imagine the Poisoner's Festival: Emi and Zane, bonding over their shared disgust for all things

Disney, touching hands when they think I'm not looking, and me hanging off to the side, the thirdiest third wheel ever.

What we need is for someone to murder Tim Riggs. Once Xavier's body is found, there will be so much work to do that Emi and Zane won't have time to smile at each other on piano benches. And after we see the crime scene, we'll be able to figure out the *how*, which will lead us to the *who* and to the prize money.

My job until then? Wrangle the lovebirds into research mode. I watch Emi lean over to Zane, bat her eyelashes, and suggest that his lips must be strong from playing the flute.

I'm doomed.

5

"WHY'S IT CALLED THE POISONER'S FESTIVAL?" ZANE ASKS, glancing toward the parking lot like he's hoping Emi will show up soon.

She's late, as usual, so Zane and I are waiting awkwardly near the ticket booth, listening to carnival music and laughter waft over the front lawn of the school. A cluster of students nearby throw darts at silver balloons nailed to a board and groan whenever they miss. Beyond them, evergreens darken the sky like giants marching to war.

"Back when James Everett was dean," I say, "he held a yearly exhibition for his students so they could see how poisons worked outside of books."

"He poisoned people? For real?"

"Animals," I say softly, trying not to picture it. "It was like a demented petting zoo."

Emi finally arrives with her typical explosion of noise and enthusiasm. "You two look bored," she says, draping arms around me and Zane. "Let's go find some fun."

The three of us walk the path, trying to decide what game to play first. Two dozen tents wind the length of the driveway, while games requiring more space—like lawn bowling and archery—are set up on neatly trimmed grass that stretches for several football fields. It looks like Dean Whitaker has finally made good on his promise to repair the stone fountain, because not only is there water pouring from the mermaid's mouth, but the basin is full of bobbing apples.

"That seems super unsanitary," I say, watching blindfolded children nod into the water like ducks.

Several little boys run by us so fast they almost knock Emi over. "Sorry!" one of them yells, but they don't slow down. Their faces and shirts are dripping with chocolate ice cream from the cones they're waving around like lightsabers.

"Yeah, because kids are usually so clean," Emi sniffs, brushing off her fanny pack.

At the third tent, we find Enzo Torres standing behind a little girl, helping her shoot a Nerf gun at cloth poppets dangling from strings.

"Have we entered some kind of alternate dimension," I say after we've hurried past him, "where Enzo is kind to children and animals?"

"He's only doing it so he can steal her prize," Emi says. "Just like he stole our forensics notes last year."

A wagon carrying several sophomores, their faces painted like butterflies, rolls past us. One of the girls tries to drink her pear cider, but the bumpy path tips it into her lap, making Zane laugh.

"Win me a goldfish," Emi tells him, pointing at a tent with pale blue stripes where a wooden basin full of water and plastic stakes is being watched over by a parent volunteer.

"As long as you promise not to poison it," Zane jokes, disentangling himself from her grasp and handing the volunteer two tickets.

"Three stakes is all it takes," the man says in a singsong, handing Zane a half-dozen yellow rings.

Zane closes one eye to help him aim. The first ring sinks into the water, but the second slides over a wood stake. The volunteer rings the victory bell.

Zane looks back for Emi's approval, but she's staring at Rose, who's lawn bowling next to a row of hedges that have been pruned, Tim Riggs–style, to look like chess pieces.

I expect him to be disappointed that Emi isn't paying attention, but he turns to me with a quick grin that makes his dimple pucker. "And here I thought I'd have to do this to the sound of shrieks," he says, tossing another ring. "Don't get me wrong," he adds quickly. "I love her enthusiasm. It can all just get a bit—"

"Loud," I finish, having had the same thought a million times.

"How did you two meet?" he asks.

"In the most Emi way possible." Thoughts of freshman year race through my head. "She came over during lunch and demanded my bologna sandwich because she was tired of the Japanese food her mom packs." *Heaven,* Emi had said before stuffing the other half of my sandwich into the lime-green turtle bag she was wearing like a baby carrier. *I have history after lunch, and war makes me hungry.*

"After I promised to trade lunches with her every day, she agreed to name our team after my *old rich white guy*." I put air quotes around the final words. "She thinks she's getting the better end of the deal, but I ate pork katsu today while she ate a bunch of chemicals between slices of bread, so . . ."

"I'm surprised Sierra's not on your team," Zane says.

"Sierra Fox?" I ask, startled. "Why would she be?"

Zane tosses his ring onto another stake, and the bell rings again. "You're friends, right?"

I frown. Had he seen us together in the hallway? If not, why would he think we're friends? "Not since middle school," I tell him.

Zane's ring bounces off the side of the basin and lands with a soft *thwap* in the grass. "So much for winning the fish," he says. After a pause, he adds, "I could have sworn someone told me you and Sierra were tight. Like, you had your own detective agency and everything."

Even though it's dark outside, the tent is strung with lights, and I'd swear the tips of Zane's ears are turning pink. Not at all his usual cool, calm, and collected self.

"The detective agency was a joke," I say. "Or at least it started that way, but then—" I stop, not wanting to get distracted from my real question. "Who told you about me and Sierra?"

"Can't remember." He shrugs. "I feel like I've met the whole school this week."

"Rose!" Emi yells, waving toward the lawn bowling game, which has just ended. When Rose arrives at our tent, Emi kisses her on each cherubic cheek. Ms. Nakamura took Emi to Paris last summer, and she'd brought back the habit. *Can't you just smell the croissants and the café au lait?* she'd asked when she kissed my cheeks the first time.

Rose turns pale blue eyes on me and Zane. "I'm headed to the food trucks if you're hungry."

I bite my lip. "Actually, I already—"

"That sounds great," Emi interrupts me. "I love the corn dogs here. They taste like they've never lived outside a machine."

I feel a pang of jealousy as Emi slides Rose's arm through hers. We walk by Dean Whitaker and Xavier, who are talking quietly near Dr. Saka's education station, where she's teaching children how to dissect earthworms. I always score off the charts on the hearing test the school nurse administers every year, so I catch a few of Dean Whitaker's words over the children's squeals of disgust. "When you're discovered in the greenhouse . . ."

Of course. He's giving Xavier instructions for playing Tim Riggs. I take a few steps closer to see if I can hear more, but Rose's sudden intake of air makes my head turn.

"What's Xavi doing here?" she says, the pink in her cheeks spreading down her neck as she stares at him.

"Why wouldn't he be?" Emi asks.

Rose doesn't answer for a second. "He and Sierra got into a giant fight at his back-to-school party last night. He accused her of cheating on him, but right in the middle of dumping her, he got super sick."

"They called an ambulance and everything," Zane adds.

"*You* were at the party?" I ask him.

"I thought I might see you and Emi there," he says, looking at me from under blond lashes.

"We're not cool enough to get invited." *Not to mention his girlfriend lied about how my mom died, and we hate each other.* "Once Xavier finds out you're one of us . . ."

Zane shrugs as if he doesn't care whether he ever sees Xavier's beach house again. "I was super bored," he says. "It's always the same: drinking and bonfires and body shots. Like they're in a teen movie montage."

"Who cares about Sierra," Emi cuts in. "Her love life is as

tired as her wardrobe." She turns to Rose. "No offense. I know you're teammates."

Rose scuffs her white sneaker against the ground. "It's not like she and I are friends," she says.

Finally, something to like about Rose.

While the others eat corn dogs and veggie nachos, I excuse myself to the bathroom, but on my way back, I walk straight into Enzo Torres, who looks like an emo ninja with frosted tips. "Watch it," he grunts without looking at me.

"Watch yourself," I say.

Something about the blond in his dark hair recalls the edge of a memory, but it's nothing I can place before his eyes flash with recognition. "Wait." He catches my arm so I can't get past him. "Have you seen Sierra?"

As soon as his fingers dig into my elbow, I freeze. Enzo was on our team for only two months last year, but it was long enough for me to discover that school rumors are true: He's the devil to Xavier's angel. Emi told me that when she yelled at him for quitting the game midsemester, he threatened to skin her cat and use it in his rituals.

"W-why is everyone asking me about Sierra?" I stutter. I love Penny, my sometimes cat, and while I may not believe in witchcraft, I definitely believe in screwed-up high school boys.

Emi appears at my side out of nowhere. "Hey, *brujo*," she says scathingly, glaring at Enzo. "If you're looking for animals to kill, you should try the woods. Maybe we'll get lucky and a bear will find you." She points to my elbow. "Dean Whitaker has a strict nonconsensual touching policy. I could ask him to explain it to you."

Enzo drops my arm like it's burning him. "Sorry, I didn't mean—"

He looks back and forth between me and Emi with bewildered eyes before taking off in the direction of the school. My body immediately unfreezes like I'm in a particularly frustrating video game.

"Why didn't you punch him in the face?" Emi asks.

My mouth drops open. "You think that was *my* fault?"

"Of course not," she says. "But Wimsey would have hit Enzo with his walking stick. Or maybe with his car. Why bother with the detective hero worship if you're just going to act like a *conejita*?"

With that thunderbolt, she heads back to the food trucks.

Humiliated tears threaten to spill from my eyes as I stand there, rooted to the spot. It's not the first time Emi's thrown my childhood nickname in my face (*"Bunnies are domesticated; you need to be wild."*), but this time, her shot hits home because I know she's right. Before my mom died, I was breaking into yards to steal back pets for Death & Fox; now I freeze before I can tell a boy to let go of my arm. The problem is I have no idea how to fix it.

Emi gives me a hug when I get back to the picnic table, which is what she always does when she wants me to know that, though her words are harsh, her heart is not.

"Love your bones," she says.

"Love your guts," I whisper back.

Zane checks his watch. "Only another hour to spend these tickets," he says, holding up a handful of white papers. "I still haven't won you a fish, Emi."

My heart gives a painful twang as I watch them smile into

each other's eyes. For the past two years, I've sidelined guys to focus on school, but seeing them together makes me wonder if that was a mistake; I wouldn't hate someone looking at me like he's looking at her.

"In lieu of a fish, I will accept a Hello Kitty plush," she tells him. "They're giving them as prizes at the strongman's booth."

We head out of the parking lot, where the food trucks are stationed, and back to the game tents. It's only when I hear the gravel crunching under my feet that I notice we're alone.

"Why is everyone near the path?" Rose asks, pointing to a dark mass of people on the other side of the main building, where the lawn borders a forest that stretches for miles on its way to the ocean.

As if Dean Whitaker heard her, his booming voice rises into the night air like a circus performer's. "Good evening, folks. The moment you've been waiting for has arrived."

"Let's find out what's going on," Emi says, hurrying toward the crowd in her rubber rain boots, which she's wearing even though no storms are forecast for days.

When we reach the grass, so many people are blocking our view that I can't even tell where Dean Whitaker is standing. Emi jumps up and down, but she's nowhere near tall enough to see over the other students, much less their parents. "When did Cape Cherry get so big?" she says. "There must be five hundred people here."

Zane, making the most of his six-foot-three frame, peers above the people in front of us and says, "Dean Whitaker and the band teacher—"

"Ms. Moss," I say.

"—are on the archery range."

"This summer," Dean Whitaker says from somewhere in front of us, "I learned that Hannah was a national archery and crossbow champion in college. And it just so happens that I grew up bowhunting with my dad in Wyoming. I thought it might be fun to have a friendly wager to see which one of us is the better shot. Best out of five wins. If I take the prize, Hannah has agreed to do parking-lot duty until Halloween. If she does"—he pauses like he's about to say something shocking—"I will dye my hair blue for two weeks."

The students in the crowd explode into whoops and shrieking laughter. Emi claps her hands with joy, and I laugh, too, imagining Dean Whitaker during our independent study class, discussing rigor mortis with hair like an Easter egg.

"I *have* to see this!" Emi attempts to slip between the people in front of her, but all that gets her is dirty looks.

"I know how we can watch," Zane says. "This way." I expect him to guide us to the right, around the chess-piece hedges, but instead he leads us toward the forest. As we skirt the edge of the gathered crowd, the ground beneath our feet gets darker and darker until I can barely see where we're going. But it's only when Zane cuts between two giant live oaks and enters the woods that I stop walking.

"It's pitch black in there," I say. "And there could be animals."

Zane pulls out his phone and turns on his flashlight. "We're not going very far. You'll see."

Rose and Emi follow him, and, after a single glance back at the cheering crowd, I do too. I've run in the woods during gym for years, but I'd get lost in an instant if I left the path. And yet Zane zigzags through the trees like he's in his own backyard.

After about a hundred more feet, Zane stops at a clump of

bushes squatting right inside the tree line. "Here," he says. He holds his phone higher, and I see that what I'd thought was a giant bush is actually a tiny hut so completely covered with ivy that it's invisible among the tangled trees surrounding it.

"No way!" Emi brushes leaves off an old ladder leaning against the hut. "Did anyone else know this was here?"

"No," I say, feeling stupid even though it's not hard to see how I overlooked it. From the lawn, the hut would look indistinguishable from any other part of the forest.

"The roof will get us above the crowd," Zane says. "And no one will be looking in this direction."

"Are you serious?" I press on the broken slats of the ladder, which are sagging with ivy. "A stiff breeze could blow it apart."

"And we could get in trouble," Rose says, her eyes darting around like an administrator might be hiding behind a tree.

Emi pushes us aside. "Dean Whitaker is a teddy bear," she says, hiking up her skirt. "Worst-case scenario, we get detention."

Rose's lips tremble as she watches Emi climb the ladder in her rain boots, but she follows her all the same. I watch as she stumbles up the rungs.

Knees knocking. Constantly checking for the ground. A small whimper I can hear over the breeze.

Conclusion: Rose is scared of heights.

Emi peeks her head over the edge. "*Vámonos*, Dulce. If you miss Moss kick Whitaker's ass, you'll never forgive yourself."

"Fine," I sigh.

Zane follows behind me as I climb the ladder. My cheeks burn as I picture how close he is to my butt.

"So, what is this place?" Emi asks after we settle onto the roof. "Does the gardener keep tools in here or something?"

Zane arches his eyebrows. "It's the icehouse." Seeing our confused looks, he says, "In the olden days, when people didn't have refrigerators, they kept blocks of ice underground so they could use them to keep their food cold. I guess the Everetts never tore this one down."

"You've gone to school here for five seconds," Emi says. "How did you find it?"

"Enzo showed me. We have study hall together, and he asked if I wanted to see something cool." Zane stares into the darkness behind us. "He knows these woods really well. We tried to get inside, but the door's padlocked."

I frown. Since when does Enzo try to make friends?

"They're starting!" Emi says.

The two teachers stand next to each other on the archery range, painted targets fifty yards in front of them. The backs of the crowd are to us, which is good, because we definitely don't have ivy camouflage.

Dean Whitaker raises his bow. Even I can see that his arms are wobbling when he lets the arrow go. It hits the outer edge of the target, far wide of the bullseye. Everyone claps politely.

"At least he hit it," Emi says, always ready to defend him.

Ms. Moss lifts her bow.

"Don't miss!" Dean Whitaker yells jovially.

She doesn't. The arrow soars through the air in a fast, straight line, hitting the center of the target with a sharp thud. This time, the clapping is surprised, as if no one can believe that sweet, apple-cheeked Ms. Moss can wield a hunting weapon with such precision.

Dean Whitaker whistles his praise. "My hair is starting to feel scared," he jokes.

His next shot hits the other side of the target, inside one of the white rings, still far from the bullseye. Ms. Moss raises the bow and lets her arrow fly . . . straight into the center.

"Are you thinking a royal blue or more of an aquamarine?" she asks Dean Whitaker, making her voice loud enough to carry through the crowd, which rumbles with laughter.

After that, Ms. Moss hits the bullseye each time, while Dean Whitaker puts his arrows into the outer white rings. He misses his last shot entirely, sending it through the trees.

The crowd groans.

"Better hope Bambi wasn't back there," Ms. Moss says with a grimace. She has only one shot left, but instead of taking a single arrow out of the quiver, she pulls three in quick succession and shoots them. Each one lands inside the center ring.

"Thinks she's Legolas," Emi grumbles as the crowd whoops with delight.

Dean Whitaker waves his arm at Ms. Moss like a magician unveiling his final trick. "We have a winner!" he says. "Apparently, not hunting for twenty years has made me rusty." He smiles. "I hope you'll enjoy my appearance on Monday."

The crowd breaks up. A stream of people heads for the tents, anxious to play their tickets before the festival closes.

Zane's thigh is touching mine on the crowded roof, a fact I've been trying to ignore, but suddenly his leg tenses. "Oh shit, it's Sheriff Calhoun." He points at the range, all his surfer-boy chill gone.

"You have a rap sheet or something?" Emi says.

"I hate cops." Zane grits his teeth. "On principle."

Dean Whitaker crosses his arms and frowns as he listens to whatever the sheriff is saying under his ugly mustache. A minute later, Mayor Fox walks up to them, snuggling into the crook of Dean Whitaker's arm like she wants to show her ex-husband how happy she and her new fiancé are together.

"Like a teddy bear marrying a cobra," Emi mutters.

It's impossible for Dean Whitaker to have heard her, but his eyes flash up to the icehouse. We all duck, but not fast enough. His mouth falls comically open when he recognizes us.

"That's our cue to go," Emi says, scuttling toward the ladder like a crab.

I take one last look at the archery range to see if Dean Whitaker is headed our way, but it's not his eyes that meet mine; it's the sheriff's. I expect to see shock or even fury on his face at spotting students scrambling dangerously across the roof of a crumbling hut, but his expression sends hot chills down my back.

He's staring at the four of us and smiling.

6

"DETENTION."

The word whooshes out of my mouth like a reverse gasp that echoes around the cafeteria.

"It's been three days, Dulce," Emi says. "Get over it."

Dean Whitaker called us to his office first thing Monday morning. "What were you *thinking*?" he said before proceeding to give us a twenty-minute lecture about safety and what would happen to the school if one of us fell off the roof. At the end, he pointed to me. "And *you*, Ms. Castillo, I thought you had better judgment."

"I'm just glad I managed not to laugh at his hair," Emi says. "He probably would have kicked me out of zero period."

"It's going on our permanent record." I hadn't realized how much I cared about that record until Dean Whitaker handed me a pink slip with the word DETENTION at the top.

"Do you seriously think UVA is going to reject you because you got one detention?"

"Sierra's cousin didn't get in because he used the wrong font for his personal essay," I say, my voice a warning. "Arial instead of Times New Roman."

Emi snorts. "They should reject you for being gullible enough to believe that story. He didn't get in because he writes like a toddler."

I open my mouth to argue but snap it shut again when Zane approaches our table and sits down. I can't believe I almost had a crush on a boy whose idea of a good time is climbing on top of buildings that should be torn down. I wonder if there's a way to turn my hormones off. I'll have to ask WebMD.

"Why'd you bring your nerd whistle to lunch?" Emi asks, pointing to the flute case lying next to Zane on the bench.

"Don't you ever think before you speak?" Zane grabs a SunChip out of her hand and eats it. The intimacy of the move makes me feel like Emi is in a movie I wish I could be in. *The kind that gets you detention,* I remind myself.

"Nope," Emi says, tossing him another chip. "If you start questioning yourself, you never stop."

"I'm auditioning for band in a few minutes," Zane tells her.

I dig into the bento box Emi's mom packed. Edamame, mushroom tempura, and rice with julienned vegetables. Every student at J. Everett has lunch at the same time, so the cafeteria is full of voices, like an orchestra warming up.

Someone knocks me in the back with their elbow, making me stab the top of my mouth with a chopstick.

"Oh shit. Sorry, Dulce." It's Xavier Torres, and his brown eyes are bright with concern. Emi and I may not rate invites to his parties, but he's always been perfectly polite to me in a politician-shaking-hands-with-the-competition way. Last year, we were partnered for chemistry and discovered we both get our organizers from a specialty stationery store in Chesapeake. After his team won the game, he handed me a new planner tied with a bow. *May we always have sticks up our asses* said the note that went with it.

"No worries." I rub the roof of my mouth with my tongue and taste nothing but rice. "No blood, no foul."

He flashes me his thousand-gigawatt smile, but as he's about to walk away, he does a double take at Zane, his face contorting into a mask of anger. The speed of the mood switch fires warning signals into my brain.

"What are *you* doing here?" he asks Zane.

Zane looks behind himself like Xavier might be talking to someone else. When he sees no one there, he turns back around. "I go to school here."

"Since when?"

"The beginning of the year." Zane frowns. "Sorry, do we know each other?"

Xavier's eyes narrow until they're snake slits. "Whatever," he says. "Just stay out of my face. Got it?"

"Happily," Zane says, looking alarmed. I don't blame him. I've never seen Xavier act so prickly. Maybe he and his brother have more in common than I thought.

Xavier checks the time on his cell phone before hurrying out the back door with his Diet Coke and apple. The fact that he's not eating lunch with Sierra means they must really have broken up.

"What was that about?" Emi asks.

"I have absolutely no idea," Zane says. "He must have confused me with someone else."

"Maybe something happened at his party," Emi says, taking a bite of my bologna sandwich. "And he was too messed up to remember who was involved." Her eyes light up. "Rose!" she calls. "Come sit with us."

"I never even talked to him that night," Zane mumbles, but Emi's attention is already gone. He looks pale, like the confrontation with Xavier shook him. My mind loops quickly through their conversation. Was it likely Xavier had snapped at a stranger? And if they did know each other, why would Zane pretend they didn't?

Rose crosses the cafeteria carrying a bulging backpack, but when she reaches our table, she doesn't sit down. "I wish I could," she says, looking wistfully at Emi like she doesn't regret her detention at all. "But next time, for sure."

"She's going to be cold in that skirt," I say, watching her walk out the same door as Xavier. "It stormed all morning."

A wave of movement across the cafeteria interrupts my words. Students are grabbing their phones, the din of voices growing louder and louder until it sounds like gnats are swarming over our heads.

"What's happening?" Zane asks.

Emi pulls her cell phone from the plush-kitten bag strapped around her waist. "Sierra's livestreaming."

"Sierra's kind of an influencer," I explain, seeing Zane's confusion. "At first, her videos were to show off her clothes—"

"And ass," Emi interrupts, pulling up the feed. "But since her mom is running for reelection this year, she's turned it into a political channel. She spends the whole time bashing Sheriff Calhoun, so it's not as boring as it sounds." Emi props her phone against a bottle of Topo Chico, and I scowl when I catch a glimpse of Sierra's curls on the screen. I've told Emi she shouldn't support my nemesis, but she said if she stopped, she'd miss me saying the word *nemesis*. It's impossible to get Emi to do anything other than exactly what she wants.

"Oh, right, the sheriff complains about her videos all the time," Zane says.

"How do you know?" I ask.

"Beth told me."

"You're friends with Sheriff Calhoun's *daughter*?" Emi asks, screwing up her face.

The tips of Zane's ears redden. "We had a lot of classes together at Cape Cherry High. She's sweeter than you might think."

Beth's longing stares in Zane's direction at Maldonado's have given me a pretty good idea of why she's nice to him.

Sierra's voice, played through dozens of phones, cuts through our conversation. "This week in 'Why Sheriff Calhoun is Trash,' I want to fill you in on his latest attempts to shut down J. Everett . . ."

My mind wanders over to Zane, whose head is nearly touching Emi's as they watch her screen together.

Who told him Sierra and I were friends? The question has been bothering me since the Poisoner's Festival. It's hard to imagine how my name would come up with a new student, and only someone who knew me in middle school would have heard about Death & Fox.

"I can't believe Dean Whitaker agreed to go on her livestream," Emi says. "Sierra's viewers are going to think he's lost his mind."

I lean forward so I can see Dean Whitaker and his blueberry hair talk about the importance of our criminology program. "Fear is the enemy of justice, which is why we must reject those who would attack our school in the name of political purity . . ."

"Oh shit." Zane jumps to his feet. "I'm going to be late for the audition."

"Break a leg," I say.

"But not your lips," Emi adds.

Zane jokingly flips her off as he hurries out of the lunchroom with his flute.

"He's already in love with me, can you tell?" Emi asks over the sound of Dean Whitaker thanking Sierra for having him on the show.

"I would have thought you'd be attached at the mouth by now."

"I know, right?" Emi sounds irritated, like the lack of smooches hasn't been her choice. "He's been super busy with his job and the farm."

"Farm?"

"Yeah, he and his mom live up on Route 45," she says. "They've got, like, twenty acres and a bunch of animals." She rolls her eyes. "He couldn't go to the movies with me on Sunday because they had to vaccinate their livestock or something."

A few minutes later, Sierra walks into the lunchroom to her usual post-livestream applause from her friends, but she doesn't even acknowledge them. Instead she hitches her bag up on her shoulder and clicks across the linoleum, head bent over her phone, until she disappears out the back door.

"What a bitchwitch," Emi says. "Can't even smile at her fan club. Oh, there's Dean Whitaker!" She waves in his direction, but he doesn't see her and sits down instead with Sierra's teammates, who do everything together, like a pack of wolves. "I wish he wouldn't have chosen Xavier to be the victim," she continues, putting her elbows on the table and sucking Topo Chico out of a rainbow straw. "It's not fair Xavier gets to be class president, co-leader of the Miss Marples, *and* have a leg up in the game."

"You can never have too much good luck or too much good hair," I say, repeating an old maxim of my mom's.

Emi answers me, but I don't hear what she says because, somewhere inside my bat ears, someone is screaming. Or at least I think they are. It's not easy to separate sounds when a hundred people are talking at once.

I close my eyes and try to tune everyone else out. "Shh," I tell Emi, who's still droning on about Xavier. "Can you hear that?"

"Hear what?" she asks. "Everyone chomping on their food? Of course I can. It's disgusting."

"No, it sounds like—" I pause, listening harder, but there's nothing except the noon bells ringing at the nearby church. If someone was screaming, they're not anymore. "Never mind. It's gone."

Twenty minutes later, after Emi has run through all the times she's caught Zane staring at her, Sierra sprints into the cafeteria from the front hallway, her dress covered in mud like she's been tromping through the woods. Her usually pale face is bright red, and the gold chains around her neck are bouncing with the effort of her breath. She has the disbelieving look of someone who's just seen Claire Everett's ghost.

Dean Whitaker notices Sierra only seconds after me, and he leaps up from the table, his face twisted with concern.

"Xavi's in the greenhouse!" Sierra screams, tripping over her feet as she stumbles toward her friends. "He's been murdered!"

She gazes around in wide-eyed horror before crumpling to the ground, spilling her books and knitting supplies all over the floor.

Everyone in the lunchroom breaks into applause. Dean

Whitaker smiles and sits back down, high-fiving the students at his table.

"That was fast," Emi says over the clapping. "Usually no one finds the body until after Labor Day." She begins stuffing SunChips into her mouth. "We should finish up so we can get to the greenhouse first. Early bird solves the murder."

"Definitely," I say, grabbing the last of the edamame with Emi's chopsticks, happy something's finally happened to take my mind off detention. Now that Tim Riggs is dead, I can complete my crime scene checklist. The packet has a few pages showing the layout of the greenhouse, but there's no diagram of the weapon. I need to remember my sketching pencils . . .

My eyes land on Sierra's shoes. A vague discomfort stirs in my brain, but it takes me a second to figure out what's wrong. One of her heels is snapped, like a twig about to fall off its branch. "It's broken," I say, standing up to get a better look. "That doesn't make sense. She'd never sacrifice a pair of Manolos for the game."

I look closer, and what I see makes my scalp prickle with ice. Bright red liquid is spreading out from behind Sierra's head as if her curls are melting.

Blood.

"Stop clapping!" I yell, but my voice isn't loud enough to carry. "She's hurt!" I try again, but the clapping continues.

Emi sees my panicked eyes and drops her sandwich. "Oh shit," she says, looking at Sierra's unmoving body. Emi is always laden with random toys, but she also never leaves home without a rape whistle attached to her necklace. She puts it to her mouth and blows, emitting an earsplitting howl.

"Oy!" she screams when everyone finally stops clapping and covers their ears. "Shut up!"

The atmosphere in the lunchroom flips on a dime. A low buzz of concern whips around the air. I rush over to Sierra, my sneakers squeaking on the floor as I kneel beside her. I grab her wrist to take her pulse, which is faint but even. Dean Whitaker runs over to us, surprisingly light on his feet. "What's wrong?" he asks, falling to his knees. "Did she hurt herself when she pretended to pass out?"

"She wasn't faking," I tell him, my words coming in gasps. "She's unconscious."

The color drains from Dean Whitaker's face, but he immediately takes charge. He points his finger at Emi, who's come over to see the drama up close. "Go to the office and call an ambulance," he says, his voice urgent but steady. "Tell them Mayor Fox's daughter has fainted and needs medical attention."

Emi runs off as fast as she can in her thick-soled boots. When she disappears from view, Dean Whitaker turns back to me, and I can see in his eyes the alarm he's trying to suppress. "If Sierra wasn't acting, that means—" He doesn't finish his sentence, but I'm already ahead of him.

If Sierra's panic was real, then what she said wasn't part of the game. Xavier Torres is dead.

7

"I'M GOING TO THE GREENHOUSE," DEAN WHITAKER TELLS Sierra, squeezing her hand like he hopes she can feel it. "I'll be back soon."

Sierra's teammates have all crowded around her unconscious body, but it's Rose who catches my eye. She's clutching her backpack against her chest and sobbing.

Sweater collar dark with tears. Breathing hard like she's been running. And her words from the festival: It's not like Sierra and I are friends.

Conclusion: Rose is way more upset about Sierra than she should be.

"I need you to come with me, Dulce," Dean Whitaker says. "If Xavier's had"—he pauses—"an accident, I might need someone to get help while I tend to him."

"Me?" I squeak, kicking myself for running over to Sierra. If I wasn't in the dean's line of sight, he would have chosen someone else. I look around the lunchroom, hoping to see another teacher, but the dean is the only adult in the room besides the lunch lady, who's peeking out from the kitchen through the slit where students put their used trays. When our eyes meet, she slams the slit shut.

"You," the dean says firmly, leaving me no choice but to follow him.

Thoughts of what we'll find in the greenhouse trigger déjà vu as we hurry down the path, images of the past overlapping with the present: Riding in the back seat of Sheriff Calhoun's car as he sped to the hospital. Stumbling into the waiting room of the ER feeling like someone was holding me underwater. My dad telling me my mom was already gone. His hollow black eyes making me think he wished he could go with her.

I shake the images out of my head to keep my body from going into freeze mode. This could all be a mistake. Maybe Xavier staged his murder scene so well Sierra thought it was real.

The game. If Xavier is dead, will they cancel it?

"Do you think . . ." I start to ask before pressing my lips together. It's selfish to be wondering about the game when Xavier might be hurt or worse. Instead I try to guess what might have happened. Tool injury? Drug overdose? Or maybe the illness that sent him to the hospital was worse than Rose and Zane knew.

Or maybe it's a joke. It wouldn't be the first time Xavier's pranked Sierra. He once announced live on air at his Channel Z internship that Sheriff Calhoun was moving out of state to pursue his real dream of owning a goat farm. She did a whole livestream about it before she figured out it was April Fool's Day.

The muscles in my body start to relax as we approach the greenhouse. That has to be it. We'll walk in, and Xavier is going to be—

"You stay out here," Dean Whitaker says, interrupting my train of thought. "If Xavier is injured, there's no reason for both of us to see it." A little shiver passes across his eyes as he pushes the door open. I don't mean to look, but as I watch the dean go in,

I catch the briefest glimpse of someone lying motionless on the ground before the door closes.

When Dean Whitaker doesn't come back out immediately, the tension returns to my muscles. Surely, if Xavier had just been staging the crime scene or teasing Sierra, I'd be able to hear him and the dean talking.

A minute later, Dean Whitaker stumbles out of the greenhouse.

Forehead dotted with sweat. Stomach heaving as he leans on the glass. Dirt clinging to his pants like he's been kneeling to take a pulse.

Conclusion: The worst has happened.

"I'm so sorry, Dulce," he says, placing a trembling hand on my shoulder. "I shouldn't have brought you down here. I just couldn't believe it was true."

Not a prank. Not an overenthusiastic acting performance. Xavier smiled at me only half an hour ago, and now he'll never smile again.

My heart begins to pound as my body realizes the truth, but there's no time to fall apart. Dean Whitaker looks like he needs to blow into a paper bag, so I try to hold it together for both of us.

"I'll stand guard and wait for you to come back," I say. "We don't want anyone touching anything, or else the coroner might not be able to figure out how he died."

"God, I didn't even think of that," he says, looking at his hands like they belong to someone else. "I touched the needle." He halts again and takes a deep breath, trying to collect himself. "You're not in any danger. The killer is already—"

"Killer?!" All my nerves pop like live wires. My eyes dart around, looking into the woods like someone might be standing there holding a bloody knife. "It wasn't an accident?"

"No," Dean Whitaker says. "But I think she—" He sniffs hard, and his demeanor changes, like there's Ritalin in the air. "I apologize," he says, his voice tough and deep again. "I'm rambling." He manages an embarrassed half smile. "I'm sure you already know this, but adults don't always feel very grown-up. You never stop wishing there was someone else to take care of things for you." He nods once, like he's made a decision. "Forget what I said. You're perfectly safe. I'll be back with the sheriff soon."

He runs up the path like an athlete, his breath coming in short bursts until he disappears. I stand there, my back to the door, trying not to imagine Xavier dead inside. *Killer?* How is that possible? I saw him walk out the back door half an hour ago.

"Is he really dead?" says a voice from the other side of the greenhouse.

I scream, a pathetic, shrill thing that shoots straight up into the cool air and then fades away.

"Sorry," Emi says, walking around the corner and peering inside the glass. "Didn't mean to scare you." She turns around and sticks her tongue out. "At least not *that* much."

"Did you call the ambulance?" I ask.

"On its way," she says. "They might have to treat Enzo Torres too. He practically collapsed when he heard me tell Mrs. Hinkle what happened to Sierra. I didn't mention his brother."

"Xavier's dead," I say. "Murdered."

"*Murdered?*" She looks shocked for a second, but then she presses her face back against the window eagerly. "How?"

"I don't know," I say. "Dean Whitaker went to call the sheriff."

"That means they'll be back soon," Emi says. "We don't have much time."

"Time for what?"

Emi walks over and cracks open the door.

"Emi, no!" I grab her arm. "We have to preserve the crime scene."

She lets out an exasperated huff. "Are you serious right now, Dulce? We're detectives! And there's a dead body inside."

"We're fake detectives," I say. "For fake murders. Investigated out of packets. This is not the same thing."

"Do you think Wimsey would stand ten feet from a murder scene and not look?"

"It's a felony!"

"Eh, I bet it's just a misdemeanor." Before I can stop her, Emi yanks her arm out of my grasp and hops inside the greenhouse.

Acid guilt floods my stomach. Dean Whitaker left me to protect the scene, and now Emi is trampling all over it. If he comes back out and sees her inside . . . I don't want to think about what will happen, but the word *expulsion* will probably be involved.

"You need to see this, Dulce," Emi calls a minute later, and to my surprise, her voice is quivering.

"Get *out* of there," I hiss, refusing to turn around so I'm not tempted to go inside.

"I know you're dying to come in here and do that fact-collecting thing," Emi says.

A little tug of want pulls behind my belly button. Of course I'd like to be in there with her. But it's illegal, and I'm pretty sure a college admissions committee won't overlook an arrest.

"If you don't get in here, I'm going to put my hands all over Xavier, and then you'll have to get me off a murder charge," Emi yells.

Goddammit, Emi. I don't think she'll actually do it, but it's clear she's not coming out of the greenhouse on her own. Maybe if I step in for a minute, she'll be satisfied and come back out. If Dean Whitaker sees me inside, I'll tell him the truth: I went in to stop Emi from contaminating evidence.

Walking through the door feels like stepping into a puff of earthy cologne, and I sneeze twice as I take in the scene.

The greenhouse is big and untidy. Potted plants line the walls like green guards, while the center is devoted to a nursery of flowers set in dozens of shallow square containers. At the back are larger plants, including a lemon tree that looks like it might burst through the glass roof. In front of the tree, a long table drips with pothos vines so overgrown they're creeping along the ground like tentacles.

Xavier's body is lying in the same place I'd seen through the door—a few feet from the entrance, facedown. There's a tiny stain on his white shirt that's too brown to be blood. Dirt, maybe? Otherwise, there's no other indication of why he's not moving or breathing.

"Why does it smell like grass?" I ask.

"Someone dug up the tobacco plants," Emi says, her face as clammy as Dean Whitaker's. She's standing at the back of the greenhouse, next to the long table, far away from Xavier's body.

"Why would a murderer do that?"

Emi shakes her head. "No idea."

A rush of wings above my head makes me look up in time to see a cardinal fly through a missing glass pane in the slanted roof. Beyond the missing pane is the window where I stood watching Enzo in the greenhouse during our team meeting. There's no one moving in the band room now, or in any of the other rooms I can see through the roof.

"That pane wasn't missing last Thursday," I say.

"Maybe a bird slammed into it," Emi says. "Or hail from the storm this morning."

I eye the dirt below the missing panel. "There's no glass. It's like someone removed it whole."

"The gardener probably cleaned it up." Emi's eyes go everywhere but Xavier, as if she's trying to pretend he's not there.

I steal another look at him, trying to make myself feel disgust, but all I can manage is curiosity. I'm beginning to understand why Wimsey was never upset when he saw a dead body in the books. Xavier feels more like a set of clues than a life that's missing. The boy who was my chemistry partner has gone, leaving behind a doppelgänger whose entire purpose for being is to help uncover who killed him. It makes me uncomfortable that I'm freaking out less than Emi, who always acts so above it all, but then again, no one ever solved a murder by fainting.

"I wonder why Dean Whitaker thinks someone killed him," I say, looking at the small whiskey-colored stain on his back again. "There's no blood."

"Because of this." Emi's fingers shake as she points at something I can't see because it's blocked by the back table. There's not much use avoiding the other shoeprints on the ground since there are so many, all crisscrossed over each other, but I do my best to walk around the cleanest marks and look at where she's pointing.

On the dirt floor is a wooden knitting needle. I bend down to get a closer look and jerk back when I see something sharp sticking out of the tapered tip.

"It's a syringe," I say. "Just like the murder weapon in the game." I look back at the pulled plants. "Guess we know why the tobacco was taken."

Emi stares at me. "You think someone injected Xavier with *nicotine*?"

Something small and black catches my eye among the tangled pothos vines. I crawl under the table and roll it out with my knuckle.

"Is this yours?" I ask, pointing to a Magic 8 Ball key chain that looks identical to Emi's.

Emi snatches her teddy bear backpack off her shoulder. "No," she says, holding out her key chain. "Mine's here."

"Who else would have one?"

To my surprise, Emi's lower lip trembles.

"Emi?"

"I gave one to—"

The distant sound of voices interrupts her answer, and all at once my mind starts screaming the word *felony* at me. Emi grabs my arm, pulling me out of my squat, and drags me toward the greenhouse door, making a wide berth to avoid Xavier's body. I shut the door behind us right as Dean Whitaker and Sheriff Calhoun appear from around a bend in the path, but it bumps off its hinge and hangs there, slightly ajar. I hope the dean thinks he forgot to close it all the way.

Dean Whitaker shoots me a confused frown when he sees Emi, but he doesn't say anything, probably because he doesn't want the sheriff to know one of us shouldn't be standing there. I can't believe I let myself get carried away inside when they could have come back at any minute.

"I'll need to interview your students and your staff. Someone might have seen something—" The sheriff's voice trails off when he notices me. His murky-gray eyes register recognition, which isn't surprising since I half lived at his house until Mayor Fox kicked him out. He liked me before Sierra and I started Death & Fox. Then he told us little girls shouldn't stick their noses where they didn't belong.

"Dulce Castillo," he drawls, looking at me like I'm a fly in his soup. "We keep meeting near dead bodies."

A stunned gasp takes my breath away.

Emi squeals as Dean Whitaker grabs the sheriff by the scruff of his uniform and pulls him backward. "If you say something like that to one of my students again," he says, while the sheriff struggles against his strong arm, "you will no longer be able to breathe through your nose. Do you understand me?"

Emi throws her hand over her mouth, whether in shock or because she's still feeling sick from seeing Xavier, I'm not sure. It's the first time I've seen Dean Whitaker lose his temper, and I finally understand why Emi likes him so much. *Not just a teddy bear,* I think. *A teddy bear willing to use his claws.*

The sheriff untangles himself from Dean Whitaker and puts up his fists even though he's at least six inches shorter than the dean and would definitely be on the broken-nose side of a boxing match. "I should arrest you for that," he growls.

Dean Whitaker pushes by Sheriff Calhoun and swings the greenhouse door open all the way. Luckily, he's too angry to notice it was already cracked. "A child has been murdered," he says. "Get in there. Do your job. Leave my students alone."

The sheriff's eyes wage a war between arresting the dean and dealing with the dead body. He rips his hat off, revealing a balding pate, and then stalks inside.

Dean Whitaker groans once the sheriff disappears behind the door. "Not my best role-model moment," he says, shaking his blue curls. "Poor Xavier. He'd be better off with the Miss Marples investigating his death than that idiot. Though I can't imagine there's much question about who—" He looks strained again. "You two should join the others in the lunchroom and wait for your parents to pick you up."

Rage swells behind my eyes as Emi and I walk slowly back to the house like the weight of what we've seen is too heavy for our legs. Not only did someone kill Xavier, they used the game to pull off their crime. They turned something special into a farce as black as bile. But why go through the trouble of imitating the game? There had to be easier ways to murder someone.

One thing I know for sure. The game will be canceled. I can picture the headlines now: "Copycat Killer on the Loose at Murder High." No doubt the sheriff will scream to anyone who will listen that the Fox Family Trust is funding a school where children die.

"Who did you give the Magic 8 Ball to?" I ask.

Emi hesitates, which is strange, because she never tries to hide anything. "Rose," she finally says. "Last Friday."

I feel a twinge of jealousy. Emi's never given me a Magic 8 Ball, and we've known each other for two years. "That's going to look bad for her," I say, not entirely unhappy that Rose might not be the saint she seems.

"Yeah, well, I made it look better." Emi pulls Rose's key chain out of her pocket.

My mouth drops open so fast it hurts my jaw. "You *stole* evidence?" I say. "How could you?"

"It's not evidence," Emi scoffs. "She must have dropped it in there sometime this week. Rose would never hurt anyone."

"You barely know her! Not to mention you committed the worst detective crime."

"The worst crime a detective can commit is *being* the murderer," Emi says reasonably. "Which I'm not. Besides, I already know who killed Xavier, and it wasn't Rose."

My thoughts sharpen. Had I missed a clue? "What do you mean you *know*?"

"Didn't you see the initials on the knitting needle?" she asks.

"I didn't look at it closely," I admit. Maybe I'm not as good at collecting facts as I thought.

"S. F.," Emi says. "It's super obvious: Sierra Fox murdered her boyfriend."

8

EAST BEACH
Two Years Ago

THE BOY CALLED PEPPER LEANED SHIRTLESS AGAINST THE seawall in a way that made me sure he was trying to look sexy, so I pretended to stare at him even though I found him about as attractive as a telephone pole.

His chest was impossibly skinny, almost concave, and covered in misshapen freckles. Every few minutes, in between smirks I thought were meant to be smolders, he took another swig of something that was tucked inside a brown paper bag and smelled like peaches.

"I haven't seen you two around Cape Cherry High," he said. "Are you freshmen?"

"Um, no." My eyes flashed over to the boathouse where Sierra was making out with Pepper's friend. "We go somewhere else."

"Cool," he said, not bothering to ask where.

Sierra and I had known that solving "The Case of the Instagram Idiots" might involve kissing our suspects, but from what I could see from my position on the beach, Sierra's lips were showing a level of commitment our two-hundred-dollar fee didn't justify.

Death & Fox Investigations had spent the past few months rescuing lost pets, reuniting women with their engagement rings, and even tracking down a bicycle that had been stolen by a creepy party clown, but this was a case that involved doing something illegal, which is why I'd lied to my mom about where we were going.

"Tiffany's Ice Cream Shoppe?" she'd asked.

"There's a new flavor," I'd said. "Coconut marshmallow."

"It's a little late to be walking on Main Street by yourselves."

"Please, Mom. We're thirteen."

She'd smiled then, as if she remembered what it was like to be a teenager. "All right, *conejita*. If you promise to be home by ten, you can go."

Pepper burped, long and loud, before laughing. "This shit is nasty," he said, shaking the bottle. "But it gets the job done." He held the bag out to me. "You should have some."

I didn't want to drink, but I knew if I didn't, I'd never get close enough to Pepper to steal his phone.

The lukewarm liquor slipped down my throat with a metallic sting. *Disgusting.* I handed back the bottle and swallowed over and over again to get the syrupy thickness out of my mouth.

Something strange started happening in my throat. For a second, I thought I was going to be sick. Then, to my horror, I burped.

Pepper burst out laughing, making heat race across my cheeks.

When Sierra had first explained the plan to flirt with the boys, I told her I thought my first kiss would be special. She said it was best to get the first one out of the way with a boy you didn't care about; that way, when you met a boy you liked, you'd have practice.

"See, what did I tell you?" Pepper said, still laughing. "It's like burp juice."

I giggled, trying to imitate the high school girls I'd seen on TV. "It's so gross," I said, but I didn't hate the tingle spreading through my arms.

A loud sound in the distance, like a transistor exploding, made me jump. Pepper shifted closer and offered up the bottle again. I took a sip, faster this time, trying to pour it straight down my throat so it didn't touch my tongue.

After another ten minutes of Pepper's brain-dead conversation, Sierra came around the corner of the boathouse, dragging Pepper's friend, Dylan, by the hand. He was taller and cuter than Pepper, and Sierra had made a beeline for him the second we arrived. Dylan didn't take his eyes off Sierra's chest as they ran through the sand.

She stumbled against the seawall, either drunk or pretending to be. "You okay?" she whispered, leaning close. It was hard to hear her over the sound of sirens in the distance. "I don't have his phone yet, but we can leave if you're too skeeved out."

The Cape Cherry High sophomore who'd hired us was being harassed online. She could tell the commenters went to her school, but she couldn't figure out who they were because they were using burner accounts. Sierra had agreed to take the case. "It's a chance to test ourselves before we start playing the game together in a few months," she'd said.

She'd DMed the accounts and within a couple hours had figured out they were run by two boys from Cape Cherry High, who she convinced to meet us at the beach. The plan was to steal their phones and find some dirt that would stop them from harassing the sophomore. Pepper and Dylan, not exactly criminal masterminds, had never questioned why a beautiful girl had randomly contacted them online; Sierra said that, like most boys, they thought they deserved girls better looking than themselves.

I smiled at Sierra and told her the truth. "I'm fine."

"Good, because Dylan and I are going to the dunes," Sierra said more loudly, pointing at the rolling mounds covered in dry sticks of beach grass a little ways up the shore. She smacked my bottom before running off. "Don't do anything I wouldn't do!" She cackled while Dylan laughed beside her. I couldn't tell if it was part of the act or if she was actually having a good time; she'd been getting more daring, and some days it felt like she was moving forward while I was standing still.

Once her curls had disappeared into the sandy dunes, Pepper moved a little nearer. "Do you want to make out?" he asked.

There it was. No romantic build up. No pretending he was interested in what I was saying. A simple acknowledgment of why we were both spending a hot night with strangers at the beach. Except he didn't know I'd already clocked the phone in the right pocket of his cargo shorts.

"Yes." I tried to sound casual, like I did this all the time, but I gasped when he wrapped his arm around my waist and drew me closer. I'd been practicing kissing on the back of my hand like Sierra had shown me in fifth grade, because even though the kiss was fake, I still wanted it to be good. *Don't forget to breathe,* Sierra had warned me. *Or you'll get dizzy.*

Except I couldn't seem to do anything but breathe as his face closed in on mine. One minute I was my own person, and the next I was connected to Pepper, sharing his air.

After all the fan fiction I'd written about Lord Wimsey and Harriet Vane making out in morgues, my first kiss was *terrible*.

Pepper knocked his lips so hard into mine they impaled my skin on my teeth. I drew back a little, but he pushed even more, like he thought pressure and passion were the same thing. His lips parted, and he stuck a tongue that felt like sandpaper into my mouth. It darted around like a mouse trying to escape an owl.

All at once, I understood that Sierra was wrong. Kissing boys wasn't fun. It hurt and tasted like rotten peaches. I wanted it to be over as fast as possible, so I leaned into him, making little sounds I hoped would distract him from noticing that my fingers were dipping into his pocket. Once I had his phone, I slid it into the back of my jeans before covering it with my tank top.

I pulled out of the kiss quickly, shoving my hand against his chest so he'd get the message. He looked surprised when he broke away, as if he'd been enjoying himself.

Before I could make an excuse to leave the beach, Sierra and Dylan came sprinting from between the dunes. Sierra skidded to a stop in front of me, sand flying everywhere. "Cops," she said, pointing to the road, where the reflection of red-and-blue lights flashed in the sky. "We have to go."

Pepper reacted faster than I did. He flung the brown paper bag into the water and took off behind Dylan without a backward glance.

"Did you get it?" Sierra asked once they were gone, her voice high and anxious as she held out Dylan's phone like it was a bomb.

"Yes," I said, jerking Pepper's phone out of my jeans. "What do we do?"

"Throw them in the ocean." Sierra flung Dylan's phone into the dark water. "We can't get caught."

I hated that we weren't going to give the sophomore the dirt she wanted, especially since Pepper struck me as the kind of guy whose phone code was 1234, but we'd at least gotten their names and knew what they looked like. That was something.

I reached my arm back and threw Pepper's phone as hard as I could. It landed with a soft *thwap* in the sand, a foot short of the water.

"You've *got* to be kidding me," Sierra growled. "No one can be this uncoordinated." She collected the phone, now a tiny tombstone sticking out of the sand, and launched it like a javelin. Far in the distance, the frothy waves swallowed it in a single gulp. Sierra grabbed my hand and pulled me toward the boathouse. "There's a path this way," she said. "We have to get to Tiffany's. Try not to fall on your face."

I was gasping for air by the time we hit Main Street, and clutching a stitch in my side. Sierra was barely winded, but she looked scared, like this was too much adventure even for her. Two hours ago, being thirteen had felt like being thirty; now it felt like being ten.

"We're fine," she said, putting on her older-sister voice. "Only a few more blocks and no one ever has to know."

The dancing-ice-cream-cone stickers on the windows at Tiffany's had never felt more like home. But just as we were about to step inside, the bright lights of Sheriff Calhoun's vehicle flashed onto the sidewalk.

"We've been here the whole time," Sierra said like she was

reciting a pledge. "We stick to that story no matter what." Her blue eyes looked into mine, wide and insistent. "Promise?"

"Promise," I said.

Sheriff Calhoun got out of the car, his blond mustache drooping in the humidity. "I've been looking everywhere for you two." He opened the back door. "Get in the car."

Sierra stepped forward. "What's wrong, Bill?"

I'd forgotten that she'd started calling her stepdad by his first name to piss him off. He'd been in the middle of divorcing her mom for almost a year because he was trying to break the prenup that protected the Fox family fortune.

Sheriff Calhoun scowled and grabbed me by the arm, like I was the one questioning him. "In the car," he repeated, shoving me inside. *"Now."*

As we drove away, Sierra spoke up from the back. "You can't arrest us," she said. "We have rights."

Sheriff Calhoun frowned in the rearview mirror. "Arrest? What are you talking about? I'm taking Dulce to the hospital."

I froze, the adrenaline from stealing Pepper's phone turning to icy fear. "W-why?" I asked, barely able to get the word out. "What happened?"

"Your mom's been in a car accident," he said. "Your dad told me she was on her way to Tiffany's. He's already waiting at the ER."

"Is she okay?" I asked, barely registering Sierra's hand, which was holding mine tight. "She's going to be fine, right?"

There was a pause, heavy and horrible. I would have accepted any answer from Sheriff Calhoun. Even a lie.

What I got was silence, and my quaking mind filled it:

My fault, my fault, my fault.

9

"DO YOU WANT TO GO TO MALDONADO'S?" MY DAD ASKS from my bedroom doorway. "It's Saturday, but there's no law saying we can't go twice this week."

He's been hovering over me like a mother hen, as if whoever murdered Xavier might sneak through my window next. He cried when I told him Sierra found Xavier's body ("*Pobrecita.* She'll never forget that."), then spent hours watching Ricardo Best on Channel Z News and yelling updates down the hall. Dean Whitaker closed the school "pending the sheriff's investigation," and less than twelve hours later, the Fox Family Trust announced that the game had been canceled, crushing all my hopes.

"I'd rather stay in," I say, petting Penny, who, in a rare exhibition of sweetness, has agreed to lie with me as I sulk. I know my dad is just trying to cheer me up, but nothing is going to make me feel better about losing the opportunity to take the trip to England my mom never will. Certainly not an eel-and-wheatgrass pizza.

"That boy might be working tonight," my dad says. "What's his name—Bane?"

"Zane," I say, not sure why he thinks I'd care. Now that the game is over, Zane and I will have no reason to hang out unless he starts dating Emi. The next time I see him will probably be in detention, which has been rescheduled, due to murder.

My ancient flip phone rings, and I make the barest effort to glance at the caller ID. It's Emi. I roll over and ignore the call. If I pick up, she'll try to make me feel better, too, and I just want to wallow in my disappointment.

Ding.

I click the ringer down so I can't hear her texting. But the screen keeps lighting up. Why isn't she taking the hint?

My dad leaves my room when the landline rings down the hall. "Hello?" I hear him say. "Sure, hold on."

He appears at my door again. "It's Emi. She promises you'll want to take a break from Sad Land and hear her news."

"What the hell," I mutter. Emi's never gone this far to get me to talk to her before. Then again, I don't make a habit of ignoring her calls.

"Penny and I are busy, Emi," I say when my dad hands me the phone. "I promised I'd pet her five hundred times, and I'm only at two hundred thirty-three."

"Okay, weirdo." Emi's voice is excited, almost fevered. "You'll never believe what's happened."

"Dean Whitaker broke off his engagement with Mayor Fox to marry your mom."

"Better than that. Are you ready?"

"Uh-huh." *Two hundred thirty-four. Two hundred thirty-five.*

"Sierra has been arrested."

I pop up on my knees so fast that Penny yowls and jumps off my bed. "You're joking."

"It's all over socials. She's going to be released pending

charges, or maybe she has to post bail? I've been reading the feeds of the students in the legal capsule, but I don't understand them. Sheriff Calhoun gave a press conference this afternoon. You didn't see it?"

"No." I fall back onto my pillows. I don't tell Emi that I haven't left my bed all day.

Half of Death & Fox Investigations, who had pinkie sworn to always serve justice and truth, arrested for murder. There's no doubt Sierra has changed for the worse since we were best friends. And yet . . .

"I can't believe it," I say.

"I know, right?" Emi gasps, like we're gossiping about a celebrity scandal. "I thought it would take the sheriff forever to put the pieces together."

"No. I mean I *can't* believe it. Sierra is a hardcore bitchwitch, but she would never murder someone." I pause, thinking of the cruel glint in her eye when she made fun of my earrings. "At least not while her mom is running for reelection."

"Sorry, babe," Emi says. "I know she used to be your bestie or whatever, but we all saw her go out the back door after Xavier, and her fingerprints were all over the knitting needle. Plus, Rose told me she was furious when Xavier broke up with her." Emi's voice gets brighter. "I can't believe I'm saying this, but I'm actually looking forward to Xavier's funeral tomorrow."

The only funeral I've ever been to is my mom's, across town at St. Monica's Catholic Church. The day before the service, Sheriff Calhoun went on Channel Z News to tearfully tell everyone that the girls' high school basketball team had been on Main Street the night my mom died. He painted a dramatic picture of how, if Deputy Armstrong hadn't crashed into her, my mom might have drunkenly mown down our town's state champions. It didn't matter that the evidence showed she'd been driving under the speed limit and without any erratic movements; Cape Cherry turned on us, and instead of the huge outpouring of support we'd expected, only a few of her closest friends came to toss roses on her grave.

My dad tried to pretend that Mayor Fox had made Sierra stay home from the funeral, but I knew better. If she'd wanted to be there, she would have jumped out of her bedroom window and fought off her family's guard dogs rather than miss it.

Unlike my mom, Xavier has an army of mourners in attendance. Emi drove Zane and Rose to the cemetery with us, but even Zane isn't tall enough to see the casket behind the rings of people in black. Thirty yards away, Enzo is leaning against an oak tree, his eyes hidden under a black cap so that I can't tell whether he's been crying. His refusal to stand with his moms by the open grave makes me think his eyes are dry. It's no secret he and his brother didn't get along, but he'd have to hate him a lot to ignore their parents at his funeral.

There's a light rain falling, which my mom would have appreciated. *The sky weeps for the dead,* she used to say whenever we'd pass by a cemetery on a wet day. I was secretly happy when it poured at her funeral; it made me feel like the sky knew she hadn't done anything wrong.

"I think everyone in Cape Cherry is here," Emi says.

I point to a row of cameras set up along the road winding through the cemetery. "Including Channel Z News."

"Bet the story made it all the way to Richmond," Zane says.

"Try national news." Emi snorts. "Hot private-school boy

gets poisoned by his even hotter girlfriend? I'm surprised Ricardo Best didn't start humping his desk."

The priest's voice lifts above the crowd. "We commend this young man's soul to God in the presence of his friends and family..."

Out of nowhere, the crowd begins to shift and mutter like a horde of angry bees.

"Oh my god, look." Rose points to the gravel road.

One of the cameramen from Channel Z News swivels his gear so fast it drops off his shoulder. He grabs the camera from the ground just in time to catch Sierra Fox cross the grass on her way to Xavier's grave. She holds her head high, as if she has nothing to be ashamed of, her curls burning like fire through the gray-and-black wetness of everything else. Anyone might think she didn't care about Xavier at all.

Her appearance has caused such outrage that even the priest has stopped talking to stare. *Karma,* I think, watching everyone's eyes judge her like she's covered in Xavier's blood. Thanks to her family, it took months for people in Cape Cherry to stop crossing roads to avoid me and my dad. Some still do.

"Sunglasses in the rain?" Emi scoffs, watching Sierra walk toward us. "Who does she think she is?"

I feel an unwanted sting of sympathy. Sierra hates oversized sunglasses. Thinks they make people look like bugs. There's only one reason she'd be wearing a pair this big and dark: She's been crying and doesn't want anyone to know.

Just before she reaches Xavier's grave, Sierra veers toward a row of mausoleums on the other side of the walking path. When the priest realizes she doesn't plan to stage a scene, he starts speaking again. For the rest of the funeral, Sierra leans against a stone statue of an angel, a mirror image of Enzo. I look over to see what he thinks of her arrival, but he's as still as the oak tree; for all I can tell, he's asleep.

After the eulogy is over, we join the line to pay our respects to Xavier's family. Before we're halfway through, someone tugs on my velvet jacket, and I'm shocked to see Sierra's half-gloved hand on my arm.

"I need to talk to you and Emi," she says.

Up close, her face is the color of sour milk, and her jaw is clenched tight, like it's all that's holding her together. I feel sorry for her in the same way I would if I saw a shark floundering on the shore. Even ex-best friends who lie about how your mom died don't deserve to be arrested for murders they didn't commit. Still, that's her problem, not mine.

"We're in line," I say, shaking off her hand.

For a second, I think she's going to leave me alone, but then she says, "Dulce, please. I need your help."

The *please* stops me. If someone told me Sierra hadn't used the word since eighth grade, I'd believe them. I glance at the line of mourners, which is creeping forward at a snail's pace. Xavier's moms don't know me, so it's not like they'll miss my condolences.

"Let's hear her out," Emi says, grabbing my hand and pulling me out of line. "I want my mom to see me on the news talking to the murderer." She turns to Rose and Zane. "You coming?"

"I don't need them," Sierra says, some of her old snappishness coming back. "Just you and Dulce."

"It's all of us or none of us." I realize too late I've agreed to come with her.

"Fine." Sierra heads toward the mausoleum with long strides, forcing me to walk at double speed to keep up.

I stop when we get to the mausoleum door. "Are we allowed to go inside?" I ask.

"It's the only way we won't be heard." Sierra points to the road. "Or have our lips read by those vultures with cameras."

The four of us look at each other before Emi shrugs. "I've never been in one of these. Maybe there will be bones. Or vampires."

"You watch too much TV," Zane says.

The mausoleum is actually a lot less creepy than I would have imagined from the outside. It's a long, clean room made of marble. Bronze crypt plates line the walls, and it smells like the refrigerated flowers relatives have stuck in the plastic holders.

"What do you want, Sierra?" I say, taking control of the conversation so she knows I'm not scared of her.

"The cops think I killed Xavi." Sierra's voice echoes off the marble as if the dead bodies are whispering.

"No shit, Sherlock." Emi laughs. "We saw the press conference. Why aren't you in jail?"

Sierra paces. "They didn't have enough evidence to hold me. But Bill—I mean Sheriff Calhoun—told my mom's lawyer that once he puts together a case, he's going to get the DA to charge me as an adult even though I'm sixteen."

"Bummer," Emi says.

"The *bummer*," Sierra spits, "is that my mom thinks I'm innocent. She says Bill is railroading me to manipulate the election. Plans to file a complaint."

The four of us exchange confused looks.

"Your problem is that your mom *doesn't* think you killed your boyfriend?" Emi asks. "Be glad you don't have my mom; she'd already be sizing me for prison clothes."

Sierra huffs with exasperation, like she's talking to children. "The evidence against me is really bad, but my mom's staff is acting like it's petty sabotage against her campaign," she says. "The first time they'll take the accusations seriously is when the jury says 'guilty.'" She pulls a rose petal off a nearby flower and smashes it between her fingers. "Besides, I know none of you care, but I loved Xavi, and I want whoever did this to go to prison forever."

"That's a sad story and everything," I say, "but what do you want from us?"

Sierra stares at me like I'm an idiot. "I want you to find out who murdered my boyfriend. I want you to prove I'm innocent."

Emi laughs so loudly I'm sure she can be heard by the reporters outside. Maybe even by astronauts in space. "Sorry," she says when she sees Sierra's glare. "It's just, the *absolute brass nuts* of asking Dulce to help clear your name after the way you've treated her." She leans against my shoulder. "I get why you two were friends. She's a chaos butterfly like me. Except evil."

A shiver of fury trails down my spine. I don't find Sierra's request to investigate Xavier's death funny at all. But before I can say there's no chance in hell I'll help her, Zane chimes in.

"What makes you think Dulce and Emi can solve a murder?" he asks. "No offense, but they're not real detectives. None of us are."

"Hey," Emi says defensively.

"Sorry." He flashes us an apologetic smile. "But it's not the same as playing the game. No one's going to hand you a packet of witness statements or pictures of the crime scene."

Emi and I exchange a brief glance. He doesn't know we snuck into the greenhouse to see Xavier's body.

"Besides," Zane continues, looking hard at Sierra, "if you really didn't do it, the sheriff won't be able to find any evidence, so what's the problem?"

"Aren't you listening?" Sierra snaps. "There's plenty of evidence. Xavi broke up with me, he was killed with my knitting needle, and the cops confiscated my phone and read my text telling Xavi I was on my way to the greenhouse, so they think I was the last person to see him alive." She crushes another petal. "Obviously, someone got there before me. But Bill won't bother looking for the actual killer. He'd rather ruin my life because he thinks my *bad attitude* is what broke up his marriage. And he hates my mom for leaving him, so putting her daughter in prison will be the icing on his revenge cake."

"But your family is rich," Rose says, and I'm surprised by the venom in her voice, not only because she usually talks like her tongue is laced with flowers, but because she was sobbing when Sierra passed out in the cafeteria. "Why don't you hire a PI?"

"I tried," Sierra admits. "He said he couldn't accept a job from someone underage. And my mom won't even consider the idea. A PI dug up a bunch of dirt on her during her first election. Conned my grandma into giving him my mom's old diaries. So she thinks they're all snakes."

"But why us?" Emi asks. "I'm not saying we couldn't do it"— she gives Zane a pointed look—"but you have the Miss Marples."

Sierra doesn't answer.

"You did ask them," Rose says slowly, her voice full of unspoken words about their team. "And they said no."

"Turns out my teammates are assholes." Sierra flicks the petals off a wilting iris. "No offense, Daisy."

"It's Rose."

Emi laughs again.

"Okay, fine," Sierra huffs. "I'm a bitch who deserves to find out the entire school thinks I killed Xavi. Can we *please* move on?" She turns to me, and for an instant, it feels like we're thirteen again, discussing a case for Death & Fox. "You're more brilliant than any PI," she says. "No one else has ever gotten second place in the game with only two players. You've done it twice." She pulls off her sunglasses so I can see her eyes. As I suspected, they're red and puffy. "If you want to hear me say the words, I will," she continues more softly. "You're better at this than me. You always were. I can't solve Xavi's murder without you."

In the before times, that would have meant the world. Now it sounds like manipulation.

When she sees that I'm unconvinced, she lets out a long sigh. "I'll pay you, then. What will it take?"

"Thirty thousand dollars," Emi says, like she's been waiting for the offer. "Same as the game. Enough for me and Dulce to take a blowout trip to England this summer."

Sierra's eyebrows hitch upward, but it's not Emi's outrageously high number that's surprised her. "You're taking your mom's trip?" she asks.

She'd been invited, of course—my mom wouldn't have dreamed of separating us for two weeks—but that was almost three years and a whole friendship ago, so I can't believe she still remembers. "All the Wimsey spots," I say curtly. "Next May, on the anniversary of her death."

Sierra winces, as if my words are tiny needles. She looks like she might say something else, but she turns to Emi instead. "I don't have that much in my bank account," she says. "But I can ask the Fox Family Trust to front me the money."

"And if they don't agree?" Emi asks. "When you answer, remember we're talking about you *not going to prison*."

Sierra draws herself up until she's even with the highest crypt plate. In her black jumpsuit and gold arm bangles, she looks like the goddess Athena. "Then I'll pay it," she says gravely, like she's issuing a royal decree. "From my trust fund when I turn eighteen."

"We'll want that in writing."

"Stop!" I say, and I'm surprised how loud my words sound, booming across the marble. The others stare at me like I've screamed at a helpless old lady, but I don't care. "You can't seriously be considering this," I hiss, pulling Emi into a corner away from the others. "You told me you thought she was guilty!"

"I've reconsidered," Emi says. "In fact, I'm thirty thousand percent sure she's innocent."

"I won't work for her."

Sierra, who must have heard me, bites her bottom lip. "Look, Dulce," she says. "I know we've had our differences—"

"Differences?" I laugh bitterly, the acid that's been burning in my bones for years crawling up my throat. "You told everyone at school that my mom was driving drunk the night she died. That it was her fault Deputy Armstrong crashed into her. But it was *ours*. If we hadn't lied and kissed those losers at the beach, she'd be *alive* right now."

Emi, who was already gearing up for her next argument, clamps her mouth shut. I'd told her about Sierra lying, but I never mentioned Pepper and Dylan. I'm just glad I haven't completely lost it and spilled the worst part of that night, the thing no one knows but me.

Sierra starts shifting her bangles up and down her arm with

nervous fingers, like she can't figure out how to defuse the bomb of my anger. "The coroner's report found alcohol in her blood—"

"Stop lying!" My words ping around the mausoleum like church bells. "You know my mom never drank. Her dad was an alcoholic, and she thought it was poison. The sheriff *lied*, and you and your mom repeated the story and turned the town against us. And for what? Did he promise your mom the second house in Charleston? Agree to stop challenging the prenup? What could have been so important that you dropped me like I was dirty?" The yelling has left me out of breath.

"The report—" Sierra says hollowly before trailing off and staring at the far wall like her vision has gone blurry. It's clear she's not going to admit what she's done, but at least she has to share the guilt I've been carrying. And now there's only three words I want her to hear before I never talk to her again.

"Fuck you, Sierra."

10

CAPE CHERRY MIDDLE SCHOOL
Two Years Ago

SCHOOL WAS THE LAST PLACE I WANTED TO GO AFTER MY mom died, but the counselor told my dad that I should return to my normal schedule as soon as possible, which was how I found myself, one week after the funeral, waiting for Sierra next to my locker.

I'd texted her nonstop for days after the night at the ER, but I hadn't received a single reply. Worse, her texts had gone from blue to green, like she'd blocked me. At first, I thought her mom had found out we'd lied and taken Sierra's phone as punishment, but when she missed the funeral, I realized something was very, very wrong. And I intended to find out what.

When Sierra finally came through the double front doors, she was with two girls she usually made fun of for being airheads. But now she was walking close to them, bouncing her shoulders against theirs like they were friends. I could have sworn she stiffened when she saw me, but it might have been my imagination, because she passed me without glancing over.

"Sierra, wait!" I called. "I need to talk to you."

When she turned around, her blue eyes were as cold as mountain ice. "I thought you'd get the message when I didn't answer your texts," she said. One of the girls next to her muffled a giggle. "But let me spell it out for you: Don't. Text. Me. Again."

The words sounded like gibberish. Don't text her? We'd been best friends since day care. Mayor Fox and my mom used to take us to the park together and watch us play Barbies in the sandbox while they complained about work.

"I know you and your dad are ashamed of what your mom did," Sierra continued. "But it isn't fair to blame my stepdad."

It felt like the air had been punched out of my lungs. "What my mom did—what are you talking about?"

"Everyone knows, Dulce," Sierra said, and the other students in the hallway murmured their agreement, as if the whole school had spent all week gossiping about what had happened and sided against me. "Deputy Armstrong was chasing another car, and your mom was so drunk she weaved into his lane. I don't know why you can't accept the truth."

Sierra winced on the word *truth*. It was a tiny movement in her shoulders, but I was sure I'd seen it.

"Can we talk alone?" I asked, desperate to make whatever was happening stop. "Just for a minute."

"I'm sorry about your mom," she said, ignoring my request. "But until you and your dad admit what she did, we're done."

"Done?" The word felt like dental putty in my mouth, thick and awkward. "You can't be— I mean, this can't be—" The tears I'd been too shocked to feel had started falling down my cheeks. "Sierra, what's *happening*?"

Another wince. This one was bigger, almost a shudder. But Sierra controlled it. "Family comes first, Dulce," she said. "You should know that."

Then she spun around and walked off with her new friends,

leaving me mortified, nauseated, and more than anything, confused. We'd always agreed that family came first. That's why we'd made sure we were family.

"Blood is thicker than water," she'd said when we took our first blood oath to never tell our parents about accidentally crashing Mayor Fox's car into the garage door. "And now we share blood."

"Will it stay in us forever?" I'd asked as she slit her finger and pressed her blood against mine.

"Definitely," she'd said. "We're part of each other always."

"Sisters," I'd said with a smile.

"Sisters."

And now she was draining her blood straight out of my body. Red trickled onto my shirt as I cried. It was only later, after someone found me on the hallway floor underneath my locker and took me to the nurse's station, that I discovered the blood wasn't imaginary; I'd sobbed so hard my nose had started bleeding.

I expected my dad to tell me to cheer up, that Sierra would get over it and apologize, but when he picked me up from the nurse's station, whimpering and covered in blood, he went pale and drove me home in silence. Later that night, he came into my room to tell me he'd talked to the principal and that I'd be doing school from home for the remaining three weeks of the year.

Months after, when I'd recovered a little from my twin shocks, I went to the beach, near where we'd met Pepper and Dylan, and lit a small bonfire. Then I took a kitchen knife and sliced straight into my palm, letting Sierra's blood pour out of me and into the orange flames.

11

"WHAT DO YOU MEAN YOU AGREED TO TAKE HER CASE?"

My dad's shift at work starts before the first bell, so except for the first and last days of the year, Emi takes me to school. She usually brings me a tea from her Starbucks run, but today, the first time J. Everett has been open since the funeral two weeks ago, she comes empty-handed because she's "been working night and day on Xavier's murder."

"It's thirty thousand dollars, Dulce," Emi says.

"Blood money." I pull my coat tighter across my chest. Emi likes to drive with the windows cracked, no matter how much I complain about the cold morning air. "From the girl whose family conspired with the sheriff to destroy any chance we had to sue him." I don't say *the girl who put me in therapy for months.*

"Have you thought about what will happen to Mayor Fox if Sierra goes down for murder?" Emi asks.

I squirm in my seat. I hadn't, but it's not hard to guess.

"She'll lose the election," Emi says. "No one will vote for a woman who raised a killer. And if she loses, who wins?"

"The sheriff's cousin," I mumble.

"The man running on the platform 'Keep Cape Cherry Pure,'"

Emi says. "The man who swears he'll have Dean Whitaker and the board of the Fox Family Trust arrested for contributing to the delinquency of minors or some shit. Say goodbye to reading what we want. Say goodbye to our internships. Say goodbye to the game."

"*Fiat justitia ruat caelum*," I say. Let justice be done though the heavens fall. James Everett's motto. "Maybe Mayor Fox going down for Sierra's crimes is fair after what she did."

"You are seriously misapplying that quote." Emi scowls. "And you said you thought Sierra was innocent."

"Innocent of murder, maybe," I say. "But not of what she did to me."

When we pull into a grassy parking space in front of the Everett house, Emi grabs her Magic 8 Ball from her teddy bear bag. "Is Dulce being completely pigheaded?" she asks.

The triangle rolls around until it stops on three words: **WITHOUT A DOUBT.**

Emi shoves the ball in my face. "The universe wants you to help Sierra."

I don't have as many flashbacks to that day in middle school as I used to, but a hint of Sierra's mocking smirk passes in front of my eyes, making me shiver.

"Not even if Nemesis herself came down and asked me."

To my surprise, Sierra returns to school at the same time as the rest of us. I thought she might lie low at home or maybe even spend some of her family money on one of those health spas where they treat grief with massages and kale smoothies, but instead she attends classes like nothing happened. If my boyfriend died, I'd probably turn up in sweats with greasy hair, but over the next few weeks, Sierra shows up looking more put together than ever—even her cat eye is flicked with a steady hand.

The only thing different is that she's no longer surrounded by friends all the time. Some J. Everett students don't even bother to keep their voices down when they gossip about her.

"They won't have lipstick where you're going," a sophomore calls as Sierra, lips a perfect scarlet, passes by our lockers. Sierra doesn't turn around, but I know she hears the sophomore's friend add, "Maybe she can make some out of soap."

Unfortunately, Emi doesn't wear enough makeup to hide how poorly the case is going. She doesn't talk about it, but sometimes I spot her in the band room sitting across from Sierra with an exasperated expression on her face.

"Tell me again," I hear her say one afternoon as I pass the door. "Start from when you did the livestream."

All of this is why I'm not prepared for Emi's good mood when she picks me up the following day.

"Tea?" she asks, a happy smile on her face. "I asked them to put an extra cinnamon stick in it."

"Um, sure." I take the paper cup she's holding out to me.

Her emotional U-turn makes me want to hear what's gone right with the case, but I know if she tells me, I'll get so mad it will ruin the rest of my day, so I sip my tea quietly, like I don't care.

"My turn to pick the music," Emi says, scrolling through her iPhone. It's a joke she tells most mornings because my flip phone is too old and useless to stream.

"Nothing too loud," I say. "My dad stayed up half the night watching the news again, so I have a headache."

Emi grins. "You'll barely hear the instruments. I promise."

I prepare myself for a band I've never heard, because Emi believes listening to the same album more than once is a waste of time. What I'm not prepared for is Sierra's voice coming through the speakers.

"At eleven thirty, I was doing my makeup in Dean Whitaker's bathroom. He lets me use it since we're almost family. That's when I got a text from Xavi."

Emi's voice answers. *"What did it say?"*

"Emi, n-no!" I stutter, my blood suddenly boiling inside the cold car. "Turn it off."

"My car, my music," Emi says with an impish grin. "What are you going to do? Jump out the window?"

For a split second, I consider opening the door and rolling out, before I decide I'd probably be run over. I may hate Sierra, but I'm not going to die to avoid listening to her.

"I'm riding the bus tomorrow," I say. "And every day after that until Sierra is locked up in jail where she belongs."

Emi touches her iPhone. "Better play this at 1.5 times speed, then."

"Xavi's text said 'Need to talk. Meet me in the greenhouse after livestream. Important. Don't be late.'"

"Did you meet him in the greenhouse often?"

"Never. He knows I hate it in there. It's so damp and smelly."

I dig in my backpack and hold up the earbuds I bring to run during gym. "I'm putting these in. So you're listening to this by yourself."

Emi shrugs. "Whatever you say."

The earbuds muffle Sierra's voice, but Emi appears to have no intention of stopping the recording. A hot blaze of curiosity fills my belly. *Goddammit, Dulce,* I think as I slip the earbud closest to the window out of my ear. If I'm going to listen, I don't have to let Emi know.

Sierra's answering a question I didn't hear. *"We had a fight at his party. He thought I was cheating on him."*

"Were you?"

There's a long pause, and then she says, *"Yes."*

"Ooh, with who?"

"Let me finish!" Sierra's voice is snappish, like she's not happy with how delighted Emi sounds. *"I left the bathroom and went into the dean's office. He was dictating something to his secretary, and after he was done, I started the livestream. He talked about the election forever—you know how he is—and I knew Xavi might think I was blowing him off, so as soon as Dean Whitaker finished, I almost ran to the greenhouse. Got mud all over my heels."*

"Yes, that's the important thing. How dirty your shoes got."

Sierra keeps going like she wasn't interrupted. *"I went into the greenhouse, and"*—her voice catches; the next words are low and shaky—*"Xavi was lying facedown on the ground, dead. He was only a few feet from the door, like he'd been trying to get outside."*

"Is that when you screamed?"

"How did you know I screamed?"

"Dulce has good hearing."

"Oh, right. When we were younger, this boy in my neighborhood hired us to find his pet mouse. Dulce heard it scurrying in the attic even though we were a whole floor below."

"Hired?"

I choke out a gasp of surprise at the new voice. "Zane's helping you?" I ask, forgetting that I'm pretending not to listen.

Emi snorts like she knew I wouldn't be able to stop. "If you can call it helping," she says. "He's cute, but he's not the brightest bulb in the pack. He must test well, because otherwise I don't know how he got into J. Everett."

Sierra is still talking over the car speakers. *"Dulce and I used to have a detective agency. Death and Fox Investigations. That's why I wanted her to look into Xavi's murder. No one else can do that fact-collecting thing like her."*

My ears warm, and for a brief second, I imagine a world in which Death & Fox never imploded. Where Sierra, instead of lying about my mom, helped me find out what really happened the night she died.

"Sorry you got stuck with the second-best Wimsey. What happened after you found Xavier's body?"

Emi has learned well over the past two years. Figure out how, and you'll figure out who. I love Wimsey's methods because there are clear rules. No psychology. No motives. Just facts.

"I was stupid. I ran over to him and felt for a pulse. Then I . . . picked up the needle."

"You go to crime *school,"* Emi says, sounding flabbergasted. *"Not touching weapons is, like, the number one rule."*

"I panicked!" Sierra's voice makes the car vibrate. *"And I was shocked because it had my initials. But someone had messed with it."*

"Yeah, I saw—I mean, I heard it had a metal tip. Like a syringe."

"It wasn't just that. Someone had decorated the needle."

"Decorated?"

"Yeah. They'd attached pink yarn to the sides. Almost like feathers."

I take my second earbud out because I'm obviously not fooling anyone. "Did you see pink yarn on the needle?" I ask Emi.

"Nope," she says. "Someone must have taken it off."

"Why did it take you so long to come back to the cafeteria after you screamed?"

"I freaked out. I ran into the woods to get sick, but it felt like I was in a maze even though they were the same trees as always. By the time I found my way back to the path, I could barely stand. That's when I returned to the house—through the front door, because it was closest."

Sierra sighs, her breath rattling through the car like she's in the back seat. *"You know the rest."*

Anyone could have gone into the greenhouse during those twenty minutes to remove the pink yarn, including the killer. But if the purpose was to frame Sierra, why come back for it? And why not just take it when they killed Xavier?

Emi says her next words slowly, like she wants Sierra to think carefully. *"I know Xavier was popular, but is there anyone who would want to kill him?"*

"Of course there is. I know exactly who killed Xavi."

I gasp at the same time Emi gasps over the speakers.

"You—what? Who?"

"Enzo Torres."

The recording falls so silent I can hear each individual tick of the frog clock that hangs above Ms. Moss's desk.

"Enzo?" I take a sip of my tea, which has lost nearly all its heat. "That's who she's blaming?"

A fourth voice, calm and self-assured, speaks for the first time. At this point, I know it a lot better than I'd like.

"It wasn't Enzo."

"Rose is helping too?" I ask, though I should have suspected it. Recently, wherever Emi goes, Rose follows.

"I know he dresses like a school shooter, but he's harmless. And he loved Xavi, even if it didn't seem like it."

Xavi? Why is Rose, the girl whose key chain mysteriously ended up a foot from the murder weapon, calling Xavier by the nickname only his brother and closest friends use? Now that I think about it, she'd called him Xavi at the Poisoner's Festival too. The word *cheater* runs through my mind, but it's quickly replaced by an image of Rose clad in a dress striped like the lesbian flag, holding hands with Mirabel García at last year's Pride pep rally.

"Did you tell Rose that Enzo threatened to skin your cat?" I ask, but Emi waves my question away as her recorded self continues interrogating Sierra.

"What makes you think Enzo killed his brother?"

"He was the—" Sierra stops. *"He was the one I—"*

"Gross! You cheated on Xavier with his brother?*"*

"It's not like we slept together! It was just a thing for a couple months. My mom's election had been getting super intense, and Enzo was really nice to me all summer when Xavi was too busy interning at Channel Z and hanging out at North Beach. But then I ditched him, and he snapped. That's why he's framing me. Revenge."

At long last, Emi and I pull into J. Everett's parking lot. She stops her Explorer next to someone's truck and unplugs her iPhone.

"That was a mean trick," I say.

"Whatever." She grabs her teddy bear backpack. "You loved it. Your brain is probably whirling with theories right now."

"So what? You think you can bombard me with interrogations and get me to join the case?"

"Is it working?"

"Not a chance," I say. "Hearing Sierra's voice that loud makes me hate her even more."

Emi pauses her exit from the car. "Have you considered that *I* want to investigate this case with you?" she asks. "That I want us to get the chance to do our Wimsey thing, since the game has been canceled?"

I look at her carefully, and to my surprise, she's not grinning or smirking. She's serious.

"You have Zane and Rose," I mumble.

"They're not you."

It's a nice thing to say, but even an avalanche of compliments won't make me help Sierra. Short of a time machine, I can't imagine a single thing that will make me change my mind.

I expect Emi to play me another interrogation the next morning, but she drives in silence. "You've made your decision," she says. "I respect that."

Her words make me suspicious because Emi never respects anything that doesn't match what she wants. But for the next two days, she doesn't try to involve me in the case, and I begin to think she's given up. Part of me is relieved, but the other part feels like an addict deprived of her supply.

On Friday afternoon, Dean Whitaker lets me out of independent study early, so I head to gym class before everyone else, hoping some solo running will clear my head.

Coach Hu is standing at the head of the trail with a clipboard, waiting for a group of juniors to come out of the woods.

"Dulce Castillo, skipping class?" she says, eyebrows raised. "That's new."

"The dean released me." I pull an old iPod I bought on Craigslist out of my hoodie pocket. "He had to go to a fundraiser."

"Spends more time on the campaign trail than here," Coach

Hu jokes. She checks her watch. "If you start now, you might be able to do the loop twice."

I connect my earbuds to the iPod, which is loaded with all my mom's favorite songs because I find it peaceful to remember her under the canopies of the live oaks. Once I hit a steady stride, I press play and almost trip over my feet when Emi's voice fills my ears.

"Our biggest obstacle in solving Xavier's murder is that we don't have access to the sheriff's case file. We have no way of knowing what's in the autopsy report or the coroner's report or the witness statements. That is, if Stepdaddy Calhoun even bothered with witnesses. Did any of you get questioned?"

I press pause and scream "Emi, you're ridiculous!" into the sky. The campus is small enough that it's possible she can hear me somewhere. No doubt she's laughing her ass off.

I can stop listening. I'm not locked in a car this time, so I've got no excuse. Except one: I don't want to.

I press play again and cringe as Sierra's voice steps into my ear. *"My mom's lawyer told me not to talk to him."*

Zane answers next. *"No one asked me for an interview."*

I frown as I pass Captain Hawthorne, the oldest tree in the woods. Why isn't Rose speaking up? Is she not with them?

I get my answer immediately.

"I don't think we should talk about this, Emi."

Emi sounds confused. *"Why not?"*

"I read my tarot cards last night, and they show danger if you keep investigating Xavi's murder."

Ugh. Of course Rose thinks tarot is real. She and my dad would get along. He could give her some of the sage he burns in our house to get rid of negative energy.

"Tarot cards?" Sierra's voice is full of the same disbelief in my head. *"You want my life to hang in the balance of cards with pretty pictures on them?"*

"You not believing something doesn't make it not true. But I've given you my warning. There's nothing else I can do."

"Actually, there is. You can tell us where you were when Xavi was killed, because I know it wasn't in the cafeteria."

"Rose isn't a suspect." Emi's tone is sharp, and I roll my eyes. If she's going to let her friends off the hook, she's never going to solve the case.

Sierra doesn't have any patience for Emi's favoritism either. *"The only people not in the cafeteria when Xavi died were me, Enzo, Rose, Zane, and Ms. Moss. Well, and some of the staff, but you already confirmed their alibis. And it's not like a stranger could have just strolled onto campus without being seen. Even if they did, how would they have known about the game?"*

"Someone could have leaked the packet," Zane suggests.

"That's an automatic disqualification if you get caught. Besides, I don't think we need to reach for a boogeyman when we have people without alibis right in front of us."

"Ms. Moss and I were together in the band room at noon," Zane cuts in quickly. *"I know because I had to pause my audition when the church bells rang."*

"Which means we need Rose's story," Sierra continues. *"I know she's pretending she and Xavi were such good friends, but he never even mentioned her."*

Good friends? Since when? This is the problem with getting only partial recordings; I'm missing context.

"I didn't say good friends." Rose sounds defensive. *"I said I know him well because I've lived next door to him my whole life."*

Neighbors. That's why Rose calls him by his nickname.

"Then tell us where you were when he was killed."

"I was reading my cards on top of the, um . . . icehouse." Rose is not a good liar, but she keeps bumbling through her story. *"I, uh, climbed up onto the roof, ate my lunch, and set out the cards. When I was done, I came in through the front door and went to the bathroom to wash my hands because the ladder made them dirty. I entered the cafeteria right when Sierra screamed about Xavi being dead. Everyone was talking like normal, and Dean Whitaker was high-fiving people, but I knew Sierra was telling the truth."*

"How?" Sierra asks. *"Everyone else thought me passing out was part of the game. But the other Miss Marples told me you were already crying. Almost like—"*

Zane finishes Sierra's sentence. *"Like you knew Xavier was dead."*

"You've got it all wrong!" Rose's words are stuffy, as if she's about to cry. *"When I was reading my cards on the icehouse, I thought about Xavi, and this horrible feeling clutched me like eagle's talons. And it really scared me. So when Sierra came in and said he'd been murdered . . . I knew."*

I stop running because my thoughts are racing faster than I am.

A Magic 8 Ball key chain in the greenhouse. Avoiding Emi's question about whether she was interviewed by the sheriff. And no witness to her alibi, which is clearly bullshit.

Conclusion: Rose is hiding something.

12

XAVIER'S BEACH HOUSE
Two Years Ago

THE CONFRONTATION WITH HER PARENTS THROBBED IN Rose's head as she stomped her way across the sand to the house next door. Xavier was lying on a unicorn float in the middle of his pool with sunglasses on. When he didn't move, Rose realized he was napping.

It was a peaceful day, with only a light breeze stirring the waves over the white picket fence that separated the beach houses from the sand. Rose had spent the morning meditating on her balcony, until her mom and dad had entered her room, each clutching a rosary.

Rose grabbed a beach towel, balled it up, and threw it directly at Xavier's face. He didn't deserve peace.

Xavier popped awake. His hands swatted in front of his nose, where the towel had hit. The sudden motion upset his balance, and the float toppled sideways, plunging him into the pool.

He came up sputtering, sunglasses askew. "What the hell, Rosie!" he said, punching the float away from his head. "Not cool."

"Not cool, huh?" His eyes went wide as he took in her unusual anger. "Let me tell you what's *not cool*, you absolute . . . asshole!" She emphasized the final word by throwing another balled-up towel at his face. He blocked it with a look of amazement. Rose rarely raised her voice and almost never cursed. But Xavier had gone too far. *"Outing me to my parents is not cool,"* she yelled.

His face fell. "Oh. That."

Rose reached for more towels, but there weren't any. A few cans of soda floated in some ice, but she hadn't abandoned her belief in nonviolence so much that she was willing to disfigure him. She collapsed onto a chaise and replayed the conversation with her parents in her head. The panic in her mom's eyes. Her dad's jaw twitching like he might cry.

"How could you, Xavi?" she whispered.

"I had to," he said. "They were talking shit about my moms."

"My parents never *talk shit*. Try again."

"I told them my family was taking a trip to San Francisco. They said we shouldn't because it was Satan's palace." Xavier rolled his eyes. "When I asked what they meant, they said they'd be praying for my moms to find God." He tossed the towels back into the basket, hard. "I'm so fucking sick of them acting like my moms need to be prayed for because they're gay. And so"—he stopped, as if he realized the depth of what he'd done, as if he felt some shame—"I told them they should add you to their prayers because you were going to the Detective's Ball with Maribel." He hurried to defend himself, like he always did when he screwed up. "And you keep saying you're going to tell them, but you haven't, and I thought it would help you if they knew."

"Don't pretend you did this for me," Rose snapped. She wasn't usually rude, but sometimes she fell back into her childhood personality, which had been a lot less Zen and a lot more *beat up Jonny Hawkins on the playground.*

"I did it for my moms," Xavier said.

The anger Rose had been trying to force down raged back into a monster. "Then let's go inside and tell them the good news," she said, standing up.

Finally, Xavier responded how she wanted. "What?" he said, his eyes round and shiny. "Why?"

"I'm sure they'd *love* to hear what you did for them," Rose said. "They'll especially love the part about how you outed a girl like them to her parents." Rose started sweeping toward the house, but Xavier grabbed her hand from the pool as she passed.

"Don't," he pleaded. "I'm sorry, okay? I shouldn't have done it. I got mad, and it came out, and"—he squeezed her hand—"I'm a dick sometimes. I know that; you know that; we all know that."

She sat back down. She didn't actually want to tell Xavier's moms what he'd done. He really was a dick sometimes, but most of the time she liked him. He'd been the first one to notice her staring at Penélope Hernández in the sixth grade and had helped her beat up Jonny when he called her a dyke.

"I had a whole speech planned," Rose said. "For *years*. Now they've freaked out. They're talking about sending me to church camp, Xavi. *Church camp.*"

"A conversion camp?" he said with horror.

"Just normal church camp. But it's still awful. My mom told me it's okay to be gay if you don't act on it."

"What the fuck does that mean?"

"I guess I'm allowed to be gay in my head." Rose sighed. "I don't know. It's stupid."

"Don't you think it's better they know?"

"That's not the point." Rose's voice grew louder. "I wanted to do it my way. It was finally something I could control in a house where I get to control nothing. And you took that from me. For my whole life, this will be how my parents found out I'm gay." She stood up, trembling with fury. "I get that we're only neighbor friends, but I thought you cared about me."

"You're making this into a way bigger deal than it is." Xavier hopped out of the pool and draped his tan body over a blue-and-white striped towel on the chaise next to hers. "For your whole life? I mean, c'mon, you're not usually so dramatic." He shot her his trademark smile. "Where's chill Rosie? Bring her back."

Rose's fury grew wings. She wasn't big on vengeance. The Buddhist texts she studied said that being angry let the mistakes of others punish you. But Xavier had stolen something from her, and it was obvious he'd only apologized so she wouldn't rat him out to his moms. To add insult to injury, he was acting as if her reaction was out of line—like she should have gotten over it the minute he said sorry.

What he'd done was unforgivable. Rose would repay.

13

THE ONLY GOOD THING ABOUT THE GAME BEING CAN-
celed is that it's given me more time to read. Now that my plan to get information through the coroner's internship has been torpedoed by the nepo baby, I need to find a different way to figure out how the police reports in my mom's case were manipulated. Which means I need to learn as much as I can about car crash investigations.

Even though there are plenty of reasons a student in the detective capsule might want access to forensics books, I don't want to be questioned by the librarian, so I sneak into the library during lunch, when it's closed.

The library is the kind my mom loved, with books lining the walls and a staircase winding up to a second level surrounded by a balcony. The dean added some modern shelves and study carrels on the first floor to make it more like a normal school library, but he left a collection of old leather chairs near the bay windows. There's a tradition of leaving the smallest chair empty, since it was supposed to be Claire Everett's favorite. Turns out even people who don't believe in ghosts are afraid of them.

After sliding under the metal chain with a plastic sign that nonsensically says CAUTION: WET FLOOR, the first thing I see is the back of Zane's head in a row of medical textbooks.

I'm about to call out a hello when I notice something strange about the small shifts in his movements. I don't suspect him of doing anything wrong, but I want to know what he's up to.

I creep into the row behind him and peer through a gap between books about DNA analysis. I blink fast to make sure I'm seeing what I think I'm seeing. Zane is taking pictures of an open book with his phone. I shift to the right to get a better view, and what I see on the page makes me emit a sound somewhere between a gasp and a giggle.

"You know there's porn on the internet, right?" I ask, too shocked to keep quiet.

Zane drops the book, along with his phone. When he spins around and sees me standing there, he turns so tomato red that even the scalp beneath his blond hair flushes.

"Oh my god, Dulce," he says, picking up his phone but leaving the book on the ground as if that will make me forget what's in it. "This is *not* what it looks like."

It's quaint, him ogling pictures of naked bodies in anatomy books instead of on his computer, though the discovery still makes me feel shaky, like I've invaded a part of his brain I'd rather have stayed dark.

"I . . . I'm taking the pictures for my internship with Dr. Yonz. You know, the cardiologist whose office is next to Maldonado's?" His voice clears a little, and he picks up the volume and shoves it back on the shelf. "The librarian said I couldn't check out any of these books, so it was the only way I could get them."

It's obvious he's lying, but I can't imagine anything short of torture will get him to admit he was searching for nudes in the school library.

"I'm actually glad you're here," he says, rounding the corner so we're not talking between books. "I've been instructed to tell you my alibi for the day Xavier Torres died."

I groan so loudly that, if we weren't alone, the librarian would have come over to shush us. "Now Emi's delivering them to me in person," I say. "What next? Enzo cornering me in the bathroom?"

Zane laughs. "Enzo's stopped showing up for classes, so I think you'll be spared that." He hops up onto one of the study carrels. "I'm not sure why she wants me to give you my story, though. I wasn't anywhere near the greenhouse at noon."

"Might as well tell me," I say, my traitorous stomach fluttering with curiosity. "Emi won't give up otherwise."

"Okay. Well, I left the lunchroom when I realized I was going to be late for my audition with Ms. Moss. I ran up the stairs with my flute and reached her room about ten minutes before noon. It could have been a few minutes later, but not more than that."

He sounds rehearsed, but that's not surprising if Emi prepped him. "Did you see anyone in the halls?" I ask.

"Only Enzo Torres as he was leaving the chem lab. Sierra says he usually eats in there instead of the cafeteria." Zane keeps going. "I went into the band room and warmed up. I think Ms. Moss had forgotten I was going to audition, because she didn't have the sheet music ready and had to dig it out of her cabinets. I started to play, but then she got a text and started packing her things in a rush. She told me her twins were ill and she needed to pick them up. I grabbed my flute and left. That was just after noon."

"Why didn't you come back to the cafeteria?"

"I came to the library to study for a trig test. I like it in here during lunch because it's quiet." He picks at a loose wood splinter on the carrel. "I don't understand why Emi's helping Sierra. She doesn't seem to appreciate it."

"One of our classmates did get murdered." I'm not sure why I'm defending Emi since I also don't think she should be helping Sierra.

"Couldn't have happened to a nicer guy." Zane's voice is bitter.

"What do you mean?" I ask sharply.

"Nothing." Zane yanks the splinter off. "He was just weird to me that day in the lunchroom. Kind of seemed like an asshole."

"He was no worse than other guys," I say, thinking of the planner he gifted me at the end of last year's competition.

"Are we all that terrible?"

I nod toward the book Zane put on the shelf. "Next time, you might want to try the *Kama Sutra*. Not as much human dissection, but still lots of nudity."

Zane puts his head in his hands. "I'm never going to live this down, am I?"

"Any idea what Emi's next step in the case is?" I try to sound casual, like I don't care.

"She asked Dean Whitaker for the camera footage from the front door, but he said no," Zane says, his eyes meeting mine again. "Sierra thinks Emi should steal it from his laptop."

"Typical Sierra," I scoff. "Letting everyone else get their hands dirty."

"You really seem to hate her."

I pause. He heard a fraction of the story in the mausoleum, but there's no reason I can't tell him more now.

"My dad and I wanted to sue the sheriff's office after my mom died," I say. "Our lawyer told us it was going to be hard to win because cops who hurt people while they're working have immunity. But he was willing to try, until Mayor Fox and Sheriff Calhoun began lying about what happened." My jaw clicks as I grind my teeth, remembering the next part. "By the time they were done smearing my mom's name, even our attorney thought she'd caused the wreck. So he dropped us." I blink back tears. "Sierra's family made sure my mom's life was worth nothing. And then Sierra made sure everyone at school thought the same."

"That's just—" Zane's hands grip the wood like he wishes he could hit something. "No wonder you didn't agree to help her. I can't believe Emi did."

"Emi follows her own arrow." I sigh. "Even if it goes straight into someone else's heart."

Zane slides off the carrel and flicks me in the shoulder like a five-year-old. "I have a tip for you."

"About Sierra?"

"About how to get a free pizza," he says. "You should order octopus. Rocco has a massive phobia of them. Won't let them in the restaurant."

Touching my arm. Reference to previous fun conversation. Screwing his boss out of a pizza.

Conclusion: Zane is trying to make me feel better about Sierra.

I smile and flick him back, hard enough that he flinches. "Thanks. I'll let my dad know."

"Remind me why we have to be at school an hour before it opens?" I yawn, balling up my jacket and putting it between my head and the cracked car window, hoping I can get five more minutes of sleep.

"I told you," Emi says. "I promised Dean Whitaker I'd input his midterm grades."

"If this is another attempt to get me to help you with Sierra—"

"It's not. Notice I haven't said anything about her for a week."

It's true; she hasn't. But she hasn't said much about anything else either. I hate to admit it, but Xavier's case is building a wall between us. If I didn't despise Sierra with such a burning passion, I'd probably give in so we could go back to being us.

A cold fog is blowing through the evergreens when we get out of the car, making them look like an out-of-focus picture. It's strange that the woods used to be Dr. Everett's backyard. The day she was kidnapped, Claire Everett had gone down the path to the greenhouse and asked the gardener for sunflowers for her friend. He'd cut some before she ran into the woods, never to be seen alive again.

I stare at the trees, unnerved by the hollow wind rustling through them like a chorus of ghosts. A killer had hidden there, watching Claire. A different one might have lain in wait for Xavier. Who's to say they're not spying on us now, tracking our investigation, ready to act if we get close?

I shudder. "We should go inside."

"In a minute." Emi takes a sip of the giant latte she insisted we pick up on the way. "I asked Rose to meet us too."

"Oh."

"You don't like her," Emi says, reading my face with a single glance.

"It's not that," I lie. "I just don't think you should trust her. She's one of the few people who could have killed Xavier, and her story doesn't explain how her key chain got into the greenhouse. There's also no way she climbed the icehouse ladder alone to eat lunch. She's scared of heights."

"Maybe being around me is making her braver." Emi shrugs.

"I didn't realize you'd been spending that much time with her." I wish the jealousy in my voice wasn't so obvious.

For once, Emi doesn't turn my insecurity into a joke. She leans into me, making our shoulders touch in a way that feels warm in the cold air. "You're my forever friend; you know that, right?" she says.

"I guess." Sierra told me the same thing before she torched our friendship.

"Sierra is a narcissistic bitchwitch," Emi says, reading my mind again. She unclips the Magic 8 Ball from her bag and shakes it. "Will I ever abandon Dulce to the horrors of living without me?" The triangle flips over until it lands on YES, DEFINITELY. I groan as she stuffs it away. "It's a liar," she says. "I may move through boyfriends like sugar packets, but my girl loyalty is endless."

A Prius pulls into the parking lot and drives toward us.

"That's not Rose's car." I frown.

"Oh, right." Emi grins. "Remember how I said this wasn't about Xavier's murder? I lied. Again."

"Emi!" I say, outraged.

"Fool you once, shame on me. Fool you four times, and I'm not the problem."

Zane parks and gets out of his car. He's wearing a long-sleeved Henley so thin I can see the outline of his abs. Emi runs over and hugs him, spilling some of her latte on his sleeve. If I'd done that, I'd replay it in my head every night for the rest of my life, but Emi simply laughs, brushes it off with the hem of her own shirt, and tells him she'll always be a part of his wardrobe now. He smiles at her, and even though I'm not usually jealous of Emi, I can see how it would be pleasant to have Zane's dimple appear because he was happy to see you.

Sierra and Rose arrive together a minute later, but it quickly becomes clear they've been arguing.

"I went to drop off some of Xavi's things at his house," Sierra says, getting out of her car and glaring at Rose, "and *she* was in his room, digging around in his stuff. His moms—who don't think I killed their son, by the way—suggested I take her to school since her car is in the shop." She turns to Emi, very pointedly ignoring me. "I already asked why she was sneaking around in there. Maybe you'll have more luck getting an answer."

There's an awkward silence while we all stare at Rose.

"I wasn't doing anything wrong," she says. "Xavi's moms let me in. I'd given him something a long time ago, and I wanted it back."

"What did you give him?" Emi asks.

Rose hesitates. "A, um, friendship bracelet."

Sierra rolls her eyes. "Please," she says derisively. "You have something to hide, and I'm going to find out what." Her crimson nail polish flashes in the fog as she holds out her hand. "Give it to me."

"What?" Rose's already-pink cheeks turn into peaches.

"The bracelet you made to honor your deep friendship with my boyfriend," Sierra says. "I want to see it."

"I couldn't find it," Rose mumbles.

I look at Emi, hoping she'll finally pick up on Rose's laughably bad attempts at lying, but instead she glares at Sierra. "The suspected killer here is you," Emi says, like she's forgotten she's trying to prove Sierra's innocence. "If you think any of us is going to believe that Rose"—she points at Rose, who's wearing a granny cardigan and whose blue cow eyes look about as hard as a piece of angel food cake—"has something to hide about Xavier's death, you're going to be a very disappointed little criminal."

Sierra spins around to me, like she's so desperate for an ally she'll even talk to the ex-best friend refusing to help her stay out of jail. "You know Rose is lying. You can't keep silent because your bestie likes having a baby doll around."

"We're wasting time," Emi says. "Let's go to the greenhouse."

"I'm staying in the car," I tell her.

"Don't be a dumb bunny," Emi says, rolling her eyes. "We're going back to the scene of the crime. You'll love it. Besides, the school isn't open yet."

Everyone looks at me. "Fine," I grumble, taking a silent vow to stand off to the side and not participate in whatever Emi has planned. "But only because it's too cold to sit still."

Sierra continues to look daggers at Rose as we walk down the path. Agreeing with her feels like shaking hands with a porcupine, but she's right: Rose's story makes no sense. She said her friendship with Xavier was casual and neighborly, but Emi and I don't even have shared bracelets or necklaces, and we're best friends.

It's much more tense in the greenhouse without Xavier's body than it was with it, maybe because an uncomfortable hush has fallen on the others. Emi pushes past the police tape and walks straight to the back, like she doesn't want to be near the place he died. I pretend to be fascinated by the orchids near the door and ignore Zane, who keeps glancing at me like he's worried I'll repeat my mausoleum performance.

"Someone was lying here," Emi says a minute later, breaking through the quiet. "There's an outline on the ground."

Rose freezes, and her eyes flash to Sierra, who's glaring at the back table like it just threatened to make her wear sweatpants. I give up the orchid pretense and walk over to find out what's causing them both such fits, but there's nothing weird behind the table, only some heavy marks in the dirt in the unmistakable shape of a body.

"Was someone taking a nap?" I ask, immediately forgetting I'd sworn to stay quiet.

"Ah, sweet-minded Dulce." Emi smiles wryly. "Picture the scene again. With less clothing."

I flush. "Oh, right."

"That doesn't mean it was Xavi," Sierra spits. "He would never cheat on me."

"Whatever," Emi says. "Everyone knows this is a prime make-out spot." She points to the thick tangle of pothos vines and then to the giant lemon tree behind her, whose leaves are pressed against the glass roof. "The tree blocks the view from the house, and the vines block the view from the door. And unlike the forest, there's almost no chance Coach Hu will catch you."

I wander back to the middle of the greenhouse and look up. If the fog wasn't so thick, I'd be able to see whether any of the lights were on in the main building. "I wish we knew how long that pane has been missing," I say, avoiding Sierra's eyes so she knows I'm speaking generally and not to her.

"Not long," Sierra says.

"I thought you never came in here," Emi counters.

Sierra kicks the dirt floor with her boot. "I did once." She pauses. "With Enzo."

"When?" Emi asks.

"Four days before the Poisoner's Festival."

"And you're sure it wasn't broken?"

"Almost positive. I looked up at the clouds while we were—" She stops, blood rushing into her pale cheeks.

"I guess Xavier wasn't the only one on his back." Emi smirks.

"Screw you, Emi."

While they bicker, I weave between the plants. I'm *not* searching for clues, but if I see something by accident . . .

I step around a monstera with leaves so massive they look prehistoric before doing a double take. Something small and pink is cradled in one of the plant's veins like a neon caterpillar. I crouch to get a better look.

"Come here," I tell Emi.

She walks over and bends down next to me. "It's a piece of pink yarn," she says.

"Ask Sierra if this is the same yarn she saw on the needle," I whisper.

Emi rolls her eyes like she thinks I'm being childish, but she does what I ask.

"It's definitely the same," Sierra says, kneeling down to look. "Love Me Knot on Main Street commissioned a small batch for Valentine's Day last year."

"How do you know?" Emi asks.

"Because I own two skeins of it."

A tangible silence fills the greenhouse. Even the birds that have been flying in and out through the empty pane are quiet, though that's probably because we've been tromping around like elephants.

"Could someone have stolen your yarn?" Emi asks Sierra.

"I keep telling you; it's Enzo," Sierra says. "The skeins were in my bedroom, along with my needles. He probably took some over the summer."

"None of us had the game packet then, which means he wouldn't have known the knitting needle was the murder weapon," Emi says. "So unless he was in your room after school started..."

"He wasn't."

Everyone looks at Sierra doubtfully.

"It's true!" she says. "Things were almost over between us by then. The last time I was with him was—"

She stops, stealing a guilty glance at me.

"That day in the hallway," I mutter, my face warming at the memory. Now I know why Enzo's gold-tipped hair looked familiar at the festival. It was him sneaking out of the janitor's closet, not Xavier.

"Enzo was weird that day," Sierra continues. "He kept saying Xavi had been sick, and that I should give him some space, but Xavi hadn't said anything to me about feeling bad. Except then, at his party, he did get sick, so I thought maybe Enzo was right."

"I heard Xavier drank too much," Zane says.

Sierra shakes her head. "He only had two shots. He didn't want to be hungover for the festival because he was hosting Channel Z News's raffle, and he doesn't"—she pauses, blinking fast like painful memories are flashing behind her eyes—"I mean he didn't like his face to look puffy on TV."

None of this explains how Enzo could have stolen the yarn. Did someone else in the Stitch 'n' Bitch Club buy a skein and leave it somewhere more accessible? Maybe Emi can go to Love Me Knot and ask if they have a record of yarn sales from February. They'll probably laugh her out of the store, but it's worth a try . . .

Stop helping, I tell myself, annoyed that Emi's plan is working. I focus on that day in middle school. Sierra looking at me like a stranger. Calling me and my dad liars. Blood running down my shirt.

The images make me so angry that I walk to the door, trembling under my skin.

"What now?" Zane asks, looking at Emi. "Does this help us narrow down who did it?"

The answer is obvious: It hasn't narrowed down anything. The pane was recently broken, but there's no evidence it has anything to do with Xavier. The outline of the body is too indistinct to make out details, and anyway, there's no way to tell if it was made before or after Xavier died.

"I'll keep thinking," Emi says.

When Sierra answers, her voice drips with enough acid to burn a hole in the dirt. "Your thoughts will be a real support when I'm doing twenty to life."

14

J. EVERETT HIGH SCHOOL
Two Years Ago

WHEN I'D IMAGINED MY FIRST WEEK AT J. EVERETT, I never dreamed I'd be spending it in a bathroom with photographs of blood spatter evidence taped to the walls. And yet there I was, eating lunch inside a bathtub overlooking the forest.

The bathroom wasn't one that had been retrofitted when the house was converted into a school, and I'd found it by accident when I tripped over a rug and fell against a wall that—to my shock—slid aside to reveal a secret door. The bathroom still had its old claw-foot tub and even a chain to pull the toilet. No renovation also meant that Dr. Everett's disturbing collection of crime scene photography hadn't been put into storage. Each picture was labeled with a date and weapon, and the blood sample in front of me, as dry and crusty as my rye bread, had spatter reaching all the way into the corners of its frame.

CHARLES HARPER, EXETER PUPIL, KNIFE. DECEMBER 22, 1954.

Christmastime, I thought, wondering why the murderer's name wasn't included. Maybe they'd never caught him. My train of thought entered the track it'd been on for months: How much blood was there when my mom died? Was it fast, or did she suffer?

Tears stung my eyes, and I let them fall. There was no way Sierra would walk in and see me crying; she'd probably already found ten boys to flirt with in the cafeteria. Before the accident, I would have been right there with her—talking excitedly about our plans to solve Death & Fox's next case, maybe even humble-bragging to the other students that our childhood joke had turned into a real business—but now all that daring was curled into a tiny corner of my mind, collecting dust.

A bang on the wall interrupted my spiraling, but before I could tell the intruder the bathroom was occupied, the door slid open.

The woman in the hallway looked at me in the tub, looked behind her, and then looked at me again.

"I thought maybe I'd come through a magic door," she said, sliding it shut. "Where crying fairies eat lunch in bathtubs."

I hurried to stand up, wiping crumbs off my jeans, but she motioned for me to sit back down. "Don't move on my account," she said, walking over to the window and cracking it before taking a cigarette out of her handbag. "I won't tell if you don't," she added with a wink.

She sat on the wide sill before lighting up and taking a few puffs. For a minute, I thought she was going to ignore me entirely. But then she crossed one leg over the other, making her skirt rustle, and looked me over. "Want to tell me why you're hiding in this bathroom?" she said.

I froze. Was I in trouble?

"It's nothing," I mumbled.

"Okay," she said, pulling out a stack of papers with bars of music on them. She continued to smoke her cigarette while she made red marks across the pages. When it was burned halfway down, she addressed me again. "I let myself have two a day now that I'm back from maternity leave." She shook her head. "I've tried nicotine patches, but there's something about the physical act of it that's relaxing. Never smoke," she warned. "It's like a ghost that won't stop haunting you."

For the first time in months, I felt the spark of calm. I didn't believe in auras or anything mystical—that was my dad's line—but if I'd had to describe her vibe, it would have been a field of poppies blowing in the breeze, someone who preferred to swim in a river than be trapped inside four walls.

"I'm Ms. Moss, by the way," she said. "But in here you can call me Hannah."

At some point in the weeks that followed, she stopped bringing papers to grade and started telling me about her new babies. "They're like air," she said. "Necessary for my survival. I'm annoyed I had to live so many years without them." She looked out at the trees, her face lined with sunshine. "I wish I'd been better to my mother before she died."

"Your mom died?" It was the first question I'd asked her; usually Ms. Moss did the talking while I listened, transfixed by the first adult in months who'd spoken to me like I wasn't some broken kid.

Her eyes met mine, and in them I read sympathy, like she was saying *oh no, you too?* "A year ago," she said. "Caught pneumonia on a cruise." Her gaze softened. "What about yours?"

"Car wreck. Three months ago."

I wasn't ready to tell her the rest, but eventually I did.

"And then Sierra told everyone in our class it was my mom's fault," I said. "And we were supposed to be on the same team, but all of that's ruined, so I don't even want to play the game anymore."

Ms. Moss nodded. "Everyone talks about how it feels for a romance to end, but they don't tell you losing a friend can be worse." She stared out the window for a minute. "What did your mom think about you coming to J. Everett?"

The day my mom had found my acceptance letter in the mail, she'd rushed inside to give it to me and then jumped up and down while I read it, certain I'd gotten in. "You're going to be like Lord Wimsey!" she'd yelled in Spanish, and then in English, and then in Spanish again.

"She was thrilled," I said.

"What do you think she'd say if she were here to guide you?"

It was easy to recall my mom's face and mannerisms. How she talked fast and moved her arms around a lot, like she was painting a picture of what she was saying.

"She'd tell me that winning was the best revenge."

"She's right," Ms. Moss said darkly. The hand gripping her skirt was missing its usual wedding ring. "I've recently learned there's only one response to betrayal."

My stomach churned, because she didn't look at all like her serene self. "What's that?" I asked.

"Let them burn," she said. "And the only way to burn down your friend is to join the game."

15

SOMETHING ABOUT THE GREENHOUSE EPISODE MUST have convinced Emi I won't get mad if she talks about Sierra's case, because she starts complaining about it all the time.

"The owner of Love Me Knot doesn't keep customer records, and I can't find anyone else at J. Everett who owns the pink yarn," she tells me during gym one day as we jog in the woods. "Sierra says the police told Xavier's parents they haven't found his phone, so they think the killer must have taken it. He didn't back anything up—apparently none of the journalism students do, to protect their sources—so all they have access to are his social media accounts." Little puffs of white air escape her lips. "There's only four weeks until the election, and the polls show Mayor Fox running behind the sheriff's cousin by twenty points." She kicks a piece of bark into a tree. "Sierra's freaking out, but it's hard doing it all alone and . . ." She looks at me. "You haven't changed your mind?"

"Nope. She doesn't deserve my help."

"You'd be helping *me*," Emi says. "And Xavier. He might have been a jerk, but he didn't deserve to die, and someone's going to get away with murder if we don't do anything." Her voice gets softer, mixing with the leaves crunching under our feet. "Wimsey would never have allowed that."

"I thought you were only pretending she was innocent," I say. "For the money."

"I was, at first, but now that I've looked at more evidence, I think your initial instinct was right. Only someone without any brain cells would kill Xavier with a branded needle *and* make it so obvious that she was meeting him in the greenhouse. She didn't even bother deleting his texts from her phone. Sierra's not that stupid."

"If she's innocent, I'm sure you'll find something that clears her," I say.

Emi shoves earbuds into her ears like she's disappointed in me. "By then it might be too late."

That night, my dad opens the door to my room and sits on the end of my bed, letting the sound of Channel Z News in with him. Ricardo Best is announcing new security measures at Cape Cherry High in response to Xavier's murder. I wish my dad would turn the television off sometimes, but ever since my mom died, he can't stand silence, even though he always joked that her constant singing felt like being married to a radio he couldn't unplug.

"Honk, honk," he says, squeezing the stuffed unicorn Emi gave me for Christmas like it's a goose. When I don't respond, he lets the unicorn fall against my bed frame. "Bad day at school?"

"Do you think it's possible to do the wrong thing for the right reason?" I ask. Emi's words about Wimsey not letting injustice pass have been weighing on me all day.

"Maybe some Tiffany's ice cream would help," my dad says. "We could go wild and eat Choco Coffee before bed."

At the word *Tiffany's*, I freeze and stop petting Penny, who's been kind enough to subject herself to my touch again. "I'm not hungry," I lie.

There have been other opportunities to tell my dad the truth. To admit my mom wasn't on her way to Tiffany's the night she died. To tell him that her death was all my fault. But I didn't tell him two years ago, and I'm not strong enough to watch his heart break now.

"Did Mom ever talk to you about Lord Wimsey?" I ask, trying to drown out Ricardo Best, who's moved on to talking about parental concern over mature content in J. Everett's science textbooks.

"Of course," my dad says. "She called him the perfect gentleman. If I forgot to take the trash out, she'd joke that Lord Wimsey wouldn't have forgotten. Or when I'd buy her daffodils, she'd congratulate me on doing my best Wimsey impression." He looks at me curiously. "Why do you ask?"

"It's a, um, project at school," I say. "I'm trying to apply his methods, but they're not working."

My dad stands up and pats my leg on top of the patchwork quilt. "He's just a character in a book, *conejita*. I wouldn't give too much weight to his methods if you've got better ones."

What would Wimsey do? It's been my go-to thought for so long. But what if seeking justice means helping the girl who made sure my mom never got any?

It's a question I can't answer.

I've been passing Ms. Moss's band room every afternoon, hoping to catch her picking up the papers the substitute has been leaving for her while she's been taking care of her sick kids. But today when I pass, there are voices coming from the room.

I peek inside and see Emi and Zane sitting at a table. Zane is writing band names on his backpack with Wite-Out, and Emi's spinning her Magic 8 Ball around in her hand like it might provide her with answers to the mystery she's supposed to be solving.

"Have you heard from Sierra?" Zane asks, capping his pen.

"Nothing for three days," Emi says. "I think she's mad we're not making more progress."

No Sierra means there's no reason I can't say hello.

"Please tell me you brought snacks," Emi says when I walk in. "This case is sucking my brain right out of my head."

I dig into my bag and toss her some Starburst. I don't want to sit down, in case I need to make a quick exit, so I perch on the windowsill. Outside, purplish storm clouds are gathering over the woods.

"Someone fixed the glass pane," Emi says, her mouth full of pink.

I half expect to see Enzo inside the greenhouse again even though Zane says he's stopped coming to school. In a book, the detective would stroke her chin and make some grand determination about Enzo's guilt or innocence based on the psychology of bailing on class, but who knows why he's absent. He might have a guilty conscience, or he might just not want to spend time where his brother was murdered.

"I wish this were a game meeting," I say.

"Same." Zane shoots me a small smile.

"If working on this case has taught me anything, it's that the game is so fake," Emi says. "The clues are provided for us. The witnesses spill their guts. And if we fail, all that happens is we don't get the prize money." She shoves her Magic 8 Ball into her bag like it's given her bad news. "Enzo would be the least likely suspect in the game," she continues. "The emo murderer—where's the twist? But he's definitely the best real-life suspect. I've texted him, shown up at his house, and even stalked him to the arcade, but he runs every time he sees me." She bites into another Starburst. "If I can't even talk to my main suspect, how am I supposed to—"

A monstrous stomping makes us eye the door in alarm. Sierra flies into the room like a Tasmanian devil—fierce and furious. She doesn't say a single word, only pounds over to Ms. Moss's desk, grabs the TV remote like it's a snake she wants to strangle, and switches on the television.

"Today, the Cape Cherry Commonwealth Attorney's Office announced it had charged sixteen-year-old Sierra Fox with first-degree murder in the death of Xavier Torres." Ricardo Best is sitting at his desk in a polished suit, like he knows this case is his best shot to go national. "Police say Ms. Fox injected her boyfriend with nicotine, a deadly poison derived from the tobacco plant, following a breakup. At a hearing Friday afternoon, Judge Orcutt set bail at five hundred thousand dollars, which was paid Saturday morning. Ms. Fox was asked to relinquish her passport and then released to the custody of her mother, Mayor Lily Fox. Representatives for her reelection campaign say—"

Sierra clicks off the TV and faces us. I'm in such a state of shock I can't take my eyes off her to see if everyone else's expressions look like mine. Somehow, despite all evidence to the contrary, I thought her wealth would save her.

"That's right, bitches," she says. "I've been *in jail*." She lifts her pant leg to show us an ankle monitor. "As of today, I'm allowed to go exactly two places: school and my house."

"At least you'll have more time to knit," Emi says, and for a second, I think Sierra might actually attack her. But then she turns her fury on me.

"You could have stopped this from happening, but you're too busy nursing a grudge from middle school."

"A *grudge*?" I pop off the windowsill. "Are you fucking kidding?"

"And you're as useless as thumbs on a slug." Sierra points a French-tipped nail at Emi.

"That's not fair," Zane says. "Emi's been trying."

Sierra's laugh is wild, hyena-like. "Trying? She hasn't even gotten the footage from the security camera. That's, like, step one."

"I've asked Dean Whitaker twice," Emi says defensively. "He told me no. Said the sheriff had already seen it and I didn't need to worry about it."

"Since when does a chaos butterfly care about the word *no*?" Sierra spits. "Have you broken into his office? Tried to hack his computer? Anything?"

"I'm working on it," Emi mumbles. "Planning those things takes time."

"What about getting the police files?" Sierra asks. "What's your plan for that?"

Emi doesn't answer.

"Yeah, that's what I thought." Sierra laughs darkly. "The problem is that, without Dulce telling you what to do, you're as chaotic as a ruler." She throws the remote back onto Ms. Moss's desk. "I can't *believe* this is the crack team that almost beat us last year."

"I did everything I could to get Dulce to help," Emi says, color rising in her cheeks. "Maybe if you hadn't been so far up Sheriff Calhoun's ass two years ago, she would have found you worth saving."

"And maybe if you weren't such a dumb twat, she'd have found you worth helping," Sierra shoots back.

"That's enough, Sierra," I say.

"The only good part of your incompetence," Sierra continues, with the bright rage of a toddler, "is that my mom has seen the light and hired a criminal defense attorney and a private investigator, so you are very, *very* fired."

"Did you really expect Emi to break laws to keep you out of jail?" I ask. "She—"

"Stop defending me," Emi snaps.

Everyone goes silent, even Sierra. I gape at Emi, feeling like I've been sucker punched. "I'm only trying to—"

"You could have tried investigating with me," she says. "I know what Sierra did to you was unforgivable, but I gave you so many chances to act like my best friend, and you didn't take a single one."

I'm dumbfounded. "B-but I told you I couldn't help her. I made that clear at Xavier's funeral."

"Screw Sierra," Emi says. "You would have been helping your friends. And saving the school. And making sure we could take our trip to England." She throws the rest of the Starburst into her bag. "I know your mom dying was horrible, but you can't keep living in the past. Some of us exist in the present. And if you can't find a way to show you give a damn, we might not exist in your future."

"How can you say that?" I whisper. As if the past will ever take its claws out of my back.

"This is all really touching," Sierra says, crossing her arms to match Emi's, "but I think you're forgetting that unless someone figures out who killed Xavi, I'm going to *actual prison*."

"Read the room," Emi says. "No one cares."

"So much for acting like Wimsey. He broke the law without a second thought. But you're too chickenshit." Sierra glowers at me. "Not that I'd expect anything different from *conejita* over here."

Hearing my mom's nickname in her mouth makes me snap.

"Don't you dare call me that!" I yell. I grab my backpack and march across the room, not even feeling bad when I knock Sierra's shoulder hard enough to send her flying into Ms. Moss's desk.

In the doorway, I spin back around to face Emi. "You want to talk about friendship?" My eyes burn into hers like lasers. "Maybe next time don't agree to help the person I hate most in the world."

16

WHEN I GET TO THE CAFETERIA THE NEXT DAY, EMI IS SIT-ting with Rose and the other Miss Marples, which is how I know she's still super mad at me, even though she's the one who sided with my nemesis. Sierra's not at the table with them, probably because all her friends think she murdered Xavier. An unkind part of me hopes she's eating lunch in my old bathtub.

I sit down near the back door, as alone as I was at the beginning of freshman year. Usually, Emi and I grab our own lunches from the fridge and switch them at the table, but she's taken my bologna sandwich without even asking. She hasn't even left me my dessert, which we always split because my dad splurges on Tiffany's cookies. A quick glance at her table makes me feel even worse: Not only has she taken the whole snickerdoodle, but she's very obviously put my half on a napkin in front of Rose.

I'm so busy thinking about what a jerk she is that when Zane sits down across from me, I almost choke in surprise.

"Ms. Moss is back from sick leave," he says, pulling a chocolate chip granola bar from his bag. "So I finally got to try out for band this morning."

"Did you make it?"

Zane smiles, making his dimple pinch. "Yeah, but Emi told me everyone does."

My eyes dart over to Emi, who's laughing so hard at something on Rose's phone that she's bright red and coughing. "I figured you'd be sitting over there," I say, trying not to let jealousy cloud my voice.

"I like this table."

In his earth-and-water eyes, I see what I've been dreading: sympathy.

"Don't try to make me feel better," I warn.

"I wasn't going to," he says.

"You have sad puppy-dog eyes."

"Sierra and Emi were out of line." He reaches his hand across the table until his fingers are on mine. A spasm shivers through me at his touch. "You stood by your principles. There's nothing wrong with that."

"But now an innocent person might go to jail," I say, pulling my hand away because I don't want to be comforted. "Sierra may be a monster, but she doesn't deserve that."

"You and Emi need to stop thinking of yourselves as Sierra's only hope," he says a little impatiently. "The sheriff can't ignore evidence no matter how guilty he thinks she is. He has to prepare a case for the prosecutor. That's probably why he interviewed Dean Whitaker last week."

"He did?" I ask. "How do you know?"

Zane takes a bite of his granola bar, making a motion like he can't talk while he's chewing. "Someone broke into one of our barns," he says after he swallows, "and I saw him when I dropped off the police report for my mom." He glances out the back window like he's thinking about the greenhouse. "Sheriff Calhoun may be an idiot, but even he should be able to figure out a case with only two suspects. Because let's be honest: It was either Sierra or Enzo."

"What about Rose?" I sneak another peek at her table.

Zane snorts. "I'd believe a golden retriever murdered Xavier before I'd believe Rose did. She's, like, Zen vegetarian girl."

Out of nowhere, an earsplitting scream rips apart our conversation. It slices through the cafeteria chatter like an arrow, stabbing my ears. For a second, there's a strange hush in the room, like we've all been stunned in place by the unexpected noise, but then people begin to shriek and leave their seats.

"What the—" Zane says, turning around.

But I'm already on my way across the cafeteria, because I was looking at Rose when she screamed, and in the instant afterward, I saw Emi collapse to the floor like a marionette whose strings had been cut. "Move," I yell, elbowing people out of my way until I reach Rose, who's holding a spasming Emi in her arms.

"Sh-she said she couldn't breathe," Rose stammers, but I don't bother listening to the rest of her gasping words.

"Help me get her on her side." I maneuver Emi into the recovery position I learned at the community center over the summer. As soon as I make sure she won't choke, I sprint out of the cafeteria, furious that no one else has run for help because they're frozen in place like ice sculptures.

When I reach Dean Whitaker's office, I don't bother knocking. His secretary squeals, "You can't go in there!" as I burst through the door. Dean Whitaker and Mayor Fox are eating lunch at a cozy table by a latticed window in the corner of the room, but the dean jumps to his feet when he sees me.

"What's wrong?" he says.

"Emi." My breath comes in short bursts, even though the cafeteria is only down the hall from his office. "She's been poisoned."

Dean Whitaker doesn't ask how I know—though it's because I learned about the symptoms in one of the forensics books I took out of the library. Instead he rushes over to a cabinet and pulls out a syringe and vial of something clear. Before I can ask what it is, he barrels out of his office, yelling at his fiancée to call 911. Mayor Fox spares me a single harsh glance before hurrying to the phone on the dean's desk. Even though she was basically my second mom for years, she feels like a complete stranger.

"The operator wants to know if Emi's conscious." Mayor Fox looks at me expectantly.

"Yes, but she's having some kind of seizure."

"Uh-huh." Mayor Fox is talking to the operator again. "Okay. Yes, the front door stays unlocked during the day."

It doesn't sound like she needs me anymore. As I run out of the room, I hear her tell the person on the phone to send the ambulance quickly.

By the time I reach the cafeteria, Dean Whitaker is already kneeling next to Emi's jerking body. He carefully extracts liquid from the vial with the syringe before injecting it into her thigh. The result is immediate. Emi's eyes flutter open, but they're glazed and confused, and her chest is still heaving.

"Don't move her!" Dean Whitaker booms at Rose, who had taken Emi's open eyes as a sign she was better.

I grab one of Emi's hands, but my own heart stutters when I feel her erratic pulse under my fingers. Fear crackles in my blood as she moans in pain.

"Atropine," Dean Whitaker explains when he sees my questioning eyes. "I got some after Xavier, just in case. It should counteract the effects of the poison."

"Should?"

Dean Whitaker's face is pale with worry. "I had to assume someone used nicotine again," he says. "Atropine will work for anything that's a depressant, but if it's something else . . ."

I don't need him to finish the sentence. If it's something else, it won't reverse the effects, and what happened to Xavier will happen to Emi.

Some students must have called 911 before Mayor Fox after all, because it takes a surprisingly short amount of time for the EMTs to come charging into the lunchroom. One of them shoves me away from Emi, and I stumble into Zane, who's come over to support Rose. His face is grim as he whispers comforting words into Rose's pink hair. She's too busy sobbing to pay attention to what the EMTs are doing, but once they strap Emi to the stretcher, I follow them out the front door.

"You're going to be fine," I tell Emi, but my voice quivers when I see how sweaty her face is under the oxygen mask. "I'll see you soon, okay?"

I try to touch her arm, but there's too much jostling, and once again, one of the EMTs pushes me away.

"I love you, Em," I call.

They shut the back doors of the ambulance with heavy thumps, cutting off my words, but I'm hoping she heard me or can at least read my mind and know how sorry I am for our fight and how desperately I want her to be okay.

As soon as the flashing lights and siren fade into the distance, my jelly legs give out on me, and I collapse onto the driveway.

Please save her, I beg my mom's spirit, even though I don't believe in any of that. *I'll do anything.*

Zane finds me there, rocking back and forth and repeating the words under my breath.

"She's going to be okay." Zane sits down and puts an arm around me. His flannel shirt is soft against my neck, like it's been washed a hundred times. "Dean Whitaker said it's a good sign she opened her eyes. If it had been the wrong drug, it probably would have sent her into a coma."

"I can't believe he risked that," I whisper.

"He didn't have a choice," he says, squeezing my shoulder. "Nicotine works so quickly that if he'd waited, she could have died."

I rock harder.

"Let me take you home," he says. "None of us is going to get any work done for the rest of the day anyway."

"But we're not allowed—" I start, and then stop, unable to believe I'm thinking about rules at a time like this. Of course I'm not staying at school.

"I'm going to the ER," I say.

Zane's nose twitches like he doesn't think that's a very good idea, but he nods and helps me off the ground.

"Why would someone poison her?" I ask once we're on the highway. Zane's Prius is smaller than Emi's Explorer, and it smells like air freshener and pizza, as if he's been playing delivery boy for Rocco. "It makes no sense."

"I mean, it has to be the same person who killed Xavier, right?" Zane says. "They must be afraid she'll solve the case."

"But she got fired. She's no threat to them."

"The poisoner must not know that."

I frown. He's right; it had to be someone who didn't know about the fight in the band room yesterday.

"Rose told me it happened right after Emi took a bite of her bologna sandwich," Zane says. "So it must have been in her food."

"That means it has to be someone at J. Everett." I clutch the seat belt as I replay Emi dropping to the ground. "I put my lunch in the fridge at eight thirty this morning. No way a stranger snuck into the building and then into the kitchen without being seen. There are too many people around all the time."

Zane nods. "And only three people don't have alibis for Xavier's murder: Enzo, Sierra, and Rose. So that narrows it down."

"But it has to be someone who's at school today," I say. "Didn't you tell me Enzo's stopped coming to class?"

"He's back. I saw him in the chem lab earlier."

And Sierra was at her locker this morning.

"How would Enzo even know that Emi was investigating his brother's murder?" I ask. "It's not like she made a school-wide announcement."

"She's been asking a lot of questions," Zane says. "Checking alibis, that sort of thing. It wouldn't be hard for Enzo to hear about it."

"At least this rules Sierra out. She obviously knows Emi's not her detective anymore."

"I guess." Zane's forehead wrinkles. "She seemed pretty furious at Emi yesterday. It could be revenge for not solving the case."

I don't believe Sierra would risk more jail time to get back at Emi, but I add her to my mental list anyway.

"Rose was sitting next to Emi when it happened," I say, unable to let her off the hook even though Zane thinks she isn't involved. "We're assuming someone tampered with her lunch in the fridge, but Rose could have waited until Emi was focused on her phone and then dropped nicotine onto her sandwich."

Her sandwich. Except, technically, it's not.

"Whoever poisoned Emi knows we switch lunches." My heart begins to pound at my temples. "I don't think Enzo or Sierra do."

"There were ten other students at that table," Zane says. "Someone would have seen. Besides, Rose must know Sierra kicked Emi off the case, right?"

Maybe not. Rose was doing yoga at a temple in Chesapeake during Sierra's meltdown, and Emi might not have rushed to share the news, especially since Sierra said so many cruel things about her.

"I'll find out," I say. "And I'll see if anyone saw her or Enzo or Sierra near the fridge between eight thirty and lunchtime. Maybe one of the lunch ladies—"

"Look, Dulce," Zane interrupts in a low voice, "I know it's tempting to throw yourself into the case after what's happened, but you should let the police handle it."

I pause, trying to figure out why his advice sounds upside down. "I thought you hated cops."

"And I thought you didn't want to help Sierra."

"Only because she's not worth it. But Emi is. She's worth anything."

When I realize I mean every single one of those words, a switch flicks in my head, and I see that Emi has been right all along. Investigating Xavier's murder has never been about Sierra; it's been about Emi and me doing what Wimsey always did: finding the truth.

"If I'd helped Sierra, I would have discovered the poisoner before they hurt Emi," I say. The thought that I could have stopped what happened makes me tremble with anger.

"You don't know that," Zane says.

"Yeah, I do. Because—" I hesitate. Once the words are out in the universe, I can't take them back. "Sierra was right. It's always me who puts together the pieces of the game. Emi has Wimsey's flair, but I've always been the brain. And I didn't use mine because I couldn't get past what Sierra had done to my family."

"I know you want to help Emi," Zane says, "but you don't want to cross Sheriff Calhoun. Trust me."

"What do you mean?"

Zane punches his blinker like he needs something to hit. "I was hoping I wouldn't have to tell you this, but last summer, one of my friends did something stupid and got arrested. Sheriff Calhoun could have given him a warning or slapped him with community service, but instead he threatened to get the DA to charge him with a felony."

Felony. There's that ugly word again. "What did your friend do?" I ask.

"It doesn't matter," Zane mumbles. "It wasn't his fault."

The stony look on his face keeps me from pushing for details. "Did you tell Emi this?"

"Of course I did," Zane says bitterly. "But you know what she's like."

I do. She wouldn't have given a vague story like that a second thought in the face of thirty thousand dollars.

"It'll be even worse if he catches you interfering," Zane says. "There are no secrets in Cape Cherry. I'm sure he knows you and your dad hired a lawyer to sue him. If he gets the chance to pay you back, he'll take it."

An hour ago, pissing off Sheriff Calhoun would have made me nervous, but now it doesn't just sound necessary, it sounds good.

When Zane pulls up to the hospital's ER department, I glance inside the glass doors and see Emi's mom in a surgical mask, waving her arms at some poor nurse like a penguin.

"I know it sucks to let Sheriff Calhoun investigate," Zane says, "but it's for the best."

Fingers wrapped tightly around the steering wheel. Eyes dead ahead, not meeting mine. Shoulders slumped with shame.

Conclusion: Zane doesn't just hate the sheriff, he's scared of him.

It's clear he isn't going to help me, not even to avenge the girl he has a crush on.

Luckily, I know someone who doesn't have anything left to lose.

17

"HOW'S EMI?" MY DAD ASKS THE NEXT MORNING WHILE he sautés spicy chorizo.

He thinks tacos will cheer me up, but the sound of Ricardo Best in the background talking about the sheriff's investigation of questionable content in J. Everett's library isn't helping my anxiety about Emi.

"I don't know," I say, flipping through the pages of a book on crime scene investigations. "Her phone must be dead."

I stayed at the ER with Emi's mom for hours until the doctor came out and told us he expected Emi to make a full recovery but that she needed to stay in the hospital for observation. I dropped into a chair and started sobbing, but it was a very different crying than the last time I'd been at the ER. Emi's mom drove me to McDonald's after, and we sat in the parking lot dipping french fries into our chocolate shakes, which was probably the first time Ms. Nakamura had ever let fast food cross the temple of her lips.

"Emi will be okay," she said every few minutes. "She's a good girl." As if nicotine only killed students who forgot to turn in their homework on time.

I don't tell my dad I'm afraid Emi's not texting me because of our fight. Her poisoning makes it seem like such a small thing, but that doesn't mean she feels the same way.

"The doctor told her mom she was complaining about the lack of streaming options, so I think she's doing better," I say. "I'm going to the hospital after school to see her."

As soon as I sneak into the sheriff's office, I add in my head. I woke up with a plan to find the poisoner, like my brain had worked it out in my sleep.

The first two periods of the day drag on and on, but my anatomy teacher lets me leave third period early, probably because she feels sorry my best friend has been poisoned. I use my freedom to bolt straight for Sierra's debate class and wait in the hall so I don't miss her. When the lunch bell rings, students stampede out of classrooms. I grab Sierra's arm before she can disappear into the crowd and drag her toward the lockers, which are wooden cubes stacked unobtrusively inside a space that used to be the maids' quarters.

"Hey!" she says, trying to brush me off. "What are you doing?"

"I have a proposition for you," I say.

"I'm flattered." She wiggles free of my grasp. "But I don't want to go to the Detective's Ball with you."

"If you're cracking jokes, your PI must be making progress."

Sierra's smirk crumbles into a scowl. "He already quit," she says. "After Enzo told him to fuck off and Dean Whitaker banned him from campus. Apparently, he tried to break into school to steal student files last night. You'd think the guy marrying my mom would want to help me stay out of jail, but he's too afraid of losing his job."

"What did your mom think of that?"

"She sounded like you," Sierra says before mimicking her

mom's marble-hard voice. *"It won't help my campaign if our PI acts like a criminal."* Sierra sniffs. "She's so under Dean Whitaker's thumb it wouldn't matter what he did. I've been trying to stop her from marrying him, but with the stress of this investigation, I think she's about to cave."

"You don't like Dean Whitaker?" I ask, startled because I thought everyone at J. Everett loved him.

"He's not good enough for her," Sierra says. "He's, like, a high school principal in some small beach town. He'll hold her career back. Besides, his name is Stanley. *Stanley.*"

"Nice to know you're still a snob." I roll my eyes. "So who's working on the case?"

"My new defense attorney, I guess." A sophomore approaches the locker next to Sierra's, but she waves him away with a flick of her fingers, and he departs with a small squeak. Apparently, there are perks to everyone at school thinking you're a killer. "Though it seems more like he's working my mom's bank account. He told me we don't need to figure out who killed Xavi—only show there's reasonable doubt that I did." She kicks a bottom locker with her boot, cracking the wood. "It's like no one understands that Xavi was my boyfriend and I want his killer caught."

I stop myself from saying *ex-boyfriend* because she actually seems upset, but I feel less bad for her a minute later when she adds, "Why are you even talking to me? Aren't I *the person you hate most in the world*?"

"Yes," I say, not caring that she looks hurt. "But Emi's one of the people I love most in the world, so you're in luck."

"In luck how?"

"I'm going to solve Xavier's murder," I say. "And you're going to help."

Sierra's face has undergone a cascade of emotions during our conversation. Anger, belligerence, disbelief. But now it collapses like she has no fight left in her. In all the years I've known her, it's the first time I've ever seen her look defeated.

"Whatever," she says. "I'll try anything."

"I still want the money."

"Obviously." She shakes her head, resigned to her fate. "Not that it matters. Your big plan to solve the case is probably passing someone a note during trig to ask if they're the poisoner."

I smile because I'm looking forward to the shock I'm about to see on her face.

"We're sneaking off campus," I say, using the cover of the other students to usher her past the dean's office and out the front door, knowing full well that, by the time someone reviews the camera footage, it'll be too late for them to stop us. "You're driving."

Leaving campus without permission is an automatic day of in-school suspension, but it turns out that when your best friend is in the hospital and a killer is on the loose, your disciplinary record stops meaning much. As we pull onto the highway, my thoughts run light and free, like Lord Wimsey flying across the ocean in a dangerous storm to save his brother from a death sentence.

"You know my ankle monitor is going to ping out of bounds when we reach the sheriff's station, right?" Sierra asks, swerving to avoid a pothole in the road.

I nod. "That's the first step of the plan."

It would be nice if I could investigate Xavier's murder without talking to Sierra, but that's not an option since we're the only two people still trying to figure out who killed him.

Thanks to me, I think, before pushing the words out of my head. Wallowing in guilt over Emi won't help me figure out the identity of the poisoner.

"Dr. Bates works for the sheriff," Sierra says. "What if you can't get her to tell us anything?"

The coroner is the second step of my plan. I've never actually met her, but she'll definitely know my name from the application I sent in for the internship.

"I'm hoping she hates her boss as much as everyone else," I say.

"Why didn't you ask Zane for help?" Sierra asks the question with the same smirk she used to give me when she teased me about boys. "He seems to follow you around like a puppy dog."

"What are you talking about?"

"Oh, please. He's always staring at you."

"He's into Emi," I say.

"Whatever you need to tell yourself."

I don't have the brain space to figure out why Sierra's social radar has malfunctioned. "I didn't ask Zane because *he* can't create the distraction I need."

Sierra's hands tighten around her steering wheel. "I don't like the sound of that."

Sierra parks at the far east end of the parking lot like I tell her to so no one will see us.

"I want you to walk in first," I say, "and act like your ankle monitor is malfunctioning."

Sierra frowns. "But it's not."

"That's why I said *act*. Ask them if they can hear the beeping, and when they say no, throw one of your fits."

"One of my *fits*?"

"Act like a princess," I continue. "While you have them distracted, I'll slip in and find the coroner's lab."

"What happens when they realize the bracelet is fine?"

"Leave the building and wait for me in the car," I say. "If they track you to the parking lot, tell them you're feeling dizzy and don't want to drive."

"What if you get caught?"

"I'll tell them I was looking for you because we're supposed to be back at school before lunch ends."

Sierra looks grudgingly impressed. "Broken ankle monitor. Princess fit. Wait in the car." She nods. "I'm ready."

We get out of her Range Rover and press ourselves close to the ugly stucco wall of the station. We would look like the worst spies ever to anyone who spotted us, but thankfully the parking lot is empty.

"Just don't let your stepdad catch you," I say. "He won't buy your act."

"Ex-stepdad," she corrects me. "And that's going to be hard."

"Why?"

"Because he's coming straight toward us." Sierra grabs my arm and drags me behind a Crown Victoria. We watch through the back window as a sunburned deputy follows Sheriff Calhoun out of the building.

"Shit," Sierra says under her breath as they walk closer. We scoot on our hands and knees around the other side of the car, using its body to block their view as they pass. "I could get rabies

155

from this," she hisses, wiping her fingers on her navy-blue jumpsuit. "Or cholera."

"At least we know he's not inside." We watch Sheriff Calhoun and the deputy leave the parking lot in a shiny Escalade SUV that seems way too expensive for a public official.

"I can't believe your mom married such a loser," I say.

"She has tragically bad taste in men." Sierra wrinkles her nose. "Although his religious stuff came later. Remember when he told me I needed an exorcism because I wanted to pierce my septum?"

I cringe at the memory. "He asked me to put some sort of necklace around your neck while you slept. I think it had saints on it."

"Yeah, he got even weirder after that," she says more quietly.

"Dean Whitaker may only be a school principal, but at least he won't try to cure your bitchwitchiness with snakes," I say, trying to lighten the mood.

"Or speak to me in tongues."

We both fall silent, like we've remembered we're not friends anymore. To cover up the awkwardness, I stand up and hurry along the sidewalk. Sierra follows behind me until we hit the double glass doors of the station.

"Don't screw up," I whisper. Without a moment's hesitation, Sierra marches through the doors. Before they close, I hear her say, "You've given me a *bum bracelet*," in a demanding voice that sounds like her mom. A few minutes later, I peek inside and see her sitting at a deputy's desk, poking her finger at the ankle monitor like she's giving it a lecture.

I bow my head and walk into the lobby, which is nearly as warm and stuffy as J. Everett's greenhouse. The station's decor is plain, with a row of plasticky visitors' chairs and a few beige cubicles where secretarial staff are supposed to be doing paperwork but are clearly eavesdropping on Sierra, who's making the kind of scene that demands popcorn.

I'm scanning the room for directions to the basement when I hear someone clear their throat behind me.

"Can I help you?"

I turn but choke on my words before I can answer. *It's him.* Deputy Armstrong. The man who hit my mom's car, staring straight at me.

Adrenaline and despair fight for dominion in my blood. It's not the first time I've seen him since my mom died; in a small town, you run into everyone, including people you wish didn't exist. But it's always been from across the road or the other side of a restaurant. This close, I can see dark circles under his pale-gray eyes, which are scanning me like I'm a suspect. I hold my breath, waiting for him to recognize me, but he doesn't. That hurts more than anything else.

"Shouldn't you be in school?" he asks in his soft drawl.

My mouth gurgles something nonsensical. I want to run away, but the carpet feels like quicksand, rooting me to the spot.

"Let me talk to Deputy Armstrong!" Sierra yells, making the deputy start and turn in confusion. I droop with relief at her rescue. "If I get in trouble because he gave me a bum bracelet, my mom is going to fire all of you."

I don't think; I just slip down the hall before Deputy Armstrong can turn back around. I was so preoccupied with avoiding Sheriff Calhoun and seeing Dr. Bates I completely forgot about him.

I'm not sure why, but I've never hated him as much as Sheriff Calhoun. Maybe because he was at the hospital that night, too, crying in the corner for hours. Even so, I don't believe his story. He says he was chasing a car that fled a stop when he crashed into my mom, but he couldn't remember the license plate or describe the vehicle, and his camera, which should have been recording, had been off for hours.

At the end of the hallway, I see a sign that says CORONER, which directs me down a flight of stairs. I expect to run into a lab tech or someone's assistant, but the dark hall is completely empty except for a bucket set up under a dripping leak in the ceiling. There are voices coming from a door casting a triangle of light onto the stained carpet. One of them sounds horribly familiar.

"But why do you take samples of the stomach if you know he died of a heart attack?"

The label above the door says AUTOPSY ROOM. I push the handle and peek in. A tall woman with a blond crew cut is standing next to a corpse. She's taking notes in a spiral binder while Zane holds a scalpel above the dead man's chest. The name tag clipped to her white lab coat says DR. BATES.

"In case the attending doctor was wrong," she says. "Do you remember what step comes next?"

I start to back away from the door, but I trip over my shoe, which squeaks like a mouse. Dr. Bates looks up at me with the same mismatched eyes I've been seeing across the lunch table for weeks. The only real difference between Zane's face and hers is the nose; his is long and straight, like Wimsey's, while hers is snubbed. They might not share a last name, but it's obvious she's his mother.

Guess I know who stole my coroner's internship.

18

XAVIER'S BACK-TO-SCHOOL PARTY
Two Months Ago

IT WAS A HOT AUGUST NIGHT, AND ZANE'S TEMPLES WERE covered with sweat as he watched Xavier Torres play beach volleyball with his friends by the light of tiki torches. Xavier's body, so fit and healthy, was the exact opposite of Ethan's. When Zane had last seen his friend in the hospital, his bloated white face—trapped under a ventilator—looked more dead than alive.

Xavier spiked the ball, and Zane used the cover of the cheering to adjust the fake pen clipped to his shirt pocket. He'd found it at a discount on some PI website; even so, it had cost every penny he'd earned in the past month. The guy he'd bought it from had promised the secret camera would last for hours—"Top in its class! Used by the FBI!"—and Zane had paid because he didn't know how long it would take to get Xavier alone.

His chance came sooner than he expected. Xavier left the volleyball match and sat down on a stone bench by the pool under a squat palm tree.

"Hey, Xavier, watch this," one of the partiers in the water called to him. "The girls are diving off the board to see whose bikini top stays on."

Xavier ignored his friend, his head buried in his phone. He frowned like it held bad news.

Zane skirted by the students taking body shots and approached Xavier. The flame of the nearby torches threw his shadow over the boy and his phone.

"Remember me?" Zane asked.

Xavier didn't even wince when he looked up at Zane's face, even though the last time they'd seen each other, they'd been sitting in plastic chairs at the sheriff's station, hands bound with zip ties. Unlike Zane, Xavier had been cleared of wrongdoing and sent home, but he'd still had to sweat it out for a few hours under the glare of the fluorescent lights until his fancy attorney showed up.

"Sure," Xavier said. "You're the guy whose dad owns that shitty houseboat on North Beach."

"You mean the guy whose friend you put in a coma."

Xavier tucked his phone into his shorts and stood up, looking annoyed that he only came up to Zane's chest. "You're confused, bro," he said. "And this is a private party. J. Everett students only."

Zane hadn't wanted Xavier to know he'd transferred until after the back-to-school party, so anytime he'd seen him in the halls over the past week, he'd ducked around a corner or into a classroom. Luckily, Zane had the kind of face people excused for everything, so even when he stepped into a freshman biology class to hide, the teacher had smiled and asked if she could help him.

"I have evidence it was you who wanted to blow up the pier," Zane said.

"Evidence, huh?" Xavier grinned, his tanned face a picture of cool unconcern. "Do tell."

"I recorded you on my phone."

"Must have been pretty slick about it," Xavier said, glancing down at Zane's hand. "Phones aren't easy to hide."

"I didn't bring it with me," Zane said. "It's somewhere safe."

Before Zane could get another word out, Xavier lunged at him with such speed that Zane stumbled backward toward the pool, catching himself only a few inches from the edge. "Safe, huh?" Xavier laughed, getting back in Zane's face. "And now you want money?"

"What else?" Zane said, though he wouldn't have touched a red cent of Xavier's. "I know you're blackmailing that teacher at school, so you should understand how this works."

Xavier stared at Zane for ten seconds, during which Zane allowed himself to hope. *Just say the words.*

"Yeah, I'm not some dumb bitch scared of her ex-husband." Xavier's smile got even wider. "And you have nothing on me. Nice try, jackass."

Zane's spirit surged with the same exhilaration he got when he went surfing. He'd done it. He'd gotten Xavier on camera admitting to the blackmail he'd bragged about over the Fourth of July. But before Zane could escape with his prize, Xavier pushed him hard in the chest—and straight into the pool.

Zane hit the water with a giant splash. A blond girl who'd just jumped off the diving board screamed and tried to get out of his way, but he hit her hip with a head-shaking jolt. When he came up spluttering, Xavier was standing at the edge of the pool.

"Dope form, bro," Xavier said. "I'd give you a seven out of ten."

Anger and chlorine burned Zane's throat and eyes as he swam in the other direction, moving bodies aside and trying to keep his chest above the water so his pen didn't get any wetter.

Students he half recognized stared as he hauled himself up the stairs, shorts and T-shirt dripping.

"Hey!" one of them shrieked, holding her hand over the top of her strawberry wine cooler.

The girl next to her hopped up onto bare feet. Her hair was pink, and she was wearing a crocheted monokini and mala beads on her wrist. Zane knew her name was Rose because they had chemistry together. "I see you've been Xavied," Rose said. "I'll help you find clean clothes."

"Thanks, but don't bother." Zane forced himself to smile and stripped off his shirt so he didn't feel so much like a drowned rat. "I was going to take a dip in the ocean anyway."

Her return smile was bright, and Zane found himself wishing his charm worked as well on Dulce, the girl from Maldonado's. Ever since he'd been shown her picture in the yearbook, he'd had the strangest urge to touch her bunny birthmark.

Zane had planned to leave the party after he'd gotten the confession, but now he wasn't sure. What if the recording had been damaged? Should he sneak inside the house to see if there was any evidence in Xavier's room?

Zane needed time to think, so he moved to the cocktail table on the other side of the pool near the beach gate, where he could make a quick exit if Xavier, who was already absorbed in his phone again, spotted him. Everything was make-your-own, and a few girls were drunkenly mixing together iced tea, orange Kool-Aid, and whiskey, a drink Zane would have found fun any other night. Behind them, Enzo Torres was measuring something into shot glasses.

One of the girls giggled as she watched Enzo stir the drinks. "Why do you always wear black?" she asked.

"Branded clothing is a billboard for capitalists," he said.

The girl stared at Enzo blankly before running after her friends. Emi had told Zane the Torres brothers hated each other. Maybe Enzo would give up some dirt on Xavier.

"Your brother's a real asshole, you know that?" Zane said.

Enzo grabbed the shot glasses off the table. "*Fiat justitia ruat caelum.*"

"What?" Zane asked. He wasn't sure what language Enzo was speaking, but it sounded familiar, like he'd read it somewhere recently.

Enzo took the shots over to Xavier. Even from the cocktail table, Zane could see the look of surprise and—was it happiness?—on Xavier's face when his brother offered him one of the shots. They drank them in one gulp and then smashed their glasses into the palm tree, laughing as if it was some kind of inside joke.

Before their laughs ended, Sierra Fox walked out of the Torres house wearing a miniskirt and a gold bikini top with matching jewelry. She marched across the limestone toward Xavier, who stood up when he saw her, a look of hot fury on his face.

"I told you not to come," Xavier shouted, his voice splitting the air like a shotgun. The pool partiers froze in place. Rose stood stupidly at the end of the diving board, watching Sierra close the distance to the bench.

"And I ignored your texts," Sierra said, spinning her thumb ring around like she was nervous. Her voice was low, but the silence of everyone else made it impossible to hide her words. "You can't break up with me without a discussion."

"I just did."

"We should do this somewhere private." Sierra grabbed his wrist.

Xavier threw her hand off like it had stung him. "Why?" he said, and Zane saw that his forehead had broken out in beads of sweat. "So your friends won't know you cheated . . . o-on . . . m-me?"

The last words came out in a choked wheeze, and Xavier clutched his chest, breathing hard.

"Xavi?" Sierra asked, sounding hesitant. "What's wrong?"

The crowd of students gasped as Xavier stumbled back toward the bench, missing it entirely as he tried to sit down.

"Xavi!" Sierra cried.

When Enzo yelled, "Call an ambulance!" everything turned to pandemonium. Xavier's friends scattered like spilled seeds. They grabbed their flip-flops and towels and made for the darkness of the beach so the cops who came with the ambulance wouldn't see them fleeing. As Zane ran for the sand, he looked back once at Xavier, who was on the ground with Sierra and Enzo bent over him.

When Zane got home and plugged the pen into his laptop, his stomach sank into black hollowness. The file had been corrupted by the pool water. He had nothing incriminating to show Channel Z News.

Zane yanked the pen out of its slot and flung it against the wall, leaving a black ink stain. "Fuck!" he yelled, not caring if his mom heard him. How had his life gone to shit in such a short period of time? A friend in a coma, criminal charges hanging over his head, and now Xavier's violence had screwed him over once again.

Zane steadied himself against his desk. There was only one option left. No matter what it took, he had to convince the blackmailed teacher to help him end Xavier's threats for good.

19

"SORRY," DR. BATES SAYS. "I THOUGHT I SHUT THE DOOR. Can I help you?"

Zane raises his head, and when he sees me, his face turns as bloodless as the corpse. "Oh crap," he says.

I run down the hall as fast as I can, which isn't very fast, because it's dark and I'm clumsy.

"Dulce, wait!" Zane calls from behind me. "I can explain."

Zane catches up to me at the staircase, where a flickering bulb is doing its best to make the hallway feel like a creepy horror movie. "I'm sorry," he says. "I should have told you."

"You *lied* to me," I say, halfway to tears.

"I know, but I had no idea someone else wanted the internship until Ms. Moss said you lost it. My mom is always complaining about how hard it is to fill, so when Sheriff Calhoun told me I should take it . . ."

He stops like he knows what he's saying isn't making things better.

"Why would the sheriff care about your internship?" I ask.

Zane hesitates as if he's deciding whether to tell me.

"You know what?" I say. "Never mind."

I turn back up the steps, but Zane touches my hand. "Don't go." His eyes are pleading under his lashes, which look dark in the low light. "I'll tell you."

I draw my hand away and cross my arms, which are trembling. I don't know Zane very well, but I still feel deeply betrayed, like I'd filed him in the category of people who wouldn't disappoint me.

"I got in trouble this summer," he says, scuffing his sneaker against the carpet. "I was hanging out with these guys who came up with a really stupid idea to blow up this old pier on North Beach. I tried to stop them, but no one listened. When the police caught us, the guy who came up with the plan blamed me."

"You told me your *friend* got in trouble," I say.

Zane's nose twitches. "I didn't want to tell you because it's embarrassing. The sheriff is threatening to charge me with felony use of an explosive device. He told me to take the coroner's internship to"—he pauses—"keep an eye on me."

"Is this why you warned me off investigating?" I ask. "To keep me from finding out you had this internship?"

"No," Zane says. "Honestly, I never thought you'd come here."

"Then why?"

"Because—"

I wait with my fingers clenched into fists. I'm seeing a whole new side of Zane, and I don't like it.

Zane says the rest in a rush. "Because the guy who planned the crime and blamed me was Xavier Torres. And I don't think you should put yourself in danger for such a piece of shit."

My heart beats three times as fast as the water dripping into the bucket while I take this in. No wonder Xavier confronted

Zane in the cafeteria the day he died; he probably thought Zane was there to make trouble.

"The guy responsible for your life sucking just happened to get poisoned two weeks after you started at J. Everett?" I say, not bothering to keep the sarcasm out of my voice. "That's quite a coincidence."

I skim over the case alibis in my head to make sure Zane's is watertight. Ms. Moss confirmed she and Zane were in the band room at noon, and she couldn't have made a mistake because the church bells can be heard all over the school, not to mention her frog clock ribbits on the hour.

"I'm in enough trouble without murdering someone," Zane mumbles.

"But won't it help your case if Xavier can't testify?"

Zane stares at the wall. "Maybe. But do you really think I'd poison Emi?"

I think about all the facts that prove he likes her. "No," I finally say. "And you'd have no reason to, since you knew she'd been fired from the case." Looking at his flushed ears makes me remember the scene in the library. "I guess you really were looking at nudes for your internship."

His lips quiver unhappily. "You're not as shy as you think you are."

"I'm not . . . what?" I say, taken aback by the abrupt switch in subject.

"You just suggested I might have murdered someone. That takes guts. Emi might be louder than you, but you're no pushover."

"Why are you telling me this?" I ask, wishing I knew how Lord Wimsey always saw through Harriet Vane's vague words to figure out what she was really saying.

"I don't know." Zane runs a hand through his already-mussed hair, like he's actually unsure. "I guess I don't think you should hide what makes you shine." His forehead crinkles. "Sorry, that sounds like a bad line. It's just"—he takes one step up the stairs so his face is right below mine, both of his eyes dark in the flickering light—"I feel like you think you're a ghost next to her, and I want you to know that you're not. Other people see you too." He takes a little breath. "I see you."

I have zero idea how to respond. I don't even know why he's saying it, unless he's trying to get me to forget he's been lying to me.

"Okay," I say.

He laughs softly and takes a step back down the stairs, breaking the moment. It's clear he hoped I'd say something different, but I'm not sure what.

"Can you forgive me for not being totally honest?" he asks much more lightly.

I get why he didn't blab his life story to us. I wouldn't want my new friends to know I might be on my way to a criminal record either. But if Zane can lie about the internship and his history with Xavier, what else might he be lying about?

"I've agreed to help Sierra find out who killed Xavier," I say, watching Zane's face fall. "Your mom might know something. If you introduce me to her, I'll *consider* forgiving you."

My hand moves to my purse, but I don't tell him about the folded document inside. That's between me and Dr. Bates.

Zane nods slowly. "Deal. I've wanted you to meet her anyway."

When we get back to the autopsy room, Dr. Bates covers the corpse's face like she's trying to protect his identity, even though he's entirely naked on the table. My dad would be making so many signs of the cross if he were here. Then he'd yell at Dr. Bates for showing a dead body to a teenage girl.

"Mom, this is Dulce," Zane says.

"Ah, the girl who loves detective novels," she says. "I'm not much for fiction myself. Prefer a good true crime podcast."

Zane's talked about me at home?

"She wants to ask you about Xavier Torres," Zane says. "She's Sierra Fox's detective."

Dr. Bates turns sharp eyes on me, and it's clear Zane didn't get his surfer chill from her.

"Aren't you a little young to be investigating a murder?" she asks.

Practical haircut. Precise handwriting in her binder. Brisk speech. Conclusion: Dr. Bates is a straight shooter.

"Yes," I say. "But no one else is willing to do it. Sheriff Calhoun wants the mayor to lose in November, so he's already decided Sierra is guilty."

"And let me guess." Dr. Bates's voice is mocking. "You're sure she's not."

"I'm not sure of anything," I admit. "But I want to find out."

"Hmm," she says with what sounds like approval. "You're a scientist. Like me."

She stares at the door for a minute, like she's trying to make a decision, then she walks over and closes it. When she turns back around, her face is grim. "If you repeat this, I'll deny it, but Sheriff Calhoun is a stain on this town and on this station. I wouldn't trust him to find his ass with both hands, much less a killer."

Zane flashes me a quick proud smile.

"Then you'll help?" I ask.

"I'll tell you what I can that won't lose me my job," she says, walking to a rusty filing cabinet. "But it doesn't look great for Sierra." She pulls out a folder and waves it in the air. "I'm old school. Don't trust computers. Too easy to hack." My stomach tingles, like it feels shy about having something in common with Zane's mom. "Here's what I can tell you," she continues, flipping the folder open. "Xavier died because three hundred milligrams of nicotine were injected into his bloodstream by a knitting needle fitted with an automatic syringe designed to release its contents on contact with the victim. The angle of the attack was steep, like someone taller than Xavier jabbed it into him."

"Taller?" I think of the three suspects. In heels, Sierra is two inches taller than Xavier. Enzo is about the same height. And Rose is barely five feet tall, maybe the shortest student at school.

"Unless Xavier was kneeling or the killer was standing on one of the greenhouse tables," Dr. Bates says. "Then it could be someone shorter."

Which rules out exactly no one.

"Is it hard to make liquid nicotine?" I ask. The research I pulled off Emi's laptop this morning says no, but Dr. Google is not the same thing as Dr. Bates, and I can't ask any of the teachers at J. Everett.

"Not hard enough," she says. "If it weren't easy to detect, people would probably be knocking off rich relatives all the time."

"Could someone with access to tobacco plants make it?"

"Sure, if they had a large number of plants. But it would be simpler to use cigarettes or even buy nicotine on the internet."

"Is there any evidence Sierra *didn't* do it?" I ask, getting desperate.

"Afraid not," Dr. Bates says, flipping another page. "At least, not in the files I have access to. There might be something in the interviews or in the police reports that could help you, but Sheriff Calhoun keeps those in his office upstairs." She trails her finger down a page full of handwritten notes. "There is one strange detail from the autopsy no one knows what to make of." She raises blond eyebrows. "This wasn't the first time someone poisoned Xavier with nicotine."

"What?" I ask, my voice rising an octave. "Someone tried to kill him twice?"

"I'm not sure," Dr. Bates says. "All I know is that six days before he was found dead, he was admitted to the ER with trouble breathing. I had a strange feeling about that when I saw it in his records, so I tested the blood they took from him that night."

"The night of the party," Zane mutters.

The same night Xavier and Sierra had a blowout fight in front of half the school. No wonder Rose was so surprised to see Xavier at the Poisoner's Festival.

"He seemed fine the next day," I say. "Wouldn't nicotine have made him really sick?"

"A small overdose would metabolize quickly," Dr. Bates says. "The doctor didn't even suspect poisoning. Thought he'd drank too much. Xavier felt better after some oxygen and fluids, so they released him the next morning."

Someone had given Xavier nicotine at the party. But how? He would have told the doctors if he'd felt someone stick him with a needle.

"Enzo and Rose were at the party, too, right?" I ask Zane, who nods.

"If Sierra didn't kill Xavier Torres, then the crime was planned by someone very clever," Dr. Bates says. "They did a wonderful job of making her look guilty."

Enzo is clever, but Rose is not. I try to picture her standing on a table in the greenhouse, stabbing Xavier while her mala beads rattle. It's a ridiculous image, like something out of a comic book.

"Any other questions?" Dr. Bates asks.

My heart begins to race double time. The truth is that I have an ulterior motive for wanting to talk to her. Except I can't do it in front of Zane.

"Could you make sure Sierra hasn't been arrested again?" I ask him. "She's supposed to be distracting the deputies, but sometimes she goes overboard."

"Sure," Zane says with an easygoing smile, like I didn't call him a could-be murderer. "I'll be back in a few minutes, Mom."

"Mr. Potts will still be here," she says, waving a hand at the naked man.

"You're so dark," he says, and for a second, I'm afraid he's talking to me. Just like in the greenhouse, being close to a corpse isn't freaking me out at all. Mr. Potts feels like the histology equipment in the corner—interesting, in a scientific sense, but not gross or creepy. I'm glad Zane's mom seems pretty normal, because otherwise I'd be wondering if there's something wrong with me.

"That wasn't very subtle," Dr. Bates says once Zane has closed the door behind him.

"He's too nice to notice I was getting rid of him," I tell her.

"I know how little say I have in the matter, but please don't involve him in this," she says. "He's in enough trouble as it is."

"Yeah, he told me."

"He has a bright future—if he stops being such a dumbass." She sighs. "I was so relieved when your dean accepted his application. Cape Cherry High threatened to kick him out when they heard what happened." She folds her hands in front of her. "What did you want to ask without Zane around?"

"Aren't we contaminating the body?" I ask, pointing to Mr. Potts.

"It's a routine autopsy." Dr. Bates glances at him. "To confirm cause of death. It's not a crime scene, and he hasn't been opened up yet, so we don't have to worry about him infecting us." She raises her eyebrows. "You sent Zane away for that?"

"N-no," I say, stumbling over my words a little. "You did the autopsy on my mom two years ago."

"That's not a question," she says, but her eyes scan my face with a new intensity, like she's trying to find a resemblance between me and someone who's been on her table. "What's your last name?"

"Castillo. Her name was Ana."

Dr. Bates's face morphs into something less stiff. "That was a sad one. I'm sorry."

I pull my dad's copy of the coroner's report out of my purse and unfold it. "You said you found alcohol in her blood, but my mom didn't drink. Ever."

"Sometimes we don't know people as well as we think we do."

"Her dad was an alcoholic," I press. "It ruined her family. She'd never even had a sip of beer."

Dr. Bates puts on her glasses and holds out her hand like something in my tone has convinced her. "Let me see." She scans through the report I hand her before frowning. "I remember this now. Her elevated blood alcohol was from the fire."

My stomach swoops like I'm falling down a flight of stairs. "W-what do you mean, from the f-fire?" I say, stammering so much I'm not sure she'll understand me.

"When Deputy Armstrong hit your mom, her gas tank exploded. Bodies exposed to high heat can register false positives on blood alcohol tests. I'm sure I noted that."

"It's not noted." I struggle to control my trembling voice. I memorized the words of the report during more late nights than I care to remember.

Dr. Bates's frown deepens as she flips through the pages. "This can't be right." She returns to the filing cabinet and thumbs through folders until she finds the one she wants and pulls a stapled document out of it. "Here it is," she says. "In a note at the bottom. *Elevated blood alcohol level. Result of extensive burning. No evidence of alcohol consumption.*" She compares it to the report I handed her. "I don't understand. This one is cut off after the first sentence."

"The sheriff announced your findings," I say, remembering how his press conference had played on Channel Z News for days. "He specifically said she'd been drinking. Everyone believed it."

Dr. Bates points to the filing cabinet. "Like I told you: old school. Zane and I don't even own a TV out at the farm. I do my work, and then I go home and feed my chickens. I try not to pay attention to the sheriff, and he does me the courtesy of not paying attention in return, mostly because he knows there's no other coroner within a sixty-mile radius."

I walk over to her desk, where she's placed the two reports side by side. "It's not a copying error," I say, tracing my finger around the black border framing the page, "because the line below the final sentence is unbroken. Someone covered up your conclusion on purpose."

A charged silence envelops us like a blanket, making the dead body a witness to what we're both thinking. Dr. Bates must feel it, too, because she pulls a sheet over Mr. Potts.

"I've no doubt Sheriff Calhoun did exactly that," she says quietly. "But he'll never admit it. Even if you accused him, he'd blame Deputy Armstrong or someone else who works here." She sits down at her desk and signs onto her computer. After a few minutes of searching, she finds the digital version of the report. "He scrubbed the digital file too," she says. "Which means mine might be the only true copy left. Bill's never been in this room; he probably doesn't know I still use paper."

"If this copy disappears, there will be no proof," I say, thinking quickly. My flip phone's camera is from the dark ages, but it's better than nothing. "Can I take a picture?" I ask, pulling it out. "Just in case the station catches on fire or something."

"Sure," she says. "But if anyone questions me, I'll say you snuck in here and stole it."

"I'll take that risk." I snap a couple of shots. I wish I could send it to my email, but my phone only works around old cell towers. There's still a few left in town—including near my house and J. Everett—but the sheriff's station has been upgraded so residents can reach it during tornadoes and lightning storms.

"I'm sorry," I say, surprised to see Dr. Bates's crushed expression as she watches me scroll through the pictures to make sure I've framed them right. "I know he's your boss."

Her laugh sounds like a bark. "I'm not worried about that corrupt old fool. I'm just wondering how many times my conclusions have been twisted like this." She hands me my useless copy of the report. "I hate to think people have been hurt because I leave my work at work."

"If you'd contradicted him, he probably would have fired you."

"True," she says thoughtfully. "Can I ask you a favor? Don't do anything with those pictures yet. Let me think about how to handle this. I know you're a very competent young lady, but it's hard for anyone to go up against the full force of the law, especially when the man in charge has ways of making problems disappear."

"Disappear?" I say, not bothering to hide the tremble in my voice this time.

"Never underestimate angry men, Dulce. It could be the last thing you do."

20

"YOU GOT IN-SCHOOL SUSPENSION?" EMI SAYS, STOPPING mid-bite of her cherry Jell-O. Her face is pale, but other than that, she looks completely normal, like she's sitting in her living room instead of the crappy patients' ward at Cape Cherry General. Half the hospital was renovated two years ago, but Emi's room is in the old wing, overlooking the twin yellow arches of the McDonald's next door. The television hanging on the wall has a crack in the top corner, like a patient threw a remote at it.

"It's fine," I say. "Are you sure you're okay?"

Emi waves my question away. To be fair, it's the fourth time I've asked her. "Two months ago, you were spiraling because you got detention," she says. "And now you don't mind if UVA sees you got suspended?"

"Two months ago, no one had tried to kill you." I deliberately keep my eyes off Rose, who's sitting in a visitor's chair at Emi's bedside, holding her non-Jell-O-eating hand. Several of Emi's plastic bracelets dangle from her wrist like they've been trading them back and forth along their arms. It feels like Rose is breaking an unspoken rule by swooping in and being Emi's comfort friend when the only reason I wasn't here earlier is that I had to stay after school to hear another lecture from Dean Whitaker.

"Well, if my poisoning is what it took for you to get a visit from the spirit of Wimsey, then it was worth it." Emi frowns. "Except for the way my heart beats like I'm running a marathon and how I might have organ damage." Then she shrugs like those things are minor details. "Sierra may be the biggest bitchwitch in the world, but I want to go to England next summer. And save J. Everett from the clutches of evil." She takes another bite of Jell-O. "I'll help once I'm better. Sierra can't fire me if I don't want to be fired."

I was afraid Emi might be so upset about our fight that she'd refuse to speak to me, but like always, she's gotten over being mad in a heartbeat.

"Sierra fired you?" Rose asks, her voice light with surprise.

Satisfaction twists my stomach. I was right: Emi hadn't told Rose about Sierra freaking out, which means she could still be the poisoner.

"The sheriff will probably close the school again now that there's been a second poisoning," I say. "But once the investigation is over, I'm going after the camera footage in the dean's office."

"I wouldn't worry about school closing." Emi's tone is suspiciously smug.

"Why not?"

"I told the cops I accidentally poisoned myself," she says, ripping the lid off a lemon Jell-O. She has five more unopened cups lined up on her tray, which I suspect she stole when a nurse's back was turned. "With nicotine I was growing in gardening class."

"You did *what?*"

"Brilliant, right? Now the cops won't interfere with your investigation." Her lips purse like the last bite of Jell-O was sour. "Hey, no fair breaking into Dean Whitaker's office without me. You have to wait."

"The election is only three weeks away," I remind her. "There's no time to lose."

"Don't do it, Dulce," Rose blurts out, her cheeks turning pink as posies. "Sierra killed Xavi. I know she did. If you keep working for her, you could be next."

An awkward silence ensues.

"Do you know that because of your tarot cards?" Emi asks gently, like Rose is a porcelain teacup swaddled in cotton.

Rose nods. "They say something terrible will happen if we keep helping Sierra."

Her tarot cards are remarkably good at diverting the investigation away from her, but I can't say that in front of Emi.

"I know you're not a believer," Rose says, watching me carefully. "But the mystical world wants to keep Emi safe. I think you can at least believe in that."

Stroking Emi's hand like it's a precious diamond. Leaning so far forward onto the bed she's almost in Emi's lap. Tears trembling at the edges of her eyes.

Conclusion: Rose doesn't have a crush on Emi; she's head over heels in love with her.

My thoughts tear in half as a new picture of Rose emerges. Unless she's faking her feelings—and faking them well—it's hard to believe she'd poison Emi. But her story about eating lunch on top of the icehouse is nonsense, and I don't buy the friendship-bracelet crap. Why lie if she wasn't involved in Xavier's murder?

Is it possible Xavier's killer and Emi's poisoner aren't the same person? No. The chances that two different people are attacking students with nicotine is astronomically low.

Or maybe Rose is innocent of both things. Everyone but me thinks the idea of her as a killer is laughable. Have I let my jealousy over Emi's new friendship bias me?

I shake the doubts out of my head. Wimsey says to ignore the psychology. I can't rule Rose out just because she might have big feelings for Emi. Criminals hurt people they love all the time.

But Rose might drop her defenses if I pretend I'm quitting the case. "Maybe you're right." I watch her sigh with relief. "Enough terrible things have happened already."

Emi frowns like she can't believe I'm giving up so quickly. I feel bad about lying, but if I don't, she'll try to investigate with me instead of recovering. If I can get all the evidence I need fast enough, maybe I can find the poisoner before she's out of the hospital—even if that person turns out to be the girl holding her hand.

"Tarot cards or not, I should have helped you when you asked." I move closer to Emi. "I was being a bad friend."

"Love your fingernails," she says, forgiving me with a silly grin.

I smile back. "Love your earlobes."

"You know what this means, right?" Rose says.

It means I'm going to have to ask the last person in the world I want to talk to for help again.

"What?" I ask.

"We'll all be alive for the Detective's Ball in two weeks."

I've been so preoccupied I forgot about the school formal on

Halloween. It's technically a Sadie Hawkins dance, but even though no one insists on any gender asking another, it's still semi-traditional for girls to ask everyone else.

"A thrilling thought," I say, because once again, I have nobody to ask. "Maybe I should pretend I got poisoned too. Can't dance if I'm busy eating Jell-O."

"You should ask Zane," Emi says.

A weird chill sends goose bumps up my arm. The hospital must have the air conditioner on high. "I don't like him like that," I tell her.

"Then you won't care if I ask him?"

I glance at Rose, but she doesn't look disappointed by Emi's proposal; in fact, I could swear she's trying not to grin. Am I wrong about her liking Emi? Is my stupid tapestry full of loose ends?

"No. Of course not."

"Speak now or forever hold your peace," Emi says in a singsong.

It's not that I can't see it: Zane in a suit, touching my lower back as we sway to the music, one hand brushing my hair behind my ear. His lips close to mine, telling me he likes my Wimsey wear. But I've known since the assembly that the right match is Emi and Zane, not me and Zane.

"Invite him," I repeat. "I don't care."

"Fine," Emi says breezily. "I'll let you know how he kisses."

On Thursday morning, I wait for Sierra in the parking lot where the food trucks were lined up during the Poisoner's Festival. She walks right past me, but when I clear my throat, she turns around. Her face scrunches up unpleasantly, like I'm some pimply-faced freshman who just catcalled her.

"Come to apologize?" she says.

"For what?" I ask.

"You left me in the sheriff's parking lot for *an hour*. I thought we'd be back before Dean Whitaker knew we were gone. My mom is furious I'm getting in trouble at school when I already have to wear this." She lifts her foot and wiggles her ankle monitor. "She asked if I *wanted* her to lose the election." Sierra throws her arms in the air, nearly getting her fingers tangled in her own mass of curls. "And for what? You didn't find anything."

Except proof the sheriff tampered with my mom's autopsy report. Every part of me wants to march into Channel Z News and demand they investigate the sheriff, but I know Dr. Bates is right; I can't beat him alone.

"Does that mean this isn't a good time to ask you to help me break into Dean Whitaker's office?"

Sierra's eyes narrow until there's almost no blue left. "Is that a joke?"

"Like you said, we need the camera footage. The video he wouldn't let Emi see. It might show Enzo's movements that day. We can finally nail him."

Zane might have seen Enzo upstairs ten minutes before noon, but no one knows where he went after that, when Xavier was in the greenhouse; if he went outside, the camera will show it.

"Why should I pay you thirty thousand dollars when I'm having to do half the work?" she snaps.

"Fine, don't help," I say. "And when I get caught, you can

comfort yourself with the knowledge that your full trust fund will be available when you get out of prison."

We glare at each other. Her bright eyes burning into mine remind me of the time in eighth grade when she accused me of purposely giving her the wrong answers on a math test so she'd look stupid in front of Austin Smith. Unlike then, I don't back down.

"Ugh, okay," she finally says. "But I don't think Dean Whitaker is going to fall for the whole broken-ankle-monitor routine."

"I have a different idea." I bite my lip. "Though you're not going to like it either."

"Let me guess. Pull the fire alarm?"

I can't help but smile a little because, if I'm being honest, I finally understand why Wimsey was always breaking the law. It's kind of fun.

"How would you feel about faking a poisoning?"

"Scientists can now pull DNA from hair samples even when the root isn't attached," Dean Whitaker says. "Amazing, right?"

"Uh-huh," I mumble, hoping he can't tell how distracted I am.

I'm in his office for our weekly independent study class. He spent the first five minutes warning me that colleges won't look kindly on my behavior issues, but now he's deep into an explanation of forensic hair analysis. To my surprise, Dean Whitaker is actually a good teacher. I would have learned more in Dr. Bates's lab, but the dean isn't the airhead playboy I always imagined. Which makes me feel a bit bad about what Sierra and I are going to do.

"What if the rootless hair is contaminated with—"

A violent knocking at the door interrupts my words. Dean Whitaker leaps up like he's been dreading more bad news. Sierra comes crashing through the doorway while Mrs. Hinkle, the school secretary, shimmies her way out of her seat and shrieks, "I will *not* have students continue to violate this office!"

"Stanley, you have to come," Sierra says, and I admit I'm impressed by her dedication to her performance. Her hair is wild, her scarlet lipstick is smeared halfway up her cheek . . . and are those real tears? "It's Gregory Yi. He's been poisoned."

"Shit," Dean Whitaker says under his breath, lunging for the same cabinet he got the atropine from two days before. Even though I know Sierra is lying, my stomach clenches with nausea because it brings back the image of Emi convulsing on the ground.

"Call 911," Dean Whitaker tells Mrs. Hinkle as he follows Sierra out the door and into the hallway, carrying the little bottle and syringe.

Mrs. Hinkle flaps her way back to her seat and busies herself with the phone. I had a plan ready if Dean Whitaker asked me to call the ambulance, but I hoped he would turn to the nearest adult instead. I take advantage of Mrs. Hinkle's distraction and shut the office door as quietly as I can before rushing over to Dean Whitaker's laptop.

The camera outside is labeled with a make and model, which made it easy to find out that it records footage onto an SD card before sending it to the cloud. I'd get caught in about five seconds if I tried to physically remove the card, but it should be easy enough to access the cloud and download the file to my thumb drive. At least according to the instructional videos I watched last night.

Luckily, Sierra had the dean's password: *Lilybug*7*. "He stays over all the time," she told me. "So I've seen him enter it at the kitchen table in the morning. It's the same one he uses to stream Netflix and Hulu, so it should work for everything."

My fingers shake hard as I type the password into his laptop, adrenaline coursing through my body like someone forgot to tell it we were supposed to be having fun.

When I press enter, the dean's desktop pops up. I breathe a sigh of relief. First hurdle jumped.

I open his browser and type in the name of the security camera's website: CamCam. A silly name, but easy to remember. I hit log in at the top right corner of the page, enter the dean's email address, and then type in *Lilybug*7*.

Brown letters appear above the box. USERNAME AND PASSWORD DO NOT MATCH.

I type it in again to make sure I didn't mishit a key but get the same error message.

Uh-oh.

Nervous energy shudders down my legs as I try to decide what to do next. I just assumed Sierra was right about the passwords all being the same, but I should have pushed her harder. Asked her to test it out at home first.

I watch the cursor blink. Maybe I don't need the cloud. Emi said the sheriff had the footage, so Dean Whitaker must have downloaded it for him. I scroll through the dean's files, searching for *camera* or *footage* or *security*. But I don't find anything.

My legs tremble harder. Sierra is going to freak when she finds out her performance was for nothing. Maybe there's a way we can steal the footage from the sheriff's office instead . . .

I stop. If Dean Whitaker didn't save the footage to a file, how *did* the sheriff get it? The dean might have handed him the SD card, but there's a much easier way to transfer files. One that wouldn't require the very lazy Sheriff Calhoun to make an extra trip to the school.

Excitement pulses in my temples. I click on the dean's mail icon and navigate to his sent messages. I type the name *Bill* into the search bar, hoping the dean addressed the email. A dozen messages pull up, with titles like *Student Admission* and *Library Book Content*, but the only one with an attachment is titled *Security Footage*, sent a week after Xavier died.

"Gotcha," I say aloud.

All I have to do now is download the attachment to my thumb drive. I pull the drive out of my back pocket and jam it into the side of the laptop, but the metal rectangle hits the computer with an unsuccessful click.

"You've got to be kidding me," I say, spinning the laptop side to side, looking for a USB port, but it's no use. The dean has one of those MacBooks with the tiny slits, and my thumb drive is a relic left over from middle school. I pull his desk drawer open to look for an adapter, but I find only pencils and a small leather-bound notebook marked LEDGER wrapped with a thick rubber band.

My thoughts race as I keep my ears open for anyone approaching the door. Mrs. Hinkle is still on the phone with 911, but the call has to be close to over. Not to mention Dean Whitaker has probably already arrived at the scene of the supposed poisoning to find no one there.

Think!

The idea that pops into my head makes it much more likely I'll get caught, but it's either that or give up. I hit forward on the dean's email to the sheriff and type in my school email address. I can delete the message after, but if the dean has his emails backed up, he'll still be able to find it.

When I press send, a notification pops up telling me the file is too big and will be turned into a Google Drive link. Another trace of what I've done. Cursing the school's file size restrictions, I confirm the transfer, but at 80 percent complete, I hear Dean Whitaker's booming voice tell Mrs. Hinkle to cancel the ambulance because someone pranked Sierra.

My heart speeds up like it wants to escape my chest.

Then the email dings. Sent.

21

THAT'S WHEN MY GLORIOUS PLAN GOES GLORIOUSLY wrong.

I delete evidence of my email in the second before the office door opens, but in my hurry to escape back to my seat, my tennis shoe gets caught in the base of the dean's swivel chair, making me stumble forward. What happens next is like one of those Rube Goldberg machines, where a marble triggers a chain reaction that can't be stopped. I try to grab the edge of the dean's desk, but my fingers get caught in the power cord stretching from his laptop to the wall. In my panic, I pull at the cord like a falling mountaineer, but the laptop, no match for my weight, flies toward me, making me land straight on my butt. Time slows down as the laptop races across the desk like a tidal wave, dragging the dean's paperweight and a coffee mug that says STUDENT TEARS along with it.

I don't even have time to cover my face as all three things come crashing to the ground. The edge of the laptop hits my leg hard enough to leave a bruise, but before I can even squeal in pain, the coffee mug shatters with an earsplitting crack, spraying cold coffee all over my jeans and the dean's keyboard.

Breathing hard, I look up and see Dean Whitaker standing on the other side of his desk, staring down at me.

If I wasn't about to be in a massive amount of trouble, the expression on his face would be funny. It's somewhere between the look of a man who's seen a poltergeist and one who's learned that someone has stolen his car. Bafflement and anger war for a minute until a single word emerges from the battle: "Dulce?"

"I tripped," I tell him, as if the important part of what's happening is that I'm on the ground and not that I'm behind his desk.

"You two set me up?" he says, putting together Sierra's deception and my stuttering horror. "There was never any third poisoning?"

"I'm sorry," I whisper. "We needed the footage."

"Footage?" he asks, his voice completely exasperated. "What on God's green Earth are you talking about?"

"The camera footage from the day Xavier died."

Dean Whitaker makes his way toward me and the laptop. I scurry around his desk like he's going to chase me, which is ridiculous because he barely even looks mad anymore. I fall onto the seat where I was learning about the pitfalls of hair texture analysis, the adrenaline leeched from my body by my failure to steal the file without getting caught.

"And why would you need that?" he asks, picking up his MacBook and then sitting down in his swivel chair to examine the damage.

"Didn't Emi tell you?"

"She asked for the footage," he says. "I assumed she was after revenge; I know you and Sierra have a difficult history." He digs in his pocket for some tissue and begins to mop up the coffee on the keyboard. "But I'm not going to help hang the girl who's going to be my stepdaughter soon."

He may not realize it, but he's just told me something important.

"There's evidence against Sierra on the footage?" I ask.

The dean goes still, his palm clutching the wet tissue. "I didn't say that—" he starts, but I cut in.

"I'm trying to *help* Sierra," I explain. "That's why she agreed to get you out of your office."

He blinks like he didn't hear me right. "You? Help Sierra?"

I'm about to clarify that I want to solve Emi's poisoning, but then I remember she told everyone she did it herself.

"Dr. Everett wrote that we can't let our feelings get in the way of justice," I say instead, quoting the dean's own class at him.

"He was a wise man," Dean Whitaker says, leaning back with a heavy sigh. "But why didn't one of you tell me what you were up to?"

"We thought you'd stop us."

"Why would I do that?" he asks. "The PI Lily hired was a common crook, and her lawyers stupidly think they can get Sierra off by planting reasonable doubt in the jury's mind. I've tried to help, but—" He stops again, grimacing like he's tasted something rotten.

"But so far, the evidence points to her," I finish.

He nods. "I wish it didn't, but it does."

The dean's words from the day we discovered Xavier's body rush back to me. He called the killer *she*. He thought it was Sierra from the beginning. I remember him looking at his hands after he came out of the greenhouse. *I touched the needle,* he said.

It was hard enough to believe that Sierra had lost her head

and picked up the murder weapon, but how could the dean of a criminology school make the same mistake?

Maybe he hadn't.

"Did you take the pink yarn off the needle when you were alone in the greenhouse?" I ask, my heart picking up speed. "Is that why you really touched it?"

The dean grows very still except for his jaw, which drums next to his ear. "How do you know about the pink yarn?"

"Sierra saw it when she found Xavier."

The dean grabs the paperweight he plucked off the floor and begins flipping the die around in his hand like he's waiting to see what number he rolls before he answers. "Yes, I took it," he says, putting the paperweight down. "I'd seen Sierra teaching Enzo Torres how to knit with the same yarn over Fourth of July weekend, and I wasn't sure how rare it was. Sometimes she buys specialty yarns from other countries, and it's not like I could ask her. I had to make a split-second decision, and that's the call I made." His face tightens. "Protecting Lily's daughter is always the call I'll make."

"But the needle had her initials on it," I say. "The sheriff would already think it's her."

The dean shakes his head. "It would be easy to convince a jury that someone stole one of her needles. She's like the rest of her Stitch 'n' Bitch Club—always carries them around in her school bag. But the pink yarn never left the house." He glances at me sharply. "I'm only telling you this because you're trying to help Sierra," he says. "I have no problem expelling you if you repeat it."

I wonder what Sierra will think when she learns what her mom's fiancé has done for her. Maybe the fact that his name is Stanley won't bother her so much anymore.

"I sent the footage to myself," I say.

The dean groans. "Teenagers always make things so complicated. If Sierra had told me, I would have shown it to you weeks ago."

"Does that mean I'm not in trouble?" I ask.

The dean's dark blue eyes go wide with disbelief. "You bet your ass you're in trouble," he says. "I can't let you break into my laptop without consequences. I'm adding another two days to your in-school suspension."

I droop with relief. He could have reported me to the sheriff. He's letting me off easy.

The dean shakes the laptop over his wastebasket. Droplets of coffee hit the trash bag with soft *plunks*. Then he pulls a can of air from the shelf behind him and blows it all over the keys while they're upside down.

"Let's see if this still works," he says, restarting the computer.

Amazingly, it does, and my stomach unclenches. I haven't ruined something expensive, and I'm only kind of in trouble. Granted, if I'd been given three days of in-school suspension a week ago, I'd be sobbing into Penny's black fur for twenty-four hours straight, but now that I've started worrying about getting arrested, school punishment doesn't seem so bad.

"I have my thoughts on what it means," he says, pulling up the video from the email, "but I'm no detective, so I'll be interested in your opinion."

My stomach does a little do-si-do. He's treating me like a real investigator.

The dean hits play. I've seen the security camera a million mornings before school. It's drilled into a brick above the front door and pointed toward the lawn so that anyone entering the main building gets recorded. The right edge captures part of the parking lot, while on the left, the forest is visible, as are the first few feet of the greenhouse path before it loops down the west side of the house and out of sight.

Dean Whitaker fast-forwards to 11:53 a.m. "This is the first movement the camera catches during lunch," he says.

The person coming out of the front door walks onto the half-circle driveway, but they don't continue to the parking lot; instead they make a left and go toward the forest before disappearing behind some trees.

It's not hard to identify them even though the footage is grainy. Enzo Torres is the only person at school who dresses in all black, and the golden tips of his dark hair are easy to see when he turns in profile.

So he *did* go outside after Zane saw him upstairs. Which means he definitely had the opportunity to kill his brother.

"He could have doubled back onto the greenhouse path," I suggest. "Out of the view of the camera."

"If he killed Xavier, he did it fast," Dean Whitaker says. "Watch."

At 11:59 a.m., only six minutes after he walked out the front door, Enzo Torres comes out of the forest and back onto the half-circle drive. Except this time, he's carrying a huge duffel bag.

"Maybe that's where he put the needle," I say. "He could have hidden the bag earlier in the day."

"I scanned through several days of footage," the dean says, "but didn't see anyone acting unusual. Besides, a duffel seems conspicuous when all he'd need is a small backpack."

Enzo pauses before he reaches the front door. The camera

doesn't record audio, but it's obvious something's caught his attention. He cocks his head to the side and makes a slight motion back toward the drive before stopping in place like he's listening.

"Sierra screamed at noon." I point to the timestamp. "About three minutes after she went out the cafeteria door. She wouldn't have had much time to kill Xavier either."

"She might have screamed before he was dead," the dean says, "to throw off the timeline." He sees my face and adds, "Not that I think she did it, of course."

Enzo obviously decides, like I did, that what he thought was screaming was nothing and enters the school with a slight frown on his face. Three minutes later, Sierra stumbles up the greenhouse path, bent at the waist. Instead of heading for the school, she turns left and plunges into the forest.

"She said she felt sick after seeing Xavier's body," I say.

"So did I." The dean moves the video forward. "Nothing happens for another ten minutes. And then—"

Sierra exits the forest.

"She's coming up the path to the front door," I say, surprised by how relieved I am that the video is matching her story. The dean shakes his head, and a second later, I understand why. Instead of coming up the half-circle drive, Sierra pauses before stomping back down the greenhouse path like someone on a mission.

There's an uncomfortable prickling on the back of my hands. "But she said she came in the front door after the forest," I say. "Why would she go back to the greenhouse?"

Dean Whitaker doesn't answer. Nothing happens for about

three minutes, and then Rose comes running up the greenhouse path. She's carrying a big backpack and keeps looking behind her like she's worried she's being followed. But it's not until her face gets closer to the camera that I get my second shock. She's crying hard, tears streaming down her face as she trips along the gravel drive, looking very unlike her usual graceful self.

"What in the world?" I say.

Two minutes later, someone darts into view of the camera. It's Sierra, and she's flat-out sprinting from the greenhouse path toward the front door, every movement of her body suggesting anguish. Her face is twisted with horror, but my eye twitches when I think about how good her mask of concern was only half an hour ago when she came to get Dean Whitaker for the fake poisoning.

When Sierra enters the school, the dean's eyes meet mine. "Do you understand why I didn't want Emi to see this?" he asks. "I didn't want her to find out Sierra had returned to the crime scene."

I nod, all the facts reeling around in my head, making me seasick. It suddenly feels like I know less about the case than I did an hour ago.

The video is still playing on the dean's laptop, and I'm happy when I see Ms. Moss come out of the house carrying her guitar case at 12:20 p.m. because it confirms Zane's story that they were both inside when Xavier was killed. Without an alibi, Zane's motive would have put him at the top of my list.

"Maybe Sierra decided she wanted to see Xavier's body one last time," I say, even though I know she finds dead things as creepy as Emi. "Or get something she dropped."

My excuses for her are pathetic.

"I'm not sure why she went back down the path," the dean says slowly. "But I do know this: She lied about what happened that day."

My phone dings almost immediately after I leave Dean Whitaker's office, its old speaker making students' heads turn in alarm.

The texts are from Sierra.

> Did the footage prove it was Enzo?
> Um, hello?
> Every minute you don't text me, I'm deducting $100 from your fee.

I put the phone back in my bag without answering. Even though he saw the footage weeks ago, Dean Whitaker obviously hasn't talked to Sierra about what's on it. *Thanks for leaving me to deal with her,* I think, looking in the direction of his office. Given our past, I'm not sure why I'm so shocked to find out Sierra's been lying to me, but it still stings.

Some freshmen I don't recognize are leaning against their lockers, laughing about a chemistry experiment that caught someone's hair on fire. For the briefest instant, I'm jealous of them. They don't care that the game's been canceled. They're not risking expulsion and arrest to solve a murder. In fact, they have no idea there's even a case to be solved. They were probably briefly upset by Xavier's death and then comforted by Sierra's quick arrest. They might even be part of the group of students lobbying Dean Whitaker to kick Sierra out of school so they don't have to attend J. Everett with a killer, having decided she's guilty until proven innocent instead of the other way around.

In my distraction, I run straight into someone's chest.

"Ouch!" a voice says.

"Oh, sorry," I apologize. Then I look up.

Enzo Torres is rubbing his shirt where my head hit him. He looks less like a *brujo* that skins cats and more like a little boy who wants his mom to kiss his boo-boo.

I wait for him to yell at me for not watching where I'm going, but instead he says, "I heard about Emi."

"You—what?" I haven't exchanged more than a dozen words with Enzo in the past year, and after our run-in at the Poisoner's Festival, I would have thought he'd want to make that silence permanent.

"I heard she's getting better," he says, adjusting his black messenger bag like he wants to give his nervous hands something to do. "But you must have been worried."

I glance around, wondering if I'm being punked, but no one else is watching us as they move through the halls toward the lunchroom. "Yeah, I was, actually." I force my eyes to meet his, and I'm surprised to see real pity there, like he both cares about my feelings and knows what it's like to worry about someone.

"Anyway," he says, and I realize my silence has made things even more awkward, "I guess I'll go." He heads for the stairs, probably on his way to the chem lab.

"Hey, Enzo," I say before his dark head disappears to the second floor.

He turns around and takes a couple steps back down. The look on his face is impossible to read, but if I had to guess, I would say it's hopeful, though I can't imagine for what. I may still be angry at him for quitting our team last year, but I can't believe I've passed him in the halls all these weeks without saying a single thing to him about Xavier.

"I'm sorry about your brother," I say, feeling even worse when Enzo's top lip twitches with emotion. "He was always nice to me when we played the game."

Enzo stares at his feet for a few seconds before nodding. Is it really possible that the boy whose eyes are filling with tears stabbed Xavier before rushing into the school with a duffel bag full of evidence?

"Thanks, Dulce," Enzo says before turning back up the stairs.

After grabbing my lunch from my locker (since Emi's poisoning, I don't store it in the refrigerator), I head to the cafeteria to eat with Zane. I've decided to forgive him for lying about the internship, because, in his place, I might have lied too. And it's not like I'm some beacon of honesty; right now, I'm lying to nearly everyone, including my best friend, who thinks I've given up the case.

"Emi still at home watching *Real Housewives* reruns?" Zane asks.

"Bingeing *Terrace House*," I say, still distracted by the fact that my number one suspect just tried to comfort me. "Her mom's treating her like a Victorian lady with tuberculosis."

Zane is quick to pick up on my mood. "Everything okay?"

"I want to ask you something," I say.

"I was hoping you might." He smiles, a little shyly, and my heart lifts. Has he somehow guessed my question? He adds, "My answer is yes, if that helps."

"Really? You'll help me break into the sheriff's station?"

"Wait, what?" Zane says, the tips of his ears turning pink. "No . . . I mean . . . break into the station?"

The final step in the case is obvious: I need someone to help me get the sheriff's case file, especially now that the camera footage has made what happened that day even less clear. Sierra has proven herself untrustworthy (again), and Emi's still recovering at home, which leaves Zane, who happens to be the best person for the job, if he'll agree to help.

"Your mom said all the interviews and reports and pictures of the scene are in the sheriff's office," I say. "I thought since she has after-hours access to the building . . ."

"You want me to steal my mom's key so we can break into Sheriff Calhoun's office?" Zane sounds like I've asked him to jump off the Eiffel Tower without a parachute.

"Yes."

"You could get arrested." His eyes widen. "*We* could get arrested."

"I have to do something." I sniff my bologna sandwich and then put it down again. "I know Sheriff Calhoun is barely working the case. He never called me for an interview even though I was with Dean Whitaker when he discovered the body. If I don't find the truth, no one will."

"Have you considered the sheriff doesn't need your statement because he already has ironclad evidence against Sierra?" Zane asks.

That thought has never occurred to me, which makes me feel stupid because all the evidence I've found points to Sierra too. Then I remember my mom.

"The sheriff manipulated my mom's autopsy results," I say.

Zane pauses on the last bite of his granola bar. "How do you know that?"

"It doesn't matter." I don't want to tell him I snuck behind his back at the coroner's office. "But he might be doing it to Sierra too. You, of all people, should want to stop him."

Zane stares at the table for a long time. Something about Xavier's murder seems to have broken his rebellious spirit, because ever since then, he's been recommending the cops he hates as a solution to the problem they created.

"I get if you don't want to risk getting into more trouble," I say when he doesn't respond. "But maybe you could lend me your mom's key?"

Suddenly, he looks up and smiles, and I swear his eyes trace my birthmark.

"I'm being such a coward, aren't I?" He crumples his granola bar wrapper and tosses it into the trash can next to the back door. "Worried about some shitty sheriff when you're offering me the chance to bring him down."

"A bit, yeah," I admit.

"Well, screw that," he says. "I'm not going to let him railroad Sierra like he's railroading me. Let's end him."

Relief and something like pride wash over me. This is the Zane I profiled at Maldonado's. Upbeat, cocky, into new things. Not the kind of guy afraid of the sheriff's shadow. For the first time in weeks, I notice how pretty his eyes are. *Adorable*, I concluded at the beginning of the semester, and now I remember why.

"Then you'll help?" I ask.

"Hell yeah, I'll help." He runs both hands through his hair like he needs somewhere to put his newfound energy. "No more tiptoeing around trouble. If you can act like Wimsey, so can I."

22

MOST SATURDAY NIGHTS I SPEND AT EMI'S STREAMING murder mysteries and giving her my opinion, on a scale of one to infinity (her rating system, obviously), of every piece of clothing that arrived for her in the mail that week. She didn't ask why I couldn't come over tonight, which probably means she's with Rose. One more reason I can't waste time coming up with the perfect plan to break into the sheriff's office. If Rose is the poisoner, she might try to hurt Emi again.

The reflection in my mirrored closet distracts me from that dark thought. In my black jeans and black turtleneck, I look just like Enzo. *All I need is an eyebrow ring,* I think. I bend forward to tuck my ponytail under the skull cap I dug out of my winter tote, then reel when I flip back up and see a ten-year-old boy staring back at me.

"Absolutely not," I mutter, quickly pulling a few strands of hair out of my scrunchie and cursing the delicate bone structure that makes me look so young.

It's not a date, dummy.

Even so, if we get caught breaking into the sheriff's station, they'll make us take mugshots, and I refuse to let Emi call me

Oliver Twist for the rest of my life. "Maybe a little makeup," I say under my breath. "Just in case." I uncap the one lipstick I own—something peachy Emi bought me in Paris for my last birthday—and apply it carefully to my lips. Emi calls them geisha lips because they look like a puffy heart. They're the one feature I like about my face.

You're not as shy as you think you are.

I'm not sure why I haven't been able to get Zane's words out of my head since the day at the coroner's office, but maybe it's because he said them as though he spends time thinking about what I'm like.

My flip phone buzzes.

Here.

Anticipation makes my fingers tingle. I put the lipstick back in my drawer and then fluff the body pillow I covered with my quilt. For months after my mom died, my dad checked on me in the middle of the night like he was afraid I might disappear too. He hasn't done it in a while, but hopefully the pillow will be enough to fool him if he does.

I crack my door and hear the predictable sound of snoring at the other end of the short hallway. I tiptoe out of my bedroom, treading the hall carpet slowly. Our house is dark, with only a sliver of moonlight shining off our family pictures to light my way. *Sorry, Mom,* I think as I pass a photo of her and my dad on their honeymoon in Oaxaca, *but this is what Wimsey would do.*

Zane is sitting in his car with the lights off when I slide into the front seat. He pulls away silently, not turning them back on until we get out of my neighborhood. Once we're on the highway, we look at each other and laugh.

"Maybe we shouldn't have worn clothes that make us look exactly like burglars," Zane says, glancing down at his black hoodie and matching sweatpants.

"If we get caught, we can say we're allergic to color," I say.

"Good thing I've been practicing breaking out in hives."

We laugh again, which makes me remember we're doing something serious.

"You're positive the back door of the sheriff's station has no camera?" I ask.

"It's broken," Zane says. "Brenda is supposed to call someone in to fix it, but she's been too preoccupied with Deputy White. Every time I pass the coat closet, I hear them making out."

When we pull around to the back of the station, he cuts the lights.

"You sure you want to do this?" he asks.

"Are *you*?"

"I've been looking forward to it all day." He shoots me a small grin. "I just don't want you to feel like you have to. Wimsey was a daredevil, but he never broke into Scotland Yard."

"How do you know?" I ask, raising my eyebrows in surprise.

"I read the books."

Half my mind has been on the crime we're about to commit, but his confession stops me mid-thought. "All eleven of them?"

He shrugs. "I wanted to know why you liked them so much."

He found time between his farm and his job to read eleven books . . . because of me?

"All I'm saying is, if you want to back out, we can find something else to do together."

The way he says *together* rings in my ears. It sounds like he means the two of us, without anyone else.

His eyes lock onto mine. The space between us is warm and heavy, like our shared breaths are landing on our skin, making it tingle and spark. Goose bumps travel up my arms, and I can see the same bumps where Zane has pushed his hoodie up to his elbows.

I break my eyes away. Whatever's happening between us must be the result of adrenaline from what we're about to do, because he's into Emi. At least I think he is. Emi told me they still haven't been on a date because he's always too busy.

"We should go inside," I say. "You're sure the sheriff is drinking at Pappy's?"

Zane nods, looking a little disappointed. "Every Saturday night."

"And you think your mom will cover for us if we get caught? Tell the sheriff she asked us to get something in the basement?"

"I hope so."

That isn't comforting, but it's better than nothing.

I expected some kind of hitch with the back door, but Zane unlocks it with his mom's massive set of keys on the second try. The hallway inside is dark and stale, like someone didn't air out the kitchen after microwaving a burrito.

"No cameras inside?" I whisper.

"I don't think so," he whispers back.

"You don't *think* so?"

"Sheriff Calhoun runs this place like a slumlord," Zane says. "The electricity goes out because Brenda forgets to pay the bills; the doors still work on knob locks; even the cells downstairs are run on the honor code because the bars won't close all the way.

He spends his whole budget on vehicles because he thinks they make him look like he's on *Cops*."

When Zane stops in front of a corner office with the blinds drawn, my stomach sinks. "Crap," I say, looking at the lock on the door. "Your mom doesn't have a key to his office, does she?"

Zane snorts and flings the door wide open. "Welcome to Sheriff Calhoun's office," he announces.

"What an idiot," I say, crossing the thin carpet with a smile.

There's hardly any crime in Cape Cherry, so it makes sense the sheriff's station is nothing more than an ugly brown building squatting on a stretch of dirt off the highway, but even I'd be pissed if I had to work all day in the cube that is Sheriff Calhoun's office. There's a small shelf of family pictures behind his metal desk, including a large photo of him fishing with Beth and her sister at Lake Hope. Not a single picture has Sierra in it even though he raised her for six years.

His computer is old, like everything else in the station. When I touch his mouse with a gloved hand, a cold blue glow brightens the room, revealing the certificate proving he graduated from cop school and a trophy for the time he caught a fat bass. *What a small, pathetic life,* I think. Twice divorced, spending every day in this beige room with nothing but a few pictures and a dirty window for company, bullying kids like Zane to make himself feel big.

I shiver away my moment of pity and focus on the screen. Sadly, the sheriff isn't sloppy enough to leave his computer unprotected, and the cursor waits for me to enter a password.

"Any chance you know it?" I ask.

"No." Zane looks startled. "Don't you have some fancy detective way of checking which keys are hit most often or something?"

I expected he wouldn't know it, which is why I have a backup plan. It's time to find out how much he really wants to take Sheriff Calhoun down.

"No, I don't," I say. "That's why I need you to text Beth and ask for her dad's password."

The ensuing silence is so heavy I might be alone in the office.

"No way," Zane finally says.

"Sheriff Calhoun isn't the careful type," I explain, thinking of how his office was unlocked. "I know Beth only sees him on weekends, but Sierra knew Dean Whitaker's password, and he doesn't even live with her."

"It's almost midnight on a Saturday," Zane says, delaying. "What if she doesn't answer?"

"She has a crush on you." I flash back to the way she pulled on his apron strings at Maldonado's. "She'll answer."

Zane stares at me for a minute before pulling his phone out of the front pocket of his hoodie. "Your friends underestimate you," he says, and I don't think it's a compliment.

Two minutes after he sends the text, his phone buzzes. He types something back, and I see him add a smiley face. Half a minute later, he's got the password.

"B-E-T-H-2-0-0-9." He spells it out before sighing. "I told her the sheriff asked my mom to get a document from his files, but that his password isn't working. If she mentions it to him . . ."

"She won't." I type the letters and numbers in. "She probably knows she shouldn't be giving it out, but she wants you to like her."

The screen lights up.

USERNAME AND PASSWORD DON'T MATCH. TWO TRIES LEFT.

"Oh, *come on*," I say, a rush of fury making me loud. "It didn't work."

Zane frowns, then checks the text again. "*BETH2009.* It's her name and birth year." He looks up. "You sure you typed it in right?"

I tap my hand nervously against the desk. If I try to type it in again and it's wrong, I'll only have one try left.

"I think so," I say. "Are you sure that's when she was born?"

"Positive," he says. "We share a birthday. September 9, 2009. 09/09/09. Not the kind of thing you forget."

"Could she be lying?" I ask.

Zane shakes his head. "If she didn't want to give me the password, she would have just ignored the text."

"Then I must have typed it in wrong," I say. "I'll try again."

This time, I watch every key as I strike it. When I'm done, I count the characters to make sure there's eight of them.

I hit enter, and the screen lights up again.

"Shit." Zane reads the message. "One try left."

"There is literally nothing worse than technology," I say, wishing I could smash the keyboard against the wall.

This is beginning to feel like déjà vu, except this time, I can't go digging around in the sheriff's sent messages to find files. If I don't figure out his password, this will all have been for nothing.

"He must have changed it," I say. "Which means we need to find it." I start turning over everything on his desk. My dad writes his passwords on Post-it notes and sticks them to random objects; maybe the sheriff does the same. I peek behind his monitor and then under his lamp and bookshelf, but there's no password.

"Is there any other way to get it?" I ask. "Maybe the IT person keeps a master list?"

Zane shakes his head again. "Brenda is all they've got," he says. "And I've had to show her how to use Word like fifty times."

I keep searching. In my desperation, I turn the sheriff's family pictures around in case he stuck a note on the back of the frames.

"I don't think it's here," Zane says, picking through the sheriff's calendar. "Maybe he keeps a password app on his phone?"

Which means we'll never find it.

I turn the fishing trip picture back around with tears of frustration in my eyes. I have no idea how I'm going to solve the case without the files.

I'm about to suggest we search Sheriff Calhoun's assistant's cubicle, but then I do a double take at the Lake Hope photo. The sheriff is standing on the sand, dangling a striped bass in the air. Beth is smiling at the camera, her fishing rod still in the water. Next to her, sitting in a folding chair, a young girl in a bathing suit peers at the photographer shyly from under a visor.

"Avery," I say.

Zane stops turning calendar pages. "What about her?" he asks.

"She's Beth's sister."

"And?"

I turn to Zane, my words alive with energy again. "The sheriff is the laziest man in the world, right?"

Zane catches on fast. "You think he used Avery's name and birthdate?"

"He definitely didn't use Sierra's." I point to the shelf of photos. "She's not in any of them."

"I'll ask Beth what year Avery was born," Zane says, fingers flying across his screen.

When Beth's text comes a minute later, Zane turns his phone to me. "2013."

This time, I announce the characters aloud as I type so I don't make any mistakes. "A-V-E-R-Y-2-0-1-3."

"You sure about this?" I ask, my finger hovering over enter. "It's our last shot."

"Too bad we don't have Emi's Magic 8 Ball," he says, sounding half-serious.

I fight the urge to close my eyes so I can't see what happens. "Let's hope signs point to yes."

The computer comes alive.

"Yes!" Zane punches the air.

It doesn't take long to find the case folder in the sheriff's database. I open it, and a cascade of files appears, all labeled with things like *mugshot* and *toxicology report*. I pull my thumb drive out of my back pocket with shaking hands. The sheriff probably hasn't bothered to review the files, but I'm sure the answers to the poisonings are there. They have to be.

After what happened in Dean Whitaker's office, I made sure to bring an adapter for the thumb drive, but it isn't necessary. I slide the drive into the USB port on the front of the ancient tower and move the documents onto it.

5 MINUTES pops up on the screen; the slumlord's operating system is glacially slow.

Zane is still texting Beth. "I have to take her to dinner now," he says. "I hope you're happy."

"Not really," I say before I can think about it. He glances up at me in surprise. "I only mean I'm sorry you had to use your friend," I add.

He puts his phone back in his hoodie and shifts a little closer in the low light. "This isn't what I thought you were going to say at lunch." He tucks a lock of hair back into my beanie, his fingertips trailing lightly across my forehead. "I hoped you were going to ask me to—"

Somewhere outside the office, a car door slams.

Zane freezes in the middle of his sentence. "Shit. Someone's here." He grabs my hand. "C'mon, we have to hide."

I check the screen.

"Two minutes left," I say.

"Are you serious right now, Dulce?" His voice is panicked. "We can't get caught in here."

There's a scratching at the front door like someone's trying to put a key into the hole and missing it over and over.

The screen moves down to one minute, as if the computer knows we're in a rush.

"Hurry, hurry," I urge it.

The person finally gets the front door unlocked and walks inside.

Done!

I yank the thumb drive out of the slot and rip the power cord from the back of the monitor because I don't have time to fumble for a way to turn the screen off. Zane drags me out of the office, but instead of heading toward the back, like I expect, he pulls me a few feet down the hallway before opening a narrow door and pushing me inside.

Footsteps clomp down the hall as he clicks the door shut. We're smooshed into such a tiny space I can feel his warm breath on my face when he sighs with relief, but he quickly sucks it in again when the footsteps get closer.

Suddenly, a loud voice bursts into song, almost making me jump out of my skin.

"It's the sheriff," Zane whispers, so softly I can barely hear him. Sheriff Calhoun isn't just singing off-key, he's slurring half the words, and I realize he must have come straight from Pappy's. Fury erupts in the blood underneath my skin. Drinking and driving. *Hypocrite.*

There's a long pause in the singing, and I hold my breath. Has he discovered the disconnected monitor?

The sheriff begins singing again, even closer now, and the hard edges of the phone inside Zane's hoodie push into my stomach as he searches in the dark for my hand as if touching my skin might make us invisible. My whole body lights up when he laces his fingers into mine, adrenaline pulsing with confusion, like it's not sure whether it should run away or lean closer to Zane, who uses his other hand to shift me deeper into what I'm now realizing must be the hall closet where Brenda and Deputy White make out.

The footsteps stop right outside, and Zane goes stock still, his face inches from mine. My eyes have adjusted to the dark, and, in the thin strip of light coming from beneath the door, I see his lips hesitate next to my cheek.

Then, and only then, do I accept what I've been too afraid to admit to myself: I like Zane. More than I've liked a guy in a very long time. It's why I felt so betrayed when he lied to me and why, whenever he's smiled in Emi's direction, I haven't just wished I was dating a guy *like* him; I've wanted the guy to *be* him.

Pain blunts the pleasure of my revelation. This might be the only time we're ever this close.

I try to engrave the details on my memory. The warmth of

his hand, which is holding mine so tight my thumb is tingling. The way his hoodie smells like lavender fabric softener and sweat. The pressure of his feet against my Doc Martens because my legs got trapped between his when we stumbled into the closet. For a moment, I transport us from the station to the dance floor: his face close to mine under the disco ball, heart humming in his wrist as we sway in the fractured light.

In the anxiety of the moment, I've forgotten to breathe, so I gently suck in some air, which tastes like coconut and salt because a lock of Zane's hair has fallen into my mouth. I brush it out with my free hand, but Zane cups my fingers against the side of his head like he's afraid the sheriff will hear my arm shifting against my body.

This time, our eyes meet, and for a split second, I'm positive he's about to brush his lips across my skin. Before I can be sure, the closet door swings open.

23

THE SHERIFF STANDS IN THE HALL, CAUGHT BETWEEN A leer and drunken confusion. "I knew I heard something," he slurs. His eyes light up with malice when he sees Zane. "You trying to double-cross me, son? Gonna have to add this to your other crimes."

"It's not what it looks like," Zane says. I'm glad he's talking, because I couldn't move my mouth if I tried. "We have permission to be here."

"No one can give you permission to be in this station alone," the sheriff says.

"Well, my mom needed . . . I mean my mom said . . ."

The metal bars of the basement's jail stamp themselves across my eyes. It's over. I've ruined everything. College, the case—all blown apart because I didn't run when Zane said run. Maybe I can at least get him out of trouble; it's the least I can do since—

"They're with me."

I feel like a saint hearing God's voice for the first time. My body unfreezes, and I slip out of the closet to find the source of our salvation.

Dr. Bates is standing in the hallway, glaring at all of us.

"With you?" the sheriff says, gaping.

"I needed some paperwork in my office," she says. "I asked Zane and Dulce to wait for me." She glances at the closet. "It looks like they decided to play seven minutes in heaven instead."

I have no idea what that is, but I can guess. Zane shoots me the tiniest shame-faced smile.

"Dressed like ninjas?" the sheriff asks, as if even in his state he can't fail to notice how out of place our clothes are.

"I asked them to take my nieces trick-or-treating next weekend," Dr. Bates says, her voice even. "They were experimenting with costumes before we drove over."

"Humph," the sheriff says. "I should write you up for this. Letting two teenagers loose unattended in the workplace. One of whom may soon have criminal charges pending against him."

"How was Pappy's?" Dr. Bates asks pointedly. "Have your usual bucket of beers?"

The sheriff's already-pink face turns the color of a beet, but none of the words he splutters make any sense.

"I'm going to take these kids home," Dr. Bates says. "Probably best to pretend we never saw each other."

The sheriff grunts, but he doesn't argue.

Dr. Bates shuttles us out the back door, where her car is parked next to Zane's.

"Mom, I can explain—"

"Zip it," she says. "I know exactly why you're here. I mean, look at you. Ninjas—my god, that man is stupid, but so are the two of you." She spins to face me. "You promised you'd keep him out of your investigation."

"I'm sorry," I say. "No one else could help me."

"How did you find us?" Zane asks.

Dr. Bates holds up her phone. "Tracked you."

I stare at the app in horror, tears rushing to my eyes like I've been slapped.

"You have a *tracker* on me?" Zane says, outraged.

"Did you seriously think I wouldn't, after what happened last summer?" she says. "Good thing I did, too, or else I'd be here bailing you out of jail." When she sees the wetness on my cheeks, she frowns. "What's wrong?"

"Nothing." I sniffle. "I'm just really sorry."

"Buck up, Dulce," she says. "I'm the mom; I have to yell. But I'm no snitch. I won't tell your dad."

She's wrong about why I'm crying, but I say, "Thank you."

Dr. Bates lowers her voice. "Tell me you at least got what you came for."

I nod.

"Good girl," she says. "But if I ever hear you pulled Zane into another one of your schemes, I'll ban you two from seeing each other. And from what I can tell, neither of you would like that very much. You hear me?"

I nod again, feeling like a bobblehead.

"By the way," she says, "my contact at Channel Z is very interested in the report we talked about last time you broke into this building. I'll know more in a few weeks."

Once she's driven away, I collapse into Zane's passenger seat like a bag of concrete.

"My mom won't say anything to your dad," he says as we pull onto the highway. "Promise."

"That's not why I'm upset," I say quietly.

"Then why?"

I've held the secret of my mom's death for so long, but I don't want to anymore. I should be telling my dad, or even Emi, but somehow I feel like, of all the people I know, Zane will judge me the least. Maybe because his past isn't clean either.

I start talking before I can change my mind. "The night my mom got killed by Deputy Armstrong," I say, "I was at the pier with Sierra, hanging out with some high school boys."

Zane nods. "Yeah, I got that from what you said in the mausoleum."

"I'd told my mom we were going to get ice cream at Tiffany's, and when Sierra and I saw police lights, we ran all the way there so no one would find out we hadn't gone in the first place.

"What I've never told anyone—not Sierra, not Emi, and not my dad—is that my mom wasn't on her way to the ice cream shop to pick us up like everyone thinks. She was on her way to the beach because she'd tracked my phone. She must have decided to surprise me at Tiffany's, seen that I wasn't where I was supposed to be, gotten concerned, and come looking."

"Oh shit," Zane says.

"I saw the tracking notification hours later," I continue. "After she was already dead." My voice trembles with a wave of tears. "If I hadn't lied to her, she wouldn't have been on Beachview Road. She would have gone the shorter way, along Main Street. Deputy Armstrong would never have crashed into her."

I'm crying so hard it takes me a minute to realize the car is slowing down. Zane stops on the grassy shoulder, gets out, and comes around to my side. I'm unsure what he's doing until he opens my door and pulls me into a hug.

"I'm so sorry, Dulce," he says.

I expect him to tell me it's not my fault or that I can't blame myself, but he doesn't. He just holds me.

After a while, my tears slow, and I push him gently away. He gives me a small dimpled smile, then goes around to the driver's side and restarts the car.

When we get back onto the road, a feeling of relief washes the rest of my tears away. My worst secret isn't a secret any longer. Its weight on my heart has been cut in half.

Ten minutes later, Zane pulls up to my house and kills the lights.

"The Detective's Ball," he says.

"What?" I ask, coming out of my reverie.

"That's what I thought you were asking me in the cafeteria."

"Oh." My cheeks, which are finally dry, flush in the low light of the streetlamp. "I mean, Emi . . ."

"Yeah, she asked me last night," he says.

"Oh," I repeat. Emi had given me plenty of warning. My disappointment isn't her fault. "Good."

Zane's words come back to me. *My answer is yes, if that helps.*

He was going to say yes. To me.

"You should come with us," he says. "We're renting a van."

"Yeah, sure," I say before I remember my actual plan for the Detective's Ball. "Wait, no. My date might drive me."

"You have a *date*?" Zane's blond eyebrows rise into little hills of surprise.

"Well, not yet," I admit. "But I have a plan."

"A plan? That doesn't sound very romantic."

"Only if you don't find interrogations romantic."

Zane looks confused, but then his lips twitch into a grin. "No way," he says. "You wouldn't."

"Whatever it takes to solve this case."

Zane laughs, and I know I'm exhausted because I wish I could bottle the sound. "Emi's face is going to be classic."

I tell Emi about my date to the dance during our long-postponed detention, which is being held in the school library.

In typical Dean Whitaker fashion, it's about as punishing as a vacation. Rose is doing yoga on a mat near the staircase, her pink hair sticking out in all directions under white Beats headphones. Zane napped in one of the study carrels until the dean asked him to help move the chairs out of the ballroom in preparation for the dance.

Since the weekend, I've been noticing small things about Zane, like how the bands he's painted in Wite-Out are some of my favorites, and how there's a dolphin charm on his beaded necklace. He gave me a little smile this morning in the hall, as if he was testing how I felt about our B&E, and I smiled back, unsure what he was thinking after my confession about my mom.

"You asked the *brujo* to the Detective's Ball?" Emi says, shoving half a Fruit Roll-Up into her mouth. "He might be a murderer!"

I barely flinched when I cornered Enzo in the chem lab and asked him to go to the dance. I thought I'd have to sell him on the idea by telling him it would make Sierra jealous, but his reaction was completely unexpected.

"Do you like black peonies?" he asked, not even bothering to say yes first.

"I guess so?" I said, even though I had zero idea what peonies looked like.

"I've been growing some in my garden at home. I'll make you a wrist corsage." He scuffed a black boot against the ground and spoke his next words quickly, like he was embarrassed. "They'll look nice with your eyes."

An image of Enzo in an apron cutting flowers to match my eyes made me feel like I was in Bizarro World, but all I said was "Okay."

And then he smiled. A real, big, happy smile that made me wonder if he was imagining dumping my dead body in the woods after the dance.

"It's the best way to question him," I tell Emi. "Unless you have another suggestion."

"How about we lock him in the janitor's closet until he tells us what we want to know?" she says.

At the word *closet*, a hot flush runs the length of my body. Emi's mom finally got tired of taking care of her, so when Emi picked me up for school, I lost no time coming clean about breaking into the dean's office and the sheriff's station, only leaving out the fluttery moments between me and Zane.

I thought Emi would be mad I lied, but all she did was raise an impressed eyebrow and say, "You've really slaughtered that *conejita*, haven't you? Maybe you should tattoo a skull and bones over your birthmark. Make it official."

"If we lock Enzo in a closet, I won't get to wear a corsage made of goth flowers," I say. "And I know you don't want to miss that. Besides, if I don't go with him, I don't go at all. It's not like anyone else is waiting for me to ask them."

Not that I'd care if they were. Since having my lips mere inches from Zane's, my daydreams about him have spun out of control. I shift in my seat, trying to figure out how to tell Emi about my crush. It'll make things awkward at the dance, but I can't secretly pine for the guy my best friend likes. Telling Zane about my mom has shown me that keeping secrets can be worse than the secrets themselves.

"Emi," I say, clearing my throat, "there's something I have to—"

She cuts me off. "Are we watching the interviews or what?"

"Now?" I say, stopped short by surprise. "I thought we were watching them at my house tonight."

Emi shrugs, twin braids bouncing off her shoulders. "I'm jealous you committed crimes without me. Watching the videos in detention will make me feel like I'm breaking a rule."

"Next time I almost get arrested, I'll be sure to bring you along."

"You better," she says. "I bet my dad would actually fly in from Tokyo if I was on trial."

I glance over at Rose. "What about her tarot-card warning?"

Emi bites her lip. "Just keep the volume down," she says.

I open my elderly laptop and plug in the thumb drive.

I briefly looked at some of the files when I got home Saturday night—Sierra's mugshot, which wasn't publicly released, was predictably beautiful—but I didn't have time to watch any of the interviews. As if he sensed I'd done something wrong, my dad kept me busy with chores on Sunday, and then, after pizza night (Halloumi cheese and chocolate sprinkles; I couldn't convince him to order octopus, so we lost again), he made me watch a double feature of two rom-coms he swore I'd love (I did not).

I click the first video, labeled *Enzo Torres*, and press play.

A man in a suit is sitting next to Enzo, who's wearing a black kilt wrapped with chains. The sheriff is across from them, with Deputy Armstrong on his left, taking notes. The camera is angled toward the witnesses, so only the sides of the sheriff's and deputy's faces are visible.

After going through some preliminary questions, the sheriff says, "I want the case against Sierra Fox to be tighter than a mosquito's ear. Not an alibi left unturned, not a single suspect left uncovered. I won't be happy unless the jury looks ready to cry at what that girl did to your brother. You understand me?"

"Well, shit," Emi says, and I know why. We've been assuming the sheriff has been neglecting the case, but it sounds like he's been working that much harder to make sure he won't be challenged. *Even more reason,* I tell myself, *to continue investigating.* Sheriff Calhoun will be looking at the evidence only to convict Sierra; we're searching for the truth.

"The DA is going to want to know who was near the greenhouse when Xavier died," the sheriff continues. "And I plan to account for everyone's movements minute by minute. I know you were in the woods between 11:53 a.m. and noon. What exactly were you doing?"

"Walking around," Enzo says. "Is that a crime?"

"Anywhere in particular?"

"No."

"Did you see Sierra Fox while you were walking nowhere in particular?"

"No."

"She must have come to your house a lot to see your brother," the sheriff says. "How would you describe her?"

Enzo taps a pen loudly against the table until his lawyer plucks it from his hand. "She's mercurial," Enzo finally answers.

The sheriff grunts. "Let's keep the words small for Deputy Armstrong."

"Rude," Emi mutters.

"Sierra's emotions change a lot," Enzo says. "She might love you one minute and hate you the next." He pauses. "At least that's what Xavi said."

"Did she have a reason to kill your brother?"

"Probably."

"What reason?"

"I don't know," Enzo says. "I'm just saying she's not the type of person to do something without a reason."

"We hear you and Xavier didn't get along."

"So?" Enzo crosses his arms. "I didn't do anything to him."

"What was in the bag you were carrying in from the woods?"

"Gardening tools."

The sheriff snorts. "You think a jury is going to believe that bullshit?"

"I object to your language," the lawyer says. "Enzo is a good kid, devastated by his brother's death. You have no reason to call him a liar."

"A good kid?" The sheriff scoffs. "Only someone with evil inside them would dress like that."

Enzo's lawyer squeaks with outrage. "Surely you're not suggesting my client's fashion choices make him a murderer."

"Hail Satan, or whatever," Enzo says in a bored voice. "Are we done here?"

The lawyer stands up like he's afraid Enzo's mouth will get him into trouble. "Unless you're going to arrest my client for wearing black, this interview is over." He nods toward the door. "C'mon, son. We're leaving."

Enzo stands up, tucks his hair behind his ear with his middle finger stuck out at an obvious angle, and then disappears from the screen.

"Walking around, my ass," the sheriff says once Enzo's gone. "We need to see if—"

The video cuts off.

"Well, that was useless," Emi says. "Also, the 1980s called. They want their Satanic Panic back."

"You're the one who says Enzo does black magic," I point out.

"Yeah, but not because he *wears black*. It's because he's always picking plants in the woods and saying weird things under his breath."

"Don't forget the cat skinning," I say.

"Who's next?" Emi asks.

"Ms. Moss." I frown. "That's weird. She didn't tell me she'd been interviewed."

"You've got to stop being sad when she doesn't treat you like her bestie," Emi says, eating the rest of the Fruit Roll-Up in a single bite.

The framing of the second video is the same as the first, except that Ms. Moss is alone, without a lawyer on her side of the table. She's tearing a Styrofoam cup into tiny pieces and stacking them in a pile next to her cell phone, which she glances at every few seconds, probably making sure the babysitter hasn't texted.

"We're interviewing everyone at James Everett High who wasn't in the cafeteria when Xavier Torres was killed," the sheriff says after getting the basics out of the way.

"Okay." Ms. Moss sounds dull, like someone's sucked all the energy out of her body.

"Can anyone vouch for your whereabouts during lunch on that day?"

"I was in my classroom alone until about ten minutes before

noon," she says. "That's when Zane Lawrence came in to audition for band."

The sheriff huffs. "I wouldn't trust that kid with a pair of scissors, much less an alibi."

"What about the front-door camera?" Ms. Moss asks, continuing to flip a piece of Styrofoam between her fingers. "It can't lie."

"It shows you were in the building until 12:20 p.m. Right after Sierra Fox ran into the cafeteria."

Ms. Moss stops flipping. "If you have evidence I was inside the school when Xavier was killed, then why am I here?"

"The killer took Xavier's phone," the sheriff says. "But we were able to access his apps, and something strange popped up on his Venmo account."

Ms. Moss's hand jerks, knocking half the Styrofoam pieces to the ground.

"It's probably nothing, but we have to cover all our bases for the DA," the sheriff says. "You understand."

"Okay," Ms. Moss repeats, leaning down to pick up the pieces.

"It shows that, every month for the last five months, you've been transferring five hundred dollars into Xavier's account."

"*Five hundred dollars?*" I say, wondering if I heard him wrong.

"That's like a million dollars in teacher money," Emi says.

"What was the money for?" the sheriff asks.

"I bought a guitar from him." Ms. Moss piles the pieces up again.

"Pretty steep on your salary."

"It's a special guitar," she says. "Pre-war. Rare. I'll probably never find one like it again." She smiles disarmingly, the dullness falling off her like shaken dust. "And I'm not very good with money, I'm afraid. My sister used to keep a piggy bank, but I spent my allowance the second my parents handed it to me."

"Did you talk to Xavier's moms about this guitar?"

Ms. Moss shrugs. "The guitar was a gift from his uncle. He was perfectly within his rights to sell it." She checks her phone. "Is there anything else? Because my neighbor is watching my kids for me, and I should be getting back."

"Well, actually—" Deputy Armstrong starts, but Sheriff Calhoun interrupts him.

"We don't need anything else," he says. "Thanks for coming in."

The deputy glances over at the sheriff once Ms. Moss leaves. "I thought you wanted it airtight—" but the sheriff cuts him off.

"She was inside the school when the kid was killed. End of story. I only asked about the Venmo transfers to make sure the defense can't claim we didn't do our job. A rich kid scamming a teacher into paying too much for a guitar isn't our problem."

"Did Xavier even play the guitar?" I ask Emi after the video ends. "He wasn't in band."

"I'll ask Sierra." Emi grabs her phone out of the holographic fanny pack around her waist.

A few seconds later, a text dings. "Apparently he was tone-deaf," Emi says, reading the message. "Couldn't play an instrument and sounded like a dying turtle when he sang."

The facts from Ms. Moss's interview twist and knot.

She's had the same guitar since freshman year. She always talks about how day care for the twins is bankrupting her. I've seen detailed budgets on her laptop, which means she's good with money, not bad.

Conclusion: Her interview answers are as off-key as Xavier's singing.

The camera footage proves Ms. Moss was inside the school until long after Xavier was killed. So why is she lying?

24

J. EVERETT HIGH SCHOOL
Two Months Ago

ZANE DIDN'T GET NERVOUS OFTEN, BUT AS HE WALKED down the hall to the band room, he felt a strange buzzing in his stomach. The feeling doubled when he saw Dean Whitaker standing in the doorway, talking to Ms. Moss. Ever since this summer, authority figures made his skin crawl.

Zane's steps faltered. Should he pretend he'd forgotten something and turn around? He didn't want anyone asking him what he was doing wandering the halls. But then the dean turned his head and spotted Zane. It was too late. He kept walking.

"The symphony director needs the permission slips by Monday," the dean said loudly, backing into the hall. "Please don't forget to collect them."

Zane tried to project confidence as the dean came toward him. "Mr. Lawrence," Dean Whitaker said, stopping. "I haven't had a chance to talk to you yet. Are you settling in well?"

"Yes, sir," Zane said. It had been good of the dean to let him into school at the last minute, although he probably hadn't had much of a choice.

"That's what I like to hear," the dean said. "You have a clean slate at J. Everett. Take advantage of it." He clapped Zane on the shoulder, then moved down the hall, whistling to himself.

Zane waited until he heard the dean go downstairs, then he knocked on the open door. "Ms. Moss, can I talk to you?" he asked.

The band teacher was at the front of the room, strumming her guitar, an empty black case open on the floor. Her hand jumped off the strings at Zane's words, like she'd been lost in thought.

"I don't see students during my planning period," she said.

"It'll only take a minute." Zane grinned in the way that always made people want to help him.

As usual, it worked. Ms. Moss leaned her guitar against the desk and ushered him in. He ignored the confusion that crossed her face when he shut the door.

"Is this about your audition?" she asked. "Because I'm happy to give you the sheet music ahead of time." She smiled softly. "It's not supposed to be stressful."

Zane slid a plastic chair in front of her and sat down. He wished he wasn't about to upset her, but he didn't have a choice. "It's about Xavier Torres," he said.

Ms. Moss winced like Xavier's name was painful, but her voice was calm when she said, "He's not in band, so I'm afraid I can't help you." She rolled her chair over to her desk, no longer smiling, and started shuffling through some papers. "I have work to do, so please come back on Thursday for your audition."

"I know he's blackmailing you."

Ms. Moss's hand froze on a book of Bach. Zane hadn't been positive she was the right teacher—both she and Dr. Saka had ex-husbands like Xavier had said at his party—but her reaction was all the confirmation he needed.

"I'm not sure what you—" she started, but Zane cut her off.

"Xavier bragged about it," he said. "Told me and my friend he wanted something to hold over his girlfriend in case she cheated on him while he was at his internship. Knew she'd freak if it went public and damaged her mom's campaign. He's a real insecure bastard."

"Did he say . . . I mean—" Ms. Moss seemed to realize the truth couldn't be poured back into the bottle. "Did he tell you why?"

There was a note of darkness in her voice, like somewhere underneath her sunshine exterior lay a jaguar ready to pounce.

Zane shook his head. "All he said is that you deserved it."

"What Xavier saw me do was perfectly legal," she said, her voice rising angrily. "And none of his business."

"Then why pay?"

"Because if people found out, Mayor Fox might lose the election." She sighed. "I can't risk destroying J. Everett, so until then, I have to pay Xavier what he wants."

"What if you didn't have to?"

Ms. Moss eyed him warily. "Why are you here?"

Zane hated thinking about what had happened to Ethan, but he knew he had to explain if he wanted her on his side.

"My parents are divorced, so I spend summers on North Beach with my dad," he said. "Me and my friends up there"—the ones his mom always called *bad influences*, though he was just as bad—"we mess around some. Nothing serious. Some vandalism. Underage drinking. A little shoplifting." He could sense he was losing Ms. Moss, who seemed to be a bit of a do-gooder despite whatever she'd done that was getting her blackmailed. "It's not a great crowd," he said quickly. "I know that now. My mom says I've always been too easygoing for my own good."

"Does Dulce know any of this?" she asked.

Right. Ms. Moss and Dulce were close. It made sense she'd be worried about her favorite student spending time with a delinquent.

"I'm not like that anymore," Zane said. "And Dulce's too smart to get involved in anything that could get her into trouble."

Ms. Moss's lips twitched unhappily. "You can't tell her about the blackmail. Promise you won't."

"I swear," Zane said. It would be an easy pledge to keep. He didn't want Dulce knowing about any of this either. "Anyway," he continued, "a few weeks before the Fourth of July, we started hanging out with some kids who were staying at this rich dude's house on the bay. Xavier was one of them. He'd been doing an internship at Channel Z News and was taking a break for the holiday. He was really suave, all smiles and wavy hair. The girls liked him, but he didn't pay any attention to them. Said he had a girlfriend back home."

"You didn't know him before?" Ms. Moss asked.

"I went to Cape Cherry High until I transferred here," Zane said. "The schools don't mix much. After I met Xavier, I was glad about that. His friends were creeps, but he had a violent streak. One night, my friend Ethan and I were tagging some tourist trap with Xavier and his crew. But I guess that wasn't exciting enough for Xavier, because he got this idea to blow up a pier on the beach."

Ms. Moss covered her mouth with her hand. "He wanted to *kill* people?"

"An abandoned pier," Zane quickly clarified. "He'd found

some explosives at a construction site and thought it would be a good place to set them off. I told Xavier no way. I don't even mess with fireworks because my uncle blew off his thumb with a Black Cat when he was young. But Ethan hero-worshipped Xavier because all the girls were after him and Ethan could barely say hi to one without passing out. So he agreed."

"I don't think I want to hear this story," Ms. Moss said, her voice tight.

"Then I'll just tell you how it ends," Zane said, wishing he didn't know the story either. "On the Fourth of July, Xavier told Ethan to take the explosives to the pier in a backpack and blow them up during the fireworks show so no one would hear." Zane flinched, remembering how Ethan had smiled as he'd strapped the backpack on. "I told Ethan not to do it. *Begged* him not to. But he didn't listen."

"And the bomb went off and killed him," Ms. Moss whispered.

Zane could see it like it was yesterday. Ethan walking across the sand toward the ocean while Xavier and his friends cheered and told him they'd save the best bottle of rum for him. Ethan turning around and flipping them all off before he entered the water, making the others whoop even louder. Watching him attach the explosives to the leg of the pier. The long minutes waiting for the bomb to explode. Then the groans of everyone on the sand when Ethan pulled the explosives off and put them back in his bag.

"No." Zane shook his head. "They didn't explode. They were duds. Probably why they'd been left behind at the site."

Ms. Moss breathed a sigh of relief.

"But even dead explosives are heavy, and on his way back to the beach, a wave pulled Ethan and his backpack under. I managed to swim out and rescue him, but he'd been under the water for too long." Zane paused. "He's been in a coma for two months. No one knows if he'll wake up."

For a moment, there was silence.

"I'm sorry, Zane." Ms. Moss's voice was small.

"Someone called the cops," Zane said, relieved to be reaching the end of the story. "Sheriff Calhoun hauled us all into the police station. Xavier lied and said I stole the explosives and made Ethan take them to the pier. His friends repeated the story. And, unfortunately, Ethan wasn't around to contradict them."

"Why aren't you in jail, then?"

"That's not important," Zane said. She wouldn't help him if she knew who he was involved with. "What is important is that Xavier almost killed my friend."

Ms. Moss looked confused. "What does any of this have to do with him blackmailing me?"

"I think we can help each other," Zane said.

"What are you suggesting?"

"We take Xavier down."

Ms. Moss's eyes went wide. "Take him down? How?"

Zane smiled. It was the smile of a gravedigger about to bury an enemy. "I have a plan."

25

"DEAN WHITAKER'S INTERVIEW IS UP NEXT," I SAY, GLANC-ing quickly at the library door to make sure he and Zane haven't gotten done stacking the chairs early. When I see that Emi, Rose, and I are still alone, I press play.

The dean, dressed in a sharp suit, is sitting across from the sheriff and Deputy Armstrong. He showed up to school the day after Xavier's murder with the blue dye washed out of his hair, as if the archery bet had never happened, so the curls being warmed by the fluorescent lights in the witness room are black.

Like he's done each time, the sheriff lists the date and the names of everyone in the room. Finally, he leans back in his chair and says, "I've been waiting for something like this to happen."

"You've been hoping a child would be murdered at my school?" Dean Whitaker says, an unmistakable chill in his voice.

"You know what I mean," the sheriff snaps. "Your school is dangerous. Poisons on every shelf. Greenhouse full of deadly plants. I'm surprised more students haven't died."

I think about Claire Everett and wonder if my dad believes that Xavier's ghost and hers are haunting the library together.

"Do you have any actual questions, or did you bring me here to reveal your ignorance?"

"He gives no fucks," Emi says, and I hear it, too, how Dean Whitaker is acting like he might stand up and walk out the door.

The side of the sheriff's mouth that I can see tenses under his mustache. "Where were you when Xavier Torres was murdered right under your nose?"

Dean Whitaker's eyes flash, but he answers without anger. "I was dictating grant requests to my secretary until half past eleven, then I appeared on Sierra's livestream." There's an awkward pause like everyone in the room is remembering that her account is dedicated to bashing Sheriff Calhoun. "When her livestream finished," the dean continues, "I went into the cafeteria and ate lunch with some of my students. I was with them until Sierra ran in and told us she'd found Xavier's body."

"Do you eat in the cafeteria a lot?" asks Deputy Armstrong in the slow, soft way he has, like a cattle rancher.

"Sometimes I do, yes," the dean says.

"Were you ever alone during that period?" the sheriff asks. "Maybe using the bathroom or sneaking out for a smoke?"

"No," says the dean. "I was with my secretary and then with Sierra in front of thousands of viewers and then with a cafeteria full of students."

"Pretty lucky for you," says the sheriff. "Most people don't have perfect alibis in a murder investigation."

"I wouldn't call anything about this tragedy lucky," says Dean Whitaker, his voice going from chilly to freezing.

"You probably see a lot of school drama as dean," Deputy Armstrong says. "Do you know who might have wanted Xavier Torres dead?"

Dean Whitaker folds his hands over his crossed legs. "I think Xavier stabbed himself while preparing for the game," he says. "He must have filled the needle with nicotine to make the scene more authentic. A horrible accident."

"You said it was a murder when you called the station," the sheriff says.

"I know." Dean Whitaker shifts a little in his seat. "But I've had more time to consider now."

"I suppose you think his phone melted into the ground?"

The dean frowns. "Xavier's phone is missing? I hadn't heard that."

"We tried to track it, but someone either turned it off or destroyed it," the sheriff says. "Either way, this was no accident."

"That's disappointing," the dean says quietly. "I would have preferred not to have a killer on my campus."

"You're a smart man," the sheriff says in a way that makes it clear he thinks the opposite. "Why would you touch what you thought was a murder weapon?"

"I wish I hadn't," Dean Whitaker says. "But I was thrown by the sight of one of my students dead, and I panicked."

"He's a good liar," I tell Emi, who knows all about him removing the pink yarn from Sierra's needle. "Sounds like he's actually sorry about it."

"Probably sorry he didn't think to bring gloves," Emi says.

"Did I tell you he called me to his office this morning?" I ask. "Said he was canceling my in-school suspensions so I could focus on the case."

"He's such a softie," Emi says. "I bet he felt bad they'd go on your permanent record."

"How long have you been engaged to Lily Fox?" Deputy Armstrong asks.

"Almost two years."

"Long time," the deputy drawls. "You ever getting married?"

"Actually, we've recently set a date," the dean says, sounding lighter. "This Christmas, in Florence."

"But Sierra's trial is scheduled to start the first week of January." Deputy Armstrong's voice is incredulous.

"Lily and I are confident you'll have arrested the real killer by then."

The sheriff rocks back in his seat, his eyes never leaving the dean. "We pulled your bank records," he says casually, like he's commenting on the rain outside.

Dean Whitaker freezes in place. His right hand, which was playing its usual pretend piano, stills into a bear claw. "What gave you the right to do that?" he asks.

"We had a warrant," the sheriff says. I can see the edge of a smile, like he's pleased to have finally gotten a reaction. "Judge Orcutt was happy to give us one when he heard you'd hassled us over the camera footage."

"What secrets do you think he's got?" I ask Emi while Dean Whitaker glares at the sheriff in silence.

Emi shrugs. "I've always gotten a sex-club vibe from him."

"Ew! And you want him to date your mom?"

"She could use some sexing."

"Gross," I groan, knocking her chair with mine and trying hard to keep the image of Emi's very straitlaced mom and Dean Whitaker out of my head.

"You've lost a lot of money at the Windgap Casino this year," says the sheriff.

Duh. The gold dice paperweights in the dean's office don't mean he loves board games. That also explains the ledger I found in his desk.

Dean Whitaker has recovered from the initial shock of having his finances pried into. "Gambling is perfectly legal in Virginia," he says. "And how I spend my money isn't your concern. But, if it were, I would point out that I lose and win large amounts every year. It always evens out."

"Did Xavier know about your gambling?"

"Of course not," Dean Whitaker says. "I don't speak to students about my private affairs."

"He didn't see you there, maybe?"

"Never," Dean Whitaker says. "The Windgap is twenty-one and over. Even if he had, I can't imagine why I'd care." He stands up like he's decided the sheriff and his deputy aren't worth any more of his time. "Please remember, as you dig into things that aren't your business, that I have an alibi for every minute between when Xavier was last seen alive and when Sierra found his body. If this harassment over my legal activities continues, I'll have no choice but to consult an attorney."

He gives his jacket a swift tug before striding out of the room. The camera cuts out two seconds later, leaving nothing but fuzz.

"What assholes," Emi says. "Why does it matter if Dean Whitaker gambles?"

"Did you know?" I ask, clicking out of the video and opening his bank records.

"I've seen a card-game website up on his laptop a couple of times." Emi shrugs. "But he might have been playing for fun."

I scan down his latest statements and whistle when I come to the end. "Doesn't seem that fun," I say. "He's lost almost three hundred thousand dollars this year."

Emi whirls the laptop around so it's facing her. "That's impossible." She scans them for herself, doing the math in her head. "Wow," she says, checking the door to the library, which is still dean-free. "He must be really bad at it."

I reach over and point at a file on the screen. "That interview doesn't have a name."

"Ooh," Emi says, clicking out of the bank records and pressing play on the video. "Maybe we have a spy at our school."

The sheriff and deputy are on the left, as usual, but the person on the right is covered with pixelated squares.

"Why are they all blacked out?" Emi asks with a frown.

I point to the label stretched across the top of the screen. "It says redacted. I guess the sheriff is protecting their identity."

Emi's eyes widen. "I was totally joking about the spy thing!"

The sheriff sounds annoyed, like someone's making him say something against his will. "Our agreement with your attorney is that, if you cooperate, we won't record your name or image and nothing you say can be used against you later. Do you understand?"

"Yes, I understand," says the pixelated person.

Emi slams her hand down on the space bar, freezing the video. "What the hell?" she says.

"What?" I ask, startled.

"That voice." Emi looks over at Rose, who's sitting in child's pose. "It's her."

I *knew* it. Well, I didn't know she gave a secret interview, but I've been positive all along that she's been lying to us. This morning in the car, I told Emi about Rose's strange behavior on the front-door footage, but she said Rose was probably upset by her tarot-card reading. Now maybe Emi will finally believe me.

"We should watch the rest of the video," I say.

"Screw that," Emi says. "If she's been keeping stuff from us, I want her to admit it right now." She marches over to Rose and taps her on the shoulder. Rose looks up with a smile that quickly begins to waver. She takes her headphones off.

"What's wrong?" she asks.

Emi points to the laptop, which I spin around. As soon as Rose sees the still frame of the video, she leaps to her feet, runs over to our table, and slams the laptop shut.

"Don't watch it!" she begs, eyes shiny with the beginning of tears. She looks back and forth between me and Emi. "How did you get the video? They promised it would stay secret."

Emi, who has followed her back to the table, says, "I think the better question is 'what are you hiding?'"

Pupils dilated. Fists clenching the holes of her granny-square jacket. Eyes darting to the door like she's thinking of making a run for it.

Conclusion: Rose is about to drop a bombshell.

"If you don't tell us, we'll watch the video," Emi says. "Either way, we'll find out."

Rose collapses into a chair and puts her headphones on the table. Her tears splash onto the wood. She's one of those girls who looks pretty when she cries, like a baby doll with a reservoir of water in her neck.

"I w-wanted to tell you the t-truth," she says, not looking at Emi. "But I've b-been so scared."

"Scared of what?" Emi interrupts, but I put out a hand to stop her.

"I don't think you hurt Xavier," I say, keeping my voice calm. "But I know you're lying about eating lunch at the icehouse."

Rose's lower lip trembles. "How do you know that?"

"You're scared of heights. And"—I glance up at Emi—"you'd need a really good reason not to eat lunch with us when Emi asked. Reading tarot cards alone isn't a good reason."

Rose doesn't deny any of those things, so I take a chance. "You went to meet Xavier, didn't you?"

"What?" Emi gasps. "You were with Xavier before he died?"

Rose sighs long and hard, like she knows it's no use lying anymore. "Xavi wanted to get back at Sierra for cheating on him," she says. "And he asked me to help."

"Help him how?" I press.

"He wanted me to pretend we were making out in the greenhouse. I was supposed to wear a hoodie so Sierra couldn't tell who I was. When she came inside at noon and saw us, she screamed."

Bombshell. Dropped.

"Are you telling me Xavier was *alive* at noon?" I say, ignoring Emi's spluttering.

"Very alive," Rose says. "And very mad at me."

"Why?"

"Xavi and I were sitting on the ground next to each other, and I was supposed to lean in and kiss him when she looked behind the table." Her watery eyes turn stone-like. "But two years ago, Xavi did something shitty to me. I don't want to talk about what," she says quickly, before I can ask. "But I thought this would be the perfect chance to get back at him."

"How?"

She looks a little queasy. "Instead of leaning over and kissing him, I pushed him onto his back and then climbed on top of him and flipped my skirt up to make it look like we were"—she sneaks a peek at Emi, whose cheeks are flushed—"well, you know."

Thanks to Emi's innuendo in the greenhouse, I do know. And now I also know what made those body marks in the dirt.

"Xavi was so surprised he didn't even react," Rose says. "Sierra screamed like she'd seen someone strangling a puppy and bolted before Xavi could explain." She twists her mala beads around her wrist. "He was furious at me. Yelling that I'd ruined everything. I told him that maybe if he hadn't—" Rose stops talking.

"Hadn't what?" Emi asks.

Rose takes a deep breath before letting it out slowly through her nose. "He outed me to my parents," she says. "That's why I did it."

There's a horrified silence. Emi looks like she wishes Xavier was still alive so she could kill him herself.

"I tried to get over it," Rose says, sounding calmer, like telling us what he did has sapped some of its power. "I thought I had, because things are much better with my parents now. They even have a pride flag hanging in the yard." She smiles a little. "It's kitschy, but it's a long way from their first response, which was made a thousand times worse by Xavi." She stares at her headphones. "Making it look like we were having sex was spur-of-the-moment pettiness—I hadn't planned it. But afterward I felt peaceful, like I'd finally balanced things." She shrugs. "Not very Zen of me, but we can't all be Buddha."

"Then what happened?"

"I was afraid Sierra would come back, so I went to the trailhead to take off the hoodie and relax with some tarot before going back to school."

"Is that when you had the premonition?" I ask. "The eagle's talons?"

Rose shakes her head. "That was a lie too," she says. "Tarot is more like a way of seeing inside yourself than a crystal ball. It can't predict the future. I made all that up"—she mumbles the next words—"to protect Emi." She blinks fast, but her tears keep coming. "After about ten minutes, I saw Sierra go back down the greenhouse path. I thought she was on her way to the cafeteria, but then I heard the greenhouse door slam. I figured she and Xavi would be too busy to notice me, so I wrapped up my reading and headed back."

"And then?"

"As I passed the greenhouse, I glanced inside. I thought if Xavi and Sierra were kissing, I wouldn't have to feel bad about what I'd done." Her words get softer. "That's when I saw Sierra standing over Xavi's body, holding a knitting needle in the air. He was facedown on the ground, and he wasn't moving. That's how I knew he was already dead."

Emi and I gape at each other, unable to believe what we're hearing. Rose starts crying harder.

"It was all my f-fault," she wails. "If I hadn't t-tricked him, Sierra wouldn't have been so mad. She wouldn't have killed him."

"Whoever did this planned it beforehand," I say. "No one carries around a needle full of nicotine in case somebody pisses them off."

Rose gazes stupidly at me. "I hadn't thought of that," she says, wiping at her tears.

"Did you actually see Sierra stab him?" I ask.

"No, but there was no one else out there," Rose says. "You can see the whole path from the trailhead. The only person who walked on it was Sierra."

"What happened after that?"

"I was terrified Sierra would do me next, so I sprinted back up the path the other way, to the front door, and hid in the bathroom. When I calmed down enough to realize I had to tell Dean Whitaker what happened, I came out, and there she was, running down the hall. She didn't see me, but I followed her into the cafeteria. I couldn't believe no one took her seriously when she said Xavi was dead." She pins me with a strange look. "Until you did."

"I was best friends with Sierra for a long time," I say. "I could tell something was wrong." Saying Sierra's name reminds me of the day we found the pink yarn in the greenhouse. "Why did you really go into Xavier's bedroom?" I ask. "I know it wasn't for a friendship bracelet."

"I'd heard the cops hadn't found his phone, so I thought he'd forgotten it at home," Rose says. "I wanted to delete our text messages so no one found out I'd planned to meet him. But the phone wasn't in his hiding spot."

"What hiding spot?" I ask.

"His air vent." She smiles a little. "We all started hiding stuff in our vents after we watched *Veronica Mars*. But it was empty. Sierra must have taken the phone after she killed him."

"I can't believe you've been lying to me this whole time," Emi says, her voice strangled with anger. "I defended you, even when everyone else said your alibi was bullshit."

"I'm so sorry, Emi," Rose says, her blue eyes wet and pleading. "But you were working for Sierra, and I was afraid she would find out I saw her kill Xavi. I planned to tell you after she was in jail."

"Not good enough," Emi says. "You should have trusted me. We've done dangerous things for Sierra because you lied. I got poisoned. Dulce could have gotten arrested. All because you're a coward."

"Emi—" Rose says, but Emi has already grabbed her backpack.

"Screw this," she says, stalking out of the library.

Rose drops her head onto her arms. "I've ruined everything."

"Did you lose your Magic 8 Ball key chain in the greenhouse?" I ask.

Her head pops off the table. "Is that where it went? The sheriff didn't ask me about it."

"Because Emi stole it from the crime scene," I say. "That's how much she thought you couldn't be the murderer." I close my laptop since there are no more interviews. "She'll forgive you."

"Really?"

"Bombard her with Starburst and Sanrio toys," I say. "And it'll be like nothing ever happened. Emi's good like that."

Rose's body relaxes, as if my words have unlocked her happy place. "Thanks, Dulce," she says, smiling. "I hope you know I'm your friend too."

I feel a sunny kind of warmth at her words. I hadn't considered Rose might actually like me, but she probably hasn't been spinning jealous murder theories in her head for weeks.

Then I think of my rapidly shrinking list of suspects and the warmth fades. Assuming Rose's story is true, she's put the crosshairs right where I hoped they wouldn't go: over Sierra.

26

AFTER THE FINAL BELL THE NEXT DAY, I FIND SIERRA tucked into the curved window nook of the art room. It's on the lower floor, overlooking the herb garden, where a squirrel is stealing food from the bird feeder. Sierra's long legs are bent like a gazelle's, her ankle monitor resting against the velvet cushion covering the window seat. Before Xavier died, she hardly went anywhere without her friends; now she's always alone. The queen bee, cut off from the hive.

She sees me approach but goes straight back to knitting the blanket lying in her lap. It looks soft and cozy, like a child's security blanket, and I wonder if she'll be allowed to take it to jail with her if she's found guilty of Xavier's murder.

I stand near a shelf full of molding clay, waiting for her to perform whatever act of rejection she needs to get out of her system. After a few minutes, she looks up and feigns surprise.

"Can I help you?" she asks.

"I don't have time for whatever game this is," I tell her.

She throws her needles down, making dust float through the strip of sunlight crossing her angry face. "You mean you don't have time for me," she says. "I haven't heard from you for a week."

"Calm down," I say a little guiltily, because I've definitely been ignoring her texts and taking extreme measures to avoid her. "I don't need to keep you informed of every little development."

"I hope you get charged with murder one day," she snarls. "Then you can tell me how *calm* you are."

I throw a folded piece of paper into her lap. "Maybe jail is where you belong."

She opens the paper and frowns. "Why are you giving me a screenshot of the sheriff's interrogation room?"

"Not the room," I say. "The pixelated person sitting across from Sheriff Calhoun. Want to guess who that is?"

She balls the paper up and throws it at me, but I dodge and it lands in a box full of yarn. "I thought you didn't have time for games," she says, but there's a note of panic in her voice.

"It's the girl you saw kissing Xavier in the greenhouse."

Color spilling out of her curls and into her razor-blade cheeks. Stammering nonsense words. Avoiding my eyes like they're the sun, bright with judgment.

Conclusion: Sierra's ego has been driving this case from the start.

She pulls her legs tight against her chest and groans. "I was afraid this would happen."

"You completely botched the timeline!" I yell.

"It was only fifteen minutes," Sierra says into her legs, her voice muffled. "I didn't think it mattered."

"Yeah, well, that small detail has cleared our number one suspect."

Her face snaps off her knees. "What do you mean?"

"Enzo was already back inside the school when Xavier died. Nowhere near the greenhouse."

"Who was she?" Sierra asks, as if I haven't blown her entire defense into space. "The girl with Xavi."

I raise my eyebrows. "Do you really care?"

"Of course I care," she says scathingly.

"You didn't see her?"

"I saw a round white ass and the back of a hoodie," Sierra spits, as if the memory disgusts her. "It's not like her butt had her name tattooed on it."

"You were cheating on him too."

"*I loved him*," she says, each word a staccato punch. "I know none of you believe that, but I did." She narrows her eyes. "You know who the girl is, don't you?"

"You have bigger problems," I say. "She saw you go back to the greenhouse. So did the front-door camera."

Sierra blinks like an owl. "I thought the camera only showed the front lawn."

"Tell me what really happened," I say, crossing my arms. "And don't lie, or I'm going to believe you did it, like everyone else does."

"Even Xavi's moms won't talk to me now," Sierra says softly. "Not since I was charged."

When she sees that I'm unmoved, she sighs. "After I saw Xavi and the girl in the greenhouse, I ran into the woods. I really did get sick and lost. When I finally found my way out, I was going to go back to the main building, but suddenly I got really, really pissed." Her voice climbs. "I'd made a mistake, but he was acting like some saint when all the time he was doing the same thing.

"I went back to the greenhouse, ready to scream at him, and

found him lying on the ground." Her words catch with something like a hiccup. "I shook him and felt for a pulse, but—" She stares past me. "You don't realize how much people move until they're dead. How they breathe and shift and how you can feel their hearts under their skin. But Xavi's body was so still. It was obvious he was gone." She shakes herself out of contemplation. "That's when I saw my knitting needle. I picked it up because I couldn't believe it had my initials on it. I'm not sure how long I stood there, stunned, but then I heard a noise near the window, and I lost my head and threw the needle across the greenhouse. The next thing I remember, I was in the cafeteria. Then everything went black."

"Didn't it occur to you the girl might have killed Xavier?"

She looks at me blankly. "She was half-naked," she says. "Why would she—" Sierra stops. "Do you mean if I'd told you the truth from the beginning, this girl would be arrested instead of me?"

I wish I could say yes, but it doesn't seem likely the sheriff would ever have arrested Rose for the murder. "I don't think she did it either," I say.

"Then it has to be Enzo!" Sierra punches the velvet cushion. "He could have found another way into the greenhouse. He's always sneaking around the grounds."

Her words remind me of what Zane said at the Poisoner's Festival: *He knows these woods really well.*

"Who else could it be?" Sierra whispers, as if she's watching her freedom slip away.

With Rose's story, I've figured out the true *how*: Someone had, between the time Rose left the greenhouse at 12:04 p.m. and the time Sierra returned to it at 12:15 p.m., snuck inside and stabbed Xavier before leaving without being seen by the camera or the other suspects. But even though I know the how, none of the *whos* make any sense. Rose had time to do it, but I don't believe someone that sensitive could kill Xavier without falling to pieces. Besides, she was checking over her shoulder for Sierra in the camera footage, like she really was scared that Sierra might follow and kill her. Not to mention she'd admitted to a motive we never would have found out about. If she faked all of that, she deserves an Oscar.

Enzo is still a possibility if he found a way out of the house, but the problem is that there are only two exits: the front door and the cafeteria door, and Enzo definitely didn't leave either of them after noon. A normal school might have a dozen ways out, but the house is old, and Dr. Everett didn't want to add exits because he thought it would make it feel too institutional. The downstairs windows are nailed shut for security reasons, and even if Enzo could have gotten out of a second-story window without breaking his neck, he would have had to climb back up without being spotted sometime before Emi saw him in the front office when she called an ambulance for Sierra.

"Maybe he'll let some information slip at the Detective's Ball this weekend," I say, but my mention of the dance makes Sierra pick up her needles and aggressively knit her blanket like she needs to vent her rage about not going. The back of the left needle is pointed toward me, and as she rotates it, something strange catches my eye. I move closer, making Sierra glance up in alarm.

"What?" she says.

"Why doesn't that needle have a yarn ditch?" I ask.

"A what?"

"Yarn ditch. You know, the indentation at the back of the needle where the yarn goes."

She looks at her needle, then back at me. "I literally have no idea what you're talking about."

Bubbles of unease fill my stomach. I shift my backpack around to my chest and pull out the pictures I printed off from the police file. I hand her the one with the murder weapon, which shows a carved line bisecting the round end of the needle. "Here." I point. "Where you put the yarn."

Sierra looks at the picture and then digs into her bag and pulls out a handful of wooden knitting needles. She turns them all over and shows me the ends, which are completely flat. "Yarn would never stay inside the ditch," she says, rolling her eyes like I'm an idiot. "Someone must have carved a line into the end of that one."

How could I not have compared the weapon with Sierra's other needles? I've always ignored her Stitch 'n' Bitch Club, angry that she replaced me with them. *This is why Wimsey was curious about everything,* I think, furious at myself. A detective never knows when their lack of knowledge will make them overlook a giant clue. The ditch just made so much sense.

"Didn't you notice the indentation when you grabbed the needle in the greenhouse?" I ask.

"Sorry," she snaps, throwing the needles back into her bag. "I guess I was too busy being horrified by Xavi's dead body."

"But why would someone carve out the line?"

"That's what I'm paying you to find out!"

"You lost the right to criticize me when you lied about your alibi," I say. "Give me one good reason I shouldn't think you did it. All you do is lie! About Xavier's murder." I glare at her. "About my mom."

There's silence in the room except for the buzzing hum of the pottery kiln in the corner. The seconds tick by as I wait for Sierra to fight back. Why isn't she?

"I get it." Sierra pulls her blanket up like she wishes she could cover her face. "I wouldn't forgive me either."

A chill branches out across my shoulders. For two years, Sierra's silence has made it seem like I'd never get closure about the breakdown of our friendship. I wish I was the type of person who could let it go—who could let *her* go—but the tapestry of my mom's death feels incomplete, like the facts are dangling just out of my reach. This finally feels like my chance to know the truth.

"Why did you do it?" I ask, heart thumping in my ears.

Sierra sinks into herself. "My mom made me."

"You never listen to your mom."

"I did that time," she says. "Bill was threatening to request split custody. He'd been my dad for six years, and he was friends with Judge Orcutt, who thought Bill was a local hero. The guy keeping the city safe. But behind closed doors, he was a terror."

"You mean he . . ." I can't bring myself to say the words.

"He didn't hit me or anything," she says. "But when he drank—and he drank a lot—he went on these religious rants. Said I was going to hell. Told my mom she was violating God's will by running for mayor instead of staying at home. He'd become a fanatic, but we were the only ones he showed it to. He said if we challenged his story about Deputy Armstrong, he'd force me to live with him part-time and prevent me from going to J. Everett."

She looks out the window like she's trying to imagine not seeing our campus every day. A wave of discomfort makes my body tense; Sierra always seemed so in control of her relationship with the sheriff—calling him by his first name, being rude to him—that I never considered he might be lurking in the shadows, playing puppeteer.

"His mania had become so bad I was terrified of spending time alone with him," she says. "And I couldn't bear the thought of going to a different school than you. So I repeated what my mom said about the alcohol. And it didn't seem so bad, because that's what the coroner's report concluded too. I figured once you saw that, you'd talk to me again. But you never did."

"Sheriff Calhoun falsified the coroner's report," I say. "The elevated blood alcohol was caused by the fire, not drinking."

Sierra clutches her blanket, but all she says is "I didn't know."

"You could have told me about the sheriff."

"You could have asked," she says. "But you didn't." Her nostrils flare. "You abandoned me as much as I abandoned you."

My temper burns through my sympathy. "That isn't the same thing at all," I say. "Once the divorce was finalized, you could have explained. You never took back all those awful things you said, even once Sheriff Calhoun couldn't get to you anymore."

Sierra stares at her ankle monitor. "I couldn't believe you had so little faith in me. We'd been friends our whole lives, and you just accepted I'd become this monster overnight. Didn't even question whether something bad was going on. If our positions had been reversed, I would have come to your house every day until I figured out what was wrong. I would have shown up to your classes and shaken the truth out of you." She takes a ragged breath. "That's why I never took back what I said. I couldn't forgive you for not fighting for our friendship."

It was so easy to believe she'd turned into a different person.

She and I had Death & Fox, but she'd become beautiful and popular, while I hadn't. Maybe I'd been waiting for the day when she moved on.

Some of my anger begins to seep away. She'd expected too much from a friend whose mom had died. But I hadn't understood her life either.

"Are you going to drop the case?" she asks.

"No," I say.

She exhales with relief. "Thank you."

"But you need to know that if you killed Xavier, I won't protect you."

Sierra's eyes meet mine, and there's a steely glint there. "If I'd killed Xavi," she says, "no one would ever have found his body."

27

CREEPY SKELETONS DANGLING FROM THE CEILING GREET me and Enzo when we walk into J. Everett's ballroom on Halloween. They're wreathed with orange marigolds because the dance's theme is Día de los Muertos. Usually, the Detective's Ball is decorated based on the setting of the game; last year, the theme was Jack the Ripper's London since the pretend murder took place in nineteenth-century England. This year's decorations should have been greenhouse flowers and topiary statues, but there was no way the administration could do that after what happened to Xavier.

Enzo's pant leg brushes against a giant smoking sugar skull, and he quickly waves the mist away from my face. "Careful not to breathe that stuff in," he says, putting his body between me and the dry ice machine. "It's toxic."

He picked me up at my house in what can only be described as a monster truck, explaining that his uncle had taken his car on a two-week vacation to Charleston and left him "this literal monstrosity." If Enzo was offended by my dad's peals of laughter as he watched us drive away, he didn't show it, and I breathed a sigh of relief when he parked the truck near the icehouse instead of in the parking lot so no one could see the moment he helped me down a mini staircase he pulled from the truck bed.

"You look really badass," Enzo says softly as we stop to let someone from yearbook staff take a picture of us inside a frame made of giant roses. I'm decked out in full Wimsey wear, as interpreted by Emi, which means super wide-legged pinstripe trousers and a matching cropped vest. Emi swore she couldn't find one that would cover my stomach, but it was obvious she was lying.

"Thanks," I say, but the music is so loud I'm not sure Enzo hears me. Most of the school is already on the dance floor, bouncing to "Monster Mash." According to Emi, Dean Whitaker never lets anyone else touch the playlist, which is probably why he's standing guard over his laptop next to Ms. Moss, who looks pale and tired in a sunny yellow dress a size too big for her.

Enzo drops me off at a table before leaving to get us sodas. The weirdest part of the evening so far hasn't been the monster truck. Or the fact that Enzo has somehow managed to put together a beautiful corsage from the black peonies and chicory in his garden. It's that he's acted like a normal guy. He was polite to my dad despite my dad's terrible jokes about getting his own eyebrow ring; he was careful to touch my elbow during the photo shoot—no "accidental" brushes of my waist or butt—and none of his compliments have sounded insincere. I assumed he'd act like a creep and make it easy to take advantage of him, but he's behaving exactly like I would have expected of Zane.

Speaking of . . . I look around the room, but I don't see his messy blond hair anywhere even though he's one of the tallest students at J. Everett.

Emi and Rose wave at me from where they're doing some kind of jerky dance that makes them look like chickens. Emi explained, as she dressed me, that Rose had given her a bouquet of Starburst candies so big she'd probably still have them by next Halloween. "She promised not to read tarot for me anymore if I forgave her, which seemed like a pretty good trade," Emi said. "Besides, which of us hasn't lied during this case?"

I glance again at Ms. Moss. She's been leaving school right after the bell every day, so I haven't been able to get her alone to ask about the guitar. She couldn't have killed Xavier, but her lies make me think she knows something about him the cops have missed. It's like how sometimes in the game witnesses have information they don't know is important. Emi and I have learned to follow up on everything, even if it doesn't seem relevant.

Ms. Moss says something to Dean Whitaker and then walks toward the frame of roses. *Now's my chance.* I stand up, wondering whether it would be better to talk to her outside or in the crowd, but before I can follow her yellow dress, Enzo arrives back at our table with a ginger ale for me and a Coke for him.

For a moment, I'm torn between Ms. Moss and Enzo, but then I realize he's the priority; Hannah may be able to give me a clue, but Enzo might actually have killed his brother. This could be my only opportunity to find out.

I sit back down, and Enzo sits across from me like he doesn't want to invade my personal space. "Do you like to dance?" he asks after a minute of silence.

"I don't know," I say. "I've never been to one of these before."

His lip quirks. "Me either. This type of thing was always more of Xavi's jam."

I was hoping to find some opening to bring up Xavier, and Enzo's given it to me in the first ten minutes.

"The shrine is kind of weird, though," Enzo adds, raising his cup to the corner of the ballroom, where a huge portrait of Xavier is propped up on a stand, surrounded by vines and pumpkins. A rumor that the dance would be canceled "out of respect" for Xavier had quickly been replaced by another rumor that his moms had told Dean Whitaker that Xavier wouldn't want his classmates to miss out on a good time.

"I'm sorry he's not here," I say.

Enzo looks into his soda. "He and I never got along, but I always hoped that maybe, when we were older—" He shrugs. "I thought he'd get cooler, you know? Not be such a dick."

"Sierra told me what happened between you and her," I say, and Enzo glances up at me sharply. "I know it was for only a couple months, but she really liked you." *Which of us hasn't lied during this case?* "She said she would never kill your brother because she couldn't hurt you like that."

Enzo looks stricken, and he plays with his skull cuff link like he's trying to collect his thoughts. "She said that?"

"She couldn't face tonight without Xavier," I say. "She's not as evil as everyone makes out."

I actually mean my words. Sierra may be a bitchwitch, but she wasn't the only one responsible for breaking up our friendship. She's also still fighting for the truth even though everything is going against her. In her place, I don't think I'd get out of bed.

"Aren't you thirsty?" Enzo asks, pointing at my ginger ale. His voice is shaking, and he's grabbing his cup so hard the edge of the plastic is splitting. "It's hot in here."

I pick up my drink, wondering how I'm going to keep pressing him when he clearly wants to change the subject, but before I can take a sip, I feel a breeze and someone sits down next to me, bringing along the scent of coconut and vodka.

"How are you two crazy kids doing?" Zane asks, grabbing my drink and downing it in a single gulp. His face is flushed, and both his eyes are bright, like he's been dancing for hours. "You look amazing, by the way," he says, brushing the shoulder of my vest. "Very Harriet Vane."

"Who?" Enzo asks, looking furious that Zane took my drink without asking.

Zane's eyebrows lift in faux surprise. "You haven't read the Lord Wimsey books? They're Dulce's favorites."

On any other night, I'd be happy Zane was looking at me with such interest and delight, but I need Enzo to myself so I can pump him for information. I'm about to suggest Zane go dance with Emi when he holds out his cup to Enzo. "Any chance you brought a flask? Mine's out."

"I don't drink," Enzo says dully.

"Sure you do," Zane says. "You took a shot of whiskey with your brother right before he collapsed at his party."

Enzo sucks in a short, quick breath, but I'm too surprised to do anything but freeze. We've been investigating for weeks, and Zane hasn't bothered to mention that Sierra's side guy handed his brother a shot before he passed out?

"Xavier had too much to drink," Enzo says. "That's all."

"Not according to my mom." Zane's words are oddly clear for someone who's polished off a flask of vodka. "She tested Xavier's blood herself. Very low in alcohol. Very high in poison."

Even in the fractured light of the disco ball, I can see the blood drain out of Enzo's face. He looks at me, then at Zane, then back at me. "Is this why Emi's been asking people questions?" he says. "You two are playing detective for Sierra?"

I don't answer, which gives him his answer.

"And this is why you asked me to the dance," he says, almost to himself, his voice edged with anger. "So your friend could crash our table and accuse me of poisoning my brother."

"No . . ." I start, but my voice is hesitant because the plan had been to accuse him of those things myself.

Enzo stands up so fast his thigh hits the table and knocks the remains of his Coke onto the paper tablecloth. But he pays no attention as it drips onto the floor.

"You know what?" he says. "Go ahead and believe the worst. Everyone else does." His voice trembles as he gazes into my eyes. "I thought you were different. I thought you liked me."

His words make my heart hurt, but they also piss me off, because he completely screwed us when he stole our forensics notes last year, and if he didn't realize I had an ulterior motive, that's on him. "Did you put nicotine in your brother's drink, Enzo?" I ask. "Because if you're letting Sierra take the blame for something you did, then you're worse than anything I could think about you."

A hiss escapes from between his teeth, and I feel Zane shift next to me, like he's ready to defend us if Enzo tries anything. But Enzo's face crumples into lines of pain, and he shoves his chair to the ground before stomping away from the table and out of the ballroom.

I sigh back into my seat. "That could have gone better."

"No way," Zane says. "You saw how he reacted. He totally poisoned Xavier's drink."

He's right; Enzo's face was too heavy with guilt not to have done it. "Why didn't you tell me sooner?" I ask.

"I completely forgot," he says, combing his fingers through his already-mussed hair. "I had to run from the cops like three minutes after it happened, and it was only when I saw him hand you the ginger ale that the memory came back to me." He bounces his leg like he has too much energy to be sitting down. "Now you know who killed Xavier. You just have to prove it."

I should feel elated. If Enzo drugged Xavier's drink, he almost definitely killed him and poisoned Emi, but—and I can't believe I'm thinking this—I'm beginning to understand why Rose keeps saying Enzo isn't the murdering type. There's a softness in him I wouldn't have believed based on his threats about hurting animals. If only I could have pushed him more, he might have been able to explain.

"That's the last we'll get out of him," I say, a little annoyed that Zane stole my only chance with Enzo. "You could have left it to me. Maybe if you'd had less to drink . . ."

"I was lying about the flask," he says. "I let Emi pour a little vodka into my soda, but that's it. I came over here because I was worried about you."

"Me? Why?"

Zane points at my empty glass. "I was afraid he might have found out you were investigating his brother's death and . . . well, you know."

My brain connects the dots. "You thought the ginger ale might be poisoned, and *you drank it?*"

"Well, yeah," he says softly, his ears turning pink.

I'm not sure who's more embarrassed, but I definitely know which of us is happier. He was willing to drink nicotine for me. I can't even begin to think through what that means.

Just then, Emi dances her way to our table. "Looks like our girl's drink is empty," she says, pointing to my cup and then to Zane.

He smiles and bites the air next to her face as he walks to the soda station.

"What a dork," she says. "Enzo bailed, huh?"

"I should probably go too," I say, flustered and hot. I can't stay here and watch Emi and Zane dance when he's put his life at risk for me. I'll tell Emi about my feelings for him tomorrow, but right now they're so intense I might lose it and start crying, and I don't want to make a scene. "There's no reason for me to stay."

"Don't be ridiculous," Emi says. "Your date's about to bring you another drink."

"My . . . what?" I look over my shoulder. "Did Enzo come back?"

"Zane," she says. "Your date."

"Are you drunk?" I ask, spinning back around. "You're being stranger than usual."

"One, yes, I am drunk. But two, I brought him for you."

"What are you talking about?"

"You've broken into Dean Whitaker's office and the sheriff's station," she says like a game show host. "Now it's time to break into Zane's heart." She cringes. "Ew, that's awful. I had a whole speech prepared and everything." At my uncomprehending look, she smiles and says, "I was going to wait for you to tell me you liked him, but since that didn't happen, I invited him to the dance for you."

"But *you* like Zane," I say.

Emi laughs. "Such a big brain and you can still be so wrong. Zane's not into me. Never was. And I don't care, because I'm into someone else." She points at Rose, who's dancing with some of her other friends to "Secret Agent Man."

"You and Rose?" I ask, shocked even though, now that I think about it, Emi has always been just as affectionate with Rose as Rose has been with her. Kissing her cheeks at the Poisoner's Festival, gifting her a Magic 8 Ball key chain, holding her hand. I can't believe I've been so preoccupied with the case that I missed the obvious.

Emi nods. "It just kind of happened. I woke up in the hospital and realized she was the first person I wanted to see." Emi rolls her eyes when my face crumples. "After you, dum-dum. You're my number one sweetie . . . Get it? Because Dulce means sweet?"

"I didn't know you liked girls," I say.

"Me either." Emi grins. "Though I can't believe I didn't think of it sooner. Twice as many kissing options!"

I shake my head. "You can't be serious about anything."

Emi gazes over at Rose with a smile I've never seen on her face before. "I'm not so sure about that." She looks back at me. "It's not weird for you, right?"

"Don't be silly," I say, poking her shoulder. "I'm just glad you're not replacing me as your best friend."

She wraps me up in a drunken hug. "If I ever do that, I promise to give you thirty days' written notice."

"Love your eyelashes."

"Love your lips," she says. "Now go kiss Zane with them."

Emi's gone when Zane returns with my ginger ale, and I have no idea how to tell him she's been playing matchmaker. Luckily, I don't have to.

"Guess we've both been jilted." Zane points to Emi and Rose, who are wrapped around each other, kissing like they've been waiting to all night.

"Yeah," I say. "I'm sorry."

He smiles softly. "I'm not."

The day in the lunchroom. *I'm going to say yes.*

"Me either," I whisper.

"Do you want to dance?" He puts the drinks on the table and holds out his hand.

As I take it, I feel like we're acting out the moment when Lord Wimsey and Harriet Vane finally admit how they feel about each other. *Please let this be real,* I think as Zane leads me over to everyone else. I'm so afraid the song will change to something upbeat and ruin the moment, but the DJ gods are smiling down on me, because the next track is from *Armageddon*, one of my dad's favorite movies to cry at.

Zane's much taller than me, so there's an awkward moment when we try to put our hands in places that make sense. Eventually, one of his arms wraps around my back while the other grabs my left hand. He pulls me close but leaves enough distance so we can see each other's faces.

He bends toward my ear. "Is this okay?"

I nod quickly, reminding myself to breathe. *In and out, Dulce.* It's hard to believe my lungs do this on their own every day, because it feels like each inhale is requiring my full attention.

There's something I want to ask Zane, but I don't want to sound like I'm fishing for a compliment, so I leave it open-ended.

"So, um, you and Emi . . ."

Zane shakes his head. "I like her," he says. "But not like that."

First Emi and Rose, now this. Apparently, my fact collecting is as useful as lipstick on a duck.

"Why didn't you say anything?" I ask.

"I thought you weren't interested," he says. "It wasn't until Emi told me what she was up to that I began to hope."

"She told you?" I groan.

"I'm happy she did." His hand wraps around mine a little tighter. "You wouldn't be in my arms right now if she hadn't."

That shuts me up.

"I didn't think you'd forgiven me for the internship thing," he says.

"I probably would have lied to my friends too," I say. "Rather than admit I'd been arrested."

"The sheriff doesn't believe my mom about the break-in." He lowers his voice. "He's threatening to add trespassing to my charges. I've started leaving by the back door to avoid him."

"I'm sorry," I say. "I'm sure your mom is still mad at me."

"She likes you. She just wishes I'd stop getting into trouble."

"The thing at the pier was Xavier's fault."

Zane shakes his head. "There have been other times."

My arm stiffens a little on his waist. "Other times?"

"I want to tell you as much truth as I can," he says. "Before I came to J. Everett, I did some shitty things. Nothing big," he adds quickly, seeing my face. "Mostly vandalism. My friends and I once took our principal's car apart and rebuilt it on the roof after he gave us detention."

"You took a car apart?"

Zane smiles. "I'm not going to say it wasn't fun," he says. "But I like the way you and Emi are more. You save all your fun for smart stuff. And I'm tired of getting in trouble."

I laugh, amazed he thinks I'm fun. "Anything else you want to confess?" I ask with a wink in my voice.

The smile leaves his face, and he stares at me like he's weighing how his next words will be received.

"You know that afternoon in the libr—" He checks himself.

A complicated series of emotions crosses his face, ending with him biting his lip. "I've wanted to kiss you ever since the first time we talked at Maldonado's," he says.

A fluttering in my back makes me feel like I might grow wings and soar into the disco ball. I grip his shirt like it'll help me stay on the ground and try to figure out how to tell him how I feel. "I lied to myself about liking you for a long time," I say. "Because I didn't want to get between you and Emi. But I think I've wanted to kiss you since I saw you in the hallway on the first day of school."

"Well, then," he says.

He bends down slowly, like he's giving me time to change my mind. But there is no way in this universe or any other that I am about to let anything ruin my first real kiss. His eyes close as his face nears, and mine do the same, as if I can't bear to look in case it's all in my head. Images flash up, unbidden. Pepper's freckled chest, the bottle of peach schnapps, Sierra's honking giggles as she runs across the sand.

Then Zane's lips touch mine and the images snap to black, leaving nothing but the feeling of his mouth. Kissing him is the opposite of Pepper in every way. Where Pepper's lips were cold and sticky, Zane's are warm and soft. He presses gently, not hard, leaving me wanting more, not less. I wrap my arms around his neck, standing on tiptoes to get closer to him, not caring that we're surrounded by the eyes of our classmates. But just as his lips part under mine, someone taps me hard on the shoulder.

I nearly scream with rage. The best moment of my whole life cut short by—

Ms. Moss?

"I'm sorry, Dulce," she says, her face stony. "But I need to talk to Zane. Now."

Zane pulls back, looking angry.

"Can't it wait?" I plead.

"Sorry, no," she says, leading Zane away by the arm.

I've never been mad at Ms. Moss before, but I have to stop myself from running after them and ripping Zane away from her. What could be so urgent that she would interrupt such an important moment for me?

I'm so focused on watching Zane and Ms. Moss walk out of the ballroom together that when a hand grabs my elbow, I actually do scream.

"Can I talk to you?" an all-too-familiar voice asks.

"What are you doing back here?" I say, barely able to make out the glare of Enzo's diamond-studded eyebrow ring through my tears. "I thought you and your monster truck bailed."

"I promise you're going to want to hear what I have to say."

I wipe a tear off my cheek. "Unless it's a confession, I really, really don't."

"And if it is a confession?"

My eyes snap to attention on Enzo's face. He always looks serious, but right now he looks grave. My thoughts fire with anticipation.

"I'm listening."

"I know Sierra didn't kill Xavier," he says. "And I can prove it."

28

"WE CAN'T TALK HERE," ENZO SAYS, LOOKING AROUND.

He touches my upper back with his fingertips, guiding me out of the ballroom and then out of the school. Part of me knows leaving the safety of the crowd is a Very Bad Idea and that if Emi or Zane knew, they'd be chasing after me, but this is exactly why I invited Enzo to the dance: to get information about his role in the murder. And so I let him lead me around the side of the house and into the herb garden, which is fragrant with rosemary and mint. The full moon is bright enough to see the grounds, but it's misting rain, which is probably why no couples are making out on the benches. The nearest one has a small gold plaque that reads IN MEMORY OF CLAIRE EVERETT, WHO WAS AS SWEET AS LICORICE AND AS WARM AS CINNAMON.

"If you try to hurt me, I'll scream," I warn, shimmying away from Enzo's arm.

"I deserve that." He stares at the dirt, his black hair on end from where he's run his hands through it. "I guess I understand why you hate me, after I abandoned the Wimseys last year."

"Why did you?" I say, unable to stop myself from asking even though we have bigger things to talk about.

"Emi started treating me like crap," he says. "I was this dream guy one minute and a moldy piece of bread the next. It really messed with my head." He looks up at me. "But I shouldn't have quit or taken my notes without explaining myself."

My first instinct is to roll my eyes at the lie, but a little birdie in my ear reminds me that Emi started laughing at him whenever he guessed a clue wrong. I didn't realize we had any part in Enzo leaving, but maybe I'm not always the best judge of how Emi treats people.

"Let me guess," I say, getting us back to the real reason we're outside. "You brought me out here to plead your innocence."

"No," he says, and my neck prickles with fear. "You and Zane were right. I poisoned Xavi's drink with nicotine."

I breathe in so fast it makes my throat burn.

"I was only trying to make him sick," he adds quickly when I start to back away in the direction of the greenhouse path. "Not kill him."

"Sick?" I ask, stopping mid-retreat. "What do you mean?"

"I thought . . ." Enzo's dark cheeks turn darker in the moonlight. "It seemed like if I could get Sierra to myself for another week, then she'd choose me instead of him. I barely put any nicotine in the whiskey, but I guess mixing it with alcohol made it stronger."

"Let me get this straight," I say. "You're claiming someone killed your brother with the same poison you *didn't* try to kill him with?"

"I know how it sounds," he says. "But it's true. The worst part is he actually seemed happy when I brought him the shot, as if, underneath all his assholery, he wanted me to like him." Enzo's eyes look wild, like he's being chased by the memories. "That night, while I waited for word from my moms, I swore I'd kill myself if he died. When he got better, I snuck into the greenhouse late one night and burned every single one of my tobacco plants. Dug them up and set fire to them in the woods."

"What about Emi?" I ask. "Did you put nicotine in her sandwich?"

Enzo frowns. "She said that was an accident."

"It wasn't."

"I didn't hurt Emi," he says. "Only Xavi."

"Poisoning your brother and threatening to skin cats," I say. "Maybe Xavier wasn't the Torres who sucked."

"Skin cats?" he asks in a voice that suggests he can't imagine anything worse. "I love cats. I've been feeding a kitten in the woods during study hall."

More lies, but I don't have time for that right now.

"What makes you think Sierra is innocent?" I ask.

"Because I saw something the day Xavi died. Something that clears her."

I snort. "What an epic love story. Boy poisons brother to get girl; boy lets girl get charged with murder."

"I *swear* I believed she'd done it," Enzo says. "For weeks, I thought she'd somehow gotten ahold of the nicotine I used for the whiskey. Then I remembered what I'd seen."

"But you still didn't speak up?"

He squints until his eyes are almost shut. "I was afraid if I got involved with the cops, my moms would find out what I'd done," he says. "They always liked Xavi more than me. Mentioned him first in their Christmas letter. Put pictures of him up on Facebook but hid mine. I didn't want to give them another reason to hate me." His expression sours. "And I was still angry at Sierra for using me to get Xavi's attention. But tonight, when you said she really liked me . . ."

"I lied," I say brutally.

Enzo nods. "That wasn't what made me change my mind. It was that you said she wasn't so bad. And I thought if you could forgive her after what she'd done to you—"

"How do you know about that?" I ask sharply.

"She got drunk one night when we were hanging out at her house and told me how she'd abandoned you after your mom died. I've never seen anyone cry like that."

My heart feels like it's being squeezed by a juicer. Sierra? Cry?

"I figured I could forgive her too," Enzo says.

"Let's pretend I believe you," I say. "What proof do you have?"

"I'll show you."

I follow him back into the house as if it's totally normal to be crime-solving with someone who just admitted to poisoning his brother. *But not killing him,* I think. Despite how improbable his story is, the facts add up. If I didn't hate psychology, I'd say that Enzo seems less like a murderer and more like a lost boy rejected by everyone. What he did is definitely messed up, but what the killer did is much worse.

We walk past the party, where I can see Zane towering over the other dancers, his head swiveling around like he's looking for someone.

Once we're upstairs, Enzo stops in front of the band room. "The day Xavi died, I was in the chem lab all morning making polymer balls for my cousins," he says, pointing down the hall to the lab.

"Zane saw you leaving when he came upstairs to audition for band."

Enzo nods. "I snuck into the woods during lunch because I'd hidden all the supplies I'd used to burn the tobacco plants, and I needed them for a family bonfire at the beach that weekend." He pauses. "What was supposed to be a family bonfire."

His explanation doesn't clear him, but it matches his movements on the camera footage. He went out, found the bag, and, six minutes later, came back to the house carrying the duffel.

"What I didn't think about until later is that I'd seen a teacher come into the lab not long before I left," he says. "She walked right over to the cabinet where all the bottles are kept."

"Bottles?"

"Solvents and cleaners," he says. "Anything you'd need in a chemistry class. But later it made me think: What if the killer hid the nicotine in plain sight?"

"Or maybe a teacher just needed something for a class?"

Enzo looks me dead in the eye. "Explain to me why a band teacher would need something from a chem lab."

And suddenly, I understand why we're outside the band room. "Ms. Moss?" I say, choking out a laugh. "Please tell me you're not suggesting *Ms. Moss* came into the lab to get nicotine to poison Xavier."

Enzo isn't deterred. "I'd never seen her in the lab before," he says. "She was acting funny, too; usually she'd say hi, but she ignored me, like she didn't want me to remember her."

"Now you're making things up."

"Go in and see," he says, pointing into the dark room.

"What?" I ask, taken aback.

"Do you think I'd accuse your favorite teacher of something like this without proof?" he says. "Go inside the room."

"No." I take two steps back. "I'm not sure what you're playing at, but I'm done."

Enzo's eyes widen, making his eyebrow ring touch his forehead. "Playing at? I thought you were Sierra's detective."

"I am."

"Then detect," he snaps. "Don't ignore evidence because it doesn't suit your narrative."

We glare at each other in the hallway.

"This is so stupid," I finally say, but I walk into the room because I know Wimsey would look at the evidence, tell Enzo why he's wrong, and then get back to dancing.

Enzo turns on his phone's flashlight and leads me around the empty music stands to the back cabinets. "Once I remembered what I'd seen, I decided to do some searching," he says. "I figured I was being paranoid—"

"Because you were," I mutter under my breath.

"But then I found this."

He opens up one of the back cabinets, which used to be full of junk.

It's empty.

"Ms. Moss must have cleared everything out," I say. Relief flows through my body, as if part of me was actually considering Enzo's theory.

"Not everything," he says. "Look down there."

I drop to my knees and Enzo follows, shining his light into the corner. When I don't see anything, I tilt my face until it almost touches the floor.

That's when I spot them, under a strip of wood that separates the cabinets: a cracked vial, the broken needle of a syringe, and a few strands of hot-pink yarn.

I reach out for them, but Enzo knocks my hand away. "Don't touch it," he says. Then he pulls plastic gloves out of his pants pocket and snaps them on.

"You just carry those around?" I ask, because this is beginning to feel like a setup.

"I pick plants in the woods for my experiments," he says. "Doing that with bare hands is very dumb, so yes, I just carry them around."

He picks up the bottle and moves it closer to my nose. The warm tobacco smell is unmistakable.

Nicotine.

"I'm sorry, Dulce," he says.

I pop off my knees and laugh. "Sorry about what? Planting evidence in the wrong room? You should have chosen someone who had the opportunity to kill Xavier. A motive would also be nice."

"Xavi was blackmailing Ms. Moss," Enzo says softly.

My heart slams into my chest with a thud, making me stop dead. "I don't believe you," I say, but facts are already beginning to scroll in my head.

The monthly Venmo transfers. The lie about the guitar. Pretending she was bad with money.

"What did Xavier have to blackmail her with?" I ask.

"A picture on his phone," Enzo says. "He considered selling it to Channel Z News, but he said it would be bad for Sierra. Then they broke up, and he decided to use it to get back at her. Two days after his party, we were sitting by the pool, and he said he'd told Ms. Moss their deal was over." He shakes his head. "He didn't even need the money. Just liked the feeling of power it gave him."

Xavier's phone? Is that why the killer took it? So the blackmail photo wouldn't get out?

"What was the picture of?" I ask.

"No idea," he says. "I never saw it. But it must have been serious, because he said Ms. Moss got nasty when he broke off their arrangement. Screamed and cried and threatened him."

"That's bullshit," I say. "Ms. Moss is the nicest person at this school. Not to mention she has an alibi."

For the first time during our tour of the band room, Enzo frowns. "An alibi?"

"I watched the footage from the front-door camera," I say. "She didn't leave the school until 12:20 p.m."

Enzo thinks for a minute. "Maybe she was working with Zane," he says slowly. "She could have given him the nicotine when he went to her room." His frown deepens. "He was in the chem lab, too, now that I think about it."

"Zane wasn't on the camera footage either," I say, but my mind is racing. "Who else came into the lab that morning?"

Enzo looks at the ceiling, ticking people off on his fingers. "Dr. Saka, Dean Whitaker, Zane, and then Ms. Moss," he says. "Only Ms. Moss took a bottle, though; the rest were putting one back."

"Every one of those people has an alibi," I say. "And none of them left the school during lunch."

"Then how did this stuff get here?" Enzo asks.

"Maybe the killer ditched it here afterward. Or planted it." I point at him. "You could have done it yourself, to throw suspicion off you."

"Right," he says. "I planted evidence inside the room hoping that you, who I didn't know was helping Sierra until tonight, would believe me. But before that, I confessed to a crime I could have kept secret forever." He rolls his eyes. "If this is my way of covering up a murder, I'm fucking terrible at it."

"Maybe you think pretending to be terrible will make me trust you, or maybe you stole one of Sierra's needles to get back at her for dumping you for Xavier, or maybe—"

I stop talking, because Enzo's phone light has flashed against the window, making me look toward the greenhouse, which is decorated with twinkle lights for the dance. Suddenly, as if Wimsey himself has walked off the page to whisper in my ear, facts begin to wrap themselves around an idea so wild I almost laugh. As the theory knits itself into a tapestry, the laugh turns into a moan. Dread spills through my body, from my head to my calves, which begin to burn like I've been running.

Oh no. No, no, no.

I rush over to the window and open it.

"What's wrong?" Enzo asks. He sounds uneasy, like he's afraid I'm going to throw myself out.

The moon is shining high over the forest. Music wafts upward like brass smoke from the ballroom below. And there, in the distance, is the new glass pane in the greenhouse roof. I hold my arm in front of my body and point. It's a direct line from the band room window to the glass pane that was, until two weeks ago, a gaping emptiness. If Xavier had been standing in front of the table full of pothos vines, he would have been inside the opening. It's only about sixty yards from the window to the greenhouse. Not much farther than the target at the archery range.

A ditch carved into the end, to pull against a wire or strap.

Pink yarn attached like feathers on the sides, to make it fly straight. A syringe that would fire on contact. *The angle was steep, like someone taller than Xavier jabbed it into him.* Dr. Bates gave me a key clue—if only I'd understood what it meant.

It seemed so obvious that someone had stabbed Xavier inside the greenhouse, but, like in all the past games, the obvious answer was the wrong one. Xavier's killer, having gotten Zane out of the band room, stood at the window, watching through the glass until Xavier was alone before she took aim and fired.

The perfect weapon, easy to smuggle out in a guitar case afterward. The perfect poison, which killed Xavier so fast he didn't have time to tell anyone that the needle came from above, as if Cupid had pivoted from love to murder. And the perfect angle and distance . . .

If you were a good enough shot.

Figure out the how, and you'll figure out the who.

I collapse into a chair and put my head in my hands. Stars pop before my closed eyes in the darkness like fireworks at a funeral.

Enzo kneels next to me, and his voice is alarmed. "Dulce, are you okay? Do you need me to get the nurse?"

I take my head out of my hands and look into the bottomless pits of his eyes. "I know what happened," I whisper.

Just then, the overhead lights flick on. Enzo and I both jump to our feet. Dean Whitaker is standing in the doorway with Emi, who's miming an apology.

"I tried to stop him," she says. "But there's only so long you can talk about seeing Claire Everett's ghost."

"Hello, Dulce," the dean says. "Doing a little more out-of-bounds snooping?"

"I can explain." The cropped vest of my Wimsey outfit is suddenly making me feel very exposed.

"Please do," he says.

"Enzo and I were"—I'm thinking fast—"kissing."

Enzo blinks like he's never seen me before while Emi tries and fails to block her laughter with her hand.

"Nice try," Dean Whitaker says. "I saw you kissing Zane Lawrence ten minutes ago. Now, tell me what you're doing up here."

"We have evidence Ms. Moss killed my brother," Enzo says.

Dean Whitaker's eyes go sharp. "What evidence?"

"There's a broken vial with nicotine in it." He points toward the cabinet. "Also, some yarn and a needle. Dulce seems to know how she did it."

"Dulce?" Dean Whitaker says. "Is that true?"

I shake my head while my thoughts run in a looped track. My idea is nonsense, the product of an overactive imagination and way too many Wimsey books.

"Ms. Moss didn't do it," I say. "I must be missing something."

I look at Emi and then away again, unable to stand the pity in her eyes. She takes a step forward but then stops like I'm a bunny that might dart away if she gets too close. Her voice is low when she says, "Wimsey didn't ignore evidence when his brother was charged with murder. He wanted all the facts to come out, even if they were bad."

"Maybe Wimsey isn't always right," I mumble.

"So you're just going to let Sierra go to prison forever even though she didn't do it?"

A gust of wind makes me shiver. I forgot my choice would have consequences either way.

"No," I sigh, making both Emi and Dean Whitaker visibly relax. "I'm not going to do that."

I beckon them over to the window. "What if someone whose identity we *don't know*"—I glare at Enzo—"shot the needle from here with a crossbow. The needle that killed Xavier had a carved notch at the end, like it had been strung against a wire. It would have been a direct shot through the glass pane that was missing. If they hit Xavier in the back, he would have been dead before he could get help."

"That's ridiculous," Dean Whitaker says, but he keeps looking at the greenhouse like he's measuring the distance. "You'd have to be a crack shot to even—" He stops, and I watch his mouth go slack, like he's remembering the archery competition at the Poisoner's Festival. "Oh," he says. "Oh, I see." His voice is sad and exhausted. "I have to call the sheriff."

"Ms. Moss couldn't have done this," I say. "You *know* her."

"I'm sorry, Dulce, but this is out of my hands." He glances around. "Don't touch anything else. This is a crime scene."

The tears that have been swimming behind my eyes break free, and I sprint past the others and out of the room with only one thought in my head: I need to warn Ms. Moss.

"Dulce, wait!" Emi calls, but I ignore her.

Ms. Moss is at the bottom of the staircase. "Is Dean Whitaker still up there?" she asks. "He said he'd be right back."

My tears turn to sobs, making it hard to speak. "I—I told them how it was done," I cry, hugging her tightly because I'm afraid it'll be the last time. "But I didn't say it was you."

She pushes me away, looking frightened. "What are you talking about? What's happened?"

"Enzo found the broken bottle," I say. "And the yarn and needle."

"Found them?" The words come out stilted, like her mouth is having trouble shaping them.

"In your cabinet. You—" I stop myself. "Someone left them there after they killed Xavier."

Ms. Moss drops onto the stairs like a felled tree. "That's impossible," she says, her face going so pale she looks dead. "I didn't leave anything in the cabinets."

"If you tell me what happened, maybe I can help you," I say. "But you have to tell me fast."

"I—" she starts, but before she can say anything more, the others come down the stairs. When she sees them, her mouth gapes open like they're evil spirits.

Dean Whitaker stops on the stair above us, looking as grim as an executioner. "I'm so sorry, Hannah, but the police are on their way."

29

THE MONDAY AFTER THE DETECTIVE'S BALL, SIERRA WALKS into the cafeteria wearing a minidress so that everyone can see her bare ankle, no longer trapped in a monitor. Her mom hosted a press conference at noon yesterday, announcing that Xavier's killer had confessed and that all charges had been dropped against her daughter. This morning's news, playing loudly in our living room, revealed an overnight poll showing Mayor Fox back in the lead, with the sheriff's cousin a very distant second.

The Miss Marples cheer when they see Sierra, as if they'd thought she was innocent the whole time, but she snubs them and strides over to me, pulling me off the bench and wrapping me in a bone-crunching hug.

"You're a genius, Dulce," she says. "Seriously, I can't thank you enough for solving the case."

"I didn't," I say, but she ignores me and hops onto the table, making everyone in the lunchroom stop talking.

"I want all of you to know that Dulce Castillo is the best fucking detective in this school and you'd be lucky to be on her team next year!"

Everyone cheers some more.

Sierra climbs off the table and winks. "Least I could do."

"I wish you'd done less," I say.

"Maybe we can go to Maldonado's this weekend," she continues as if she hasn't heard me. "Hash out the details of your payment." She smiles like we're friends again. "Pizza's on me."

She leaves, either unaware of or indifferent to my misery in the midst of her own happiness.

I hear her yell, "Told you bitches I didn't do it!" before she sits down with her friends, who seem perfectly ready to hand back her crown.

"My mom told me Ms. Moss confessed as soon as she got into the interview room," Zane says, watching Sierra with distaste. "Said she killed Xavier because he was blackmailing her over a photo he'd taken. Refused to say of what."

"I don't believe it," I say.

Emi shrugs. "Everything fits."

"It doesn't fit," I argue. "How did she know Xavier would be in the greenhouse?"

"The game packet," Emi says. "The greenhouse was the scene of the crime. She must have watched for him out her window. Knew he'd have to go in alone eventually."

"How did she get the nicotine?" I ask. "*She* wasn't growing plants in the greenhouse."

"Probably bought it on the internet."

"And snuck some into my bologna sandwich?" I think of all those hours eating lunch in the blood spatter bathroom with her. "No way. She doesn't know we switch."

Emi pauses in the middle of biting into an apple. "Ms. Moss confessed, Dulce," she says. "It's over."

But it isn't over for me. People falsely confess all the time.

Someone must have something on Ms. Moss for her to tell these lies. Her story might make sense, but every part of me is screaming that it's not true. Someone's taken the facts and arranged them in the wrong order.

"Not completely over," Rose says, pointing at a sheriff's deputy who's just poked his head into the cafeteria.

"Probably here to take our porn away." Emi flips him off when he leaves.

"Our porn?" I ask. "What are you talking about?"

"The sheriff is so mad he can't put Sierra in jail he's decided to open an official investigation into the 'pornography' in our library books." Emi rolls her eyes. "My mom heard Ricardo Best talking about it on the news last night and freaked out. Like the dean has us trading nudes in study hall."

My eyes flash over to Zane before I can help it. I expect him to give me an embarrassed smile, but he's staring hard at his hands. Maybe after our kiss at the dance, he's hoping I won't remember what I saw in the library.

"How do the cops even know about the textbooks?" Rose asks. "I doubt the librarian is a snitch."

Zane stands up, scratching his seat loudly against the floor. "I just remembered," he says. "I left my chemistry textbook in the car."

Rose frowns when Zane doesn't say goodbye to me. "Is he okay?" she asks.

"Probably off to find the nudes," Emi jokes.

But I don't laugh. Rose is right: Zane is acting weird. And it started when he saw the deputy.

My heart begins to stutter under my ribs. "Emi," I say, my voice hushed, "how *did* the sheriff know?"

She waves a hand in the air. "No idea. It just looked like a blurry photo to me. You couldn't even tell it was a nude. I tried to tell my mom that, but—"

"Photo?" I say, my heart beating harder. "Show me."

Emi giggles. "Trying to get ideas for date night?"

"I'm serious, Emi."

She glances at my face, and her smile disappears. "Okay, okay." She pulls out her phone and scrolls to a YouTube video of last night's news segment. "They show it here, but like I said, you can barely see anything."

I take the phone and press play. A minute into Ricardo Best's report, a photo pops up on-screen. It's blurry, like someone's put a filter on it, but I can still make out enough of the original to recognize it.

It's the picture Zane snapped with his phone in the library.

I get into the front seat of Emi's car after school while Rose slides into the back. I'm glad she's with us because I don't feel like talking. In between my nonstop thoughts about Ms. Moss, I've been trying to figure out how Sheriff Calhoun could have gotten Zane's library photo. Zane obviously didn't give it to him—showing the sheriff a pornographic picture wouldn't exactly help Zane's criminal case—but there's no doubt in my mind it's the same one.

I've come up with two scenarios. One, Zane's mom saw the picture and turned it over as a concerned parent (Hadn't Ricardo Best used that language in one of his news broadcasts? I wish I'd paid more attention.). Or two, Sheriff Calhoun is using the station's Wi-Fi to steal data from phones that connect to it. The problem is that Dr. Bates doesn't seem like the type to tattle to a boss she hates, and I'm not sure the sheriff is tech savvy enough to steal a photo from an open Wi-Fi connection.

I shake thoughts of the photo out of my mind. Ms. Moss is sitting alone in a jail cell right now, and I'm the only person who knows she doesn't belong there. I hoped clearing Sierra would mean the end of the investigation, but I can't give up on the teacher who's done so much for me.

"I'm not going home," I tell Emi before she can turn in the direction of my house. "I want to see Ms. Moss."

Emi exchanges a look with Rose in the rearview mirror. "I don't think they let people see prisoners, Dulce."

"That's why I'm going to sneak in," I say. "If I get caught, I'll tell them I'm there to see Dr. Bates. She'll cover for me." *And maybe tell me whether she took the photo from Zane's phone.*

"I don't—" Emi starts, but Rose interrupts her.

"I think it's a great idea," she says.

Emi raises her eyebrows. "Are we already at the suck-up-to-my-best-friend stage of the relationship?"

Rose ignores her and asks, "Wasn't there ever a time in those books you two like when the detective thought the police had the wrong suspect?"

"Harriet Vane," I say, pushing my advantage. "Wimsey never believed she poisoned her boyfriend, and he was right; she was innocent."

"Fine." Emi gives up. "But if you can't get anything from her, will you agree to drop it?"

I think for a minute. The news said Ms. Moss is being

transferred to a prison in Richmond later this week. If I don't find out the truth now, I never will. "Yes," I say. "If Ms. Moss tells me to my face that she killed Xavier, I'll consider the case closed."

When Emi pulls into the sheriff's station, I direct her to the back, where Zane parked the night we broke in.

"You two should stay here," I say. "She'll be more likely to tell me the truth if I'm alone."

Since it's daytime, the door is unlocked, and I slip in unnoticed. I wait for someone to stop me as I pass the beige cubicles, but the only thing I hear is a bunch of muffled voices singing "Happy Birthday." I dart past the half-cracked door of the kitchen and catch a glimpse of streamers and cake.

Silently thanking whoever was born today, I hurry down the stairs. The basement hallway is empty too. The lights in the autopsy room are off, so I guess I won't be asking Dr. Bates about the photo. Her absence will be a problem if I get caught, but I don't have time to worry about that.

"Please don't let there be a guard," I mutter under my breath as I pass a sign that says JAIL. An arrow next to it leads me past the morgue, cool air tickling my ankles as I walk by holding my breath, thoughtlessly mimicking my dad, who thinks you can inhale ghosts.

In true slumlord fashion, there's not only no guard, there's also no door—just a gap where one should be. Ms. Moss is lying on a cot inside a cell, staring up at a tiny window fitted with a black grate.

She doesn't move at the sound of my footsteps, so I lean against the bars and whisper, "Ms. Moss?"

"Dulce?" she says. Her voice is thick, like she hasn't spoken in hours. "Is that you?"

She struggles into a sitting position, swaying a little as she does.

"Are you okay?" She looks pale and disheveled.

"I'm fine," she says. "They gave me some medicine to calm me down, so I'm a little . . . what's the word?"

"Out of it?"

"Woozy."

"Ms. Moss, we don't have much time," I say, because I have zero idea how long office birthday parties last. "I need you to tell me who really killed Xavier."

She gives me a look of such sympathy that I recoil. "I'm sorry, Dulce," she says. "But I killed him."

No.

For a minute, it's the only word in my head, like the rest of me has disassociated from reality. I'd built a brick wall around the possibility that Hannah had done it, but now, for the first time since Saturday night, weeds begin to push through the cracks.

"I—I don't believe that," I say.

"I know. And that's such a comfort. But it's still true."

The wall crumbles as I read her face. It's as open and honest as always. The word *no* fades into the distance, replaced by its horrible opposite: *yes.*

"But *why?*" I cry before quickly lowering my voice. "I know Xavier was blackmailing you over that photo, but it's just not . . . you."

As I stare at the broken figure of Ms. Moss wavering on the

cot, the urge to see my mom overwhelms me. I'd do anything to have her wrap me in her arms and tell me everything's going to be okay. That somewhere, someone has written the story wrong and that Wimsey will sweep in and present me with the real solution.

"I didn't mean to," she whispers.

"What?" I say, jolted out of my yearning. "How can you accidentally shoot someone?"

She looks at me, and her eyes are steady despite the medicine. "Will you keep it a secret?"

There's no way I can agree to that, but I need her to tell me the truth.

"I've kept secrets worse than anything you can say," I lie, a pit in the center of my stomach because I know I'm taking advantage of her disoriented state.

"Xavier saw me with someone," she says. "Someone I shouldn't have been with. He told me I needed to pay him five hundred dollars every month or he'd sell the picture to Channel Z News. I thought I could stop after the election, but then *he* came to me with a plan."

"Who did?"

She speaks like she's in her own world. "He said we could blackmail Xavier back. Put him to sleep and then plant drugs on him so he'd get kicked out of school and everyone would think he'd faked the picture in retaliation." She shakes her head. "I wanted to wait for November, but then Xavier broke off our deal, so I had to agree. I went to the chemistry lab, where he'd put the sleeping medicine in the farthest bottle to the left. Left like love, he'd said, to help me remember. When I saw Xavier in the greenhouse, I pulled my dad's old crossbow out of my guitar case, where I'd hidden it.

"I filled the needle he'd given me," she says. "He's good with tools, and he knew how to make it like the syringe you take down animals with. He told me to touch it with gloves so I didn't leave fingerprints. After I had the needle loaded, I opened the window and took aim."

"Is that when you shot Xavier?"

Ms. Moss's head is drooping a bit, like it's hard for her to hold it up. "There was a girl in there," she says. "Rose Martin. I had to wait for her to leave. And then it took another minute for Xavier to move to the right place. As soon as he did, I let the needle fly." She looks into the distance like she's watching the memory. "It soared through the broken pane like any arrow would. He'd added some pink yarn to the back so it would fly true. I told you he was good at things like that."

"Yeah, you did." My impatience is hard to hide. "But you haven't told me who he is."

"I watched Xavier fall," she says. "And then I packed up to leave. I took one last look out the window, and that's when I saw Sierra in the greenhouse. That part wasn't supposed to happen. He was supposed to put the drugs in there to make it look like Xavier had passed out after getting high. I didn't know what to do, so I stuck to the plan. That's what he said: 'If anything goes wrong, stick to the plan.' I almost ran into Sierra coming through the front door, but I stepped into a classroom as she passed so she didn't see me. Then I drove away."

"Were your kids really sick?" I ask.

She shakes her head. "I heard about the murder on the news and lost my mind for a while. A terrible mistake. All my fault."

"I don't understand. If you shot him with sleeping medicine, how did he die of nicotine poisoning?"

"I must have grabbed the wrong bottle," she says. "Left for love, but I must have forgotten."

"You remember now," I point out. "Do you really think you forgot then?"

"I was nervous. Enzo was sitting near the cabinet of bottles in the chem lab, and I was afraid he might catch me, so I panicked." She begins to cry softly. "And now that poor boy is dead, and my babies will grow up without me."

The wrong bottle. I don't believe for a second that she messed up, but then how did Xavier die?

My mind spins the facts I know about that day into a web, and I travel the strands, back and forth, up and down, searching for the answer. If the center of the web is Ms. Moss grabbing the farthest bottle on the left like she was supposed to, then what could have turned sleeping medicine into nicotine?

The answer, when I reach it, is so obvious I can't believe I didn't see it immediately.

"Ms. Moss, I don't think you messed up the bottles," I say. "I think someone switched them."

There's a beat. "Switched . . . them?"

"He tricked you. He pretended he was giving you sleeping medicine when really he put poison in that bottle. He never intended to plant drugs on Xavier. He wanted him dead."

"No," she says. "He was in trouble with the law. He wouldn't want more."

I freeze. "With the sheriff?"

She nods. "He said he'd made a mistake and the sheriff might charge him."

My stomach twists like a snake eating itself.

Zane was worried about Xavier testifying against him. He and his mom run a farm, where they use darts to give animals medicine. He dropped a bottle off in the chemistry lab that day.

Conclusion: Zane framed Ms. Moss.

I shudder away my suspicions. I can't fall apart now. I'm too close. "Ms. Moss, the person you're talking about made you kill Xavier Torres," I say. "You need to tell me who it is."

She shakes her head so hard that her hair, which is already matted and puffy, flops around like a mop. "No," she says, fighting the idea. "He's been trying to help. He told me he could get me out of here."

"He's lying. He wants you to take the blame for what he did."

"But he said . . ."

"He lied." I hope, if I repeat it enough times, it'll get through her fog. "And if you don't tell me who he is, he's going to get away with this murder."

There's another pause.

"If you're right, he'll kill me too," she says, her voice a little clearer. "Or my kids."

"Your kids are with your sister in Vermont," I remind her. "They said so on the news. He can't get to them."

She starts muttering like she's about to have a breakdown. "It's too late. My poor babies."

I'm trying to think of what else I can do to convince her when an angry voice behind me says, "What the hell are you doing in here?"

I spin around. Sheriff Calhoun is standing in the doorway. I was so intent on interrogating Ms. Moss that I didn't hear his boots, which must have been muffled by the carpet.

"I wanted to tell Ms. Moss goodbye," I say stupidly. "Before she goes to Richmond."

The sheriff's hand closes over my wrist. "I'm not sure what makes you think you can sneak around this station, but—"

His grip immediately takes me back to the night my mom died, when he grabbed my arm to push me into his car. As if no time has passed at all, my whole body goes rigid.

"What's wrong with you?" he says, trying to pull me away from the bars.

If he gets me out of the room, I'll never know what happened. *Unfreeze!* I scream inside my head, and when that doesn't work, I start observing facts.

The sheriff has white icing in his mustache. There's a fat spider in the corner with a pouch full of eggs. Ms. Moss is humming a nursery rhyme about the spider, like her kids are in the room.

The recitation makes my body unclench, but that just makes it easier for the sheriff to drag me away from the cell. "Do you remember when we had lunch in the beautiful bathroom?" I call, taking my last chance to reach Ms. Moss. "What did you say to do if someone betrayed you?"

A dreamy look crosses her face. "Where fairies eat lunch in the tub."

"Stop talking to the prisoner," Sheriff Calhoun says, dragging me harder, but I keep fighting against him.

I've lost her, but I have to keep trying. "The killer betrayed you, Ms. Moss. What did you say to do?" The sheriff jerks my arm, almost pulling it out of its socket. "Ow, you bastard!" I scream, and my pain seems to snap Ms. Moss out of her stupor.

"I told you to let them burn," she whispers.

"Let's burn him, Hannah. Let's burn him to the fucking ground."

The clouds part, and a ray of light streams through the basement window, illuminating her face. She jumps up from the cot and runs to the cell bars, reaching an arm out with a desperate look in her eye. I make a sudden swinging motion that takes the sheriff by surprise, forcing him to drop my wrist. He lunges after me, but my desire makes me quick. I grab Ms. Moss's hand, and she pulls me against the bars, the cold metal digging into my cheek.

She says only three words before Sheriff Calhoun yanks me away from her, but they're enough:

"Check the icehouse."

30

THE SHERIFF DIGS HIS FINGERS INTO MY ARM AS HE DRAGS me down the hallway. "You think you're tough shit, don't you, little girl?" he growls. "Think you can go into my office and touch my things?"

I go numb under his hand, but then he says, "Pull immature pranks like unplugging my monitor," and I sigh with relief. He doesn't know I stole the files. If he did, I'd probably be sitting in the cell with Ms. Moss.

The sheriff keeps talking, and I remember now how he never seemed to stop when he was married to Mayor Fox. Just a stream of nonsense strung together, like the words were important because they were coming from his mouth. But I barely hear them because all I can think about is how Zane's alibi is falling to pieces. If he set up Ms. Moss, he could have committed the murder from the comfort of the library.

Impossible, I think. Zane may have told one lie about his past, but that doesn't make him a bad person.

"Strange to see you with Zane that night," Sheriff Calhoun says like he read my mind. "I wouldn't have called you the forgiving type."

A nervous chill runs down the arm he's holding. "F-forgiving type?" I stutter. "What would I need to forgive Zane for?"

The sheriff grins under his mustache. "He never mentioned he was working for me?"

I stop dead, and Sheriff Calhoun stops too. "He and I made an arrangement," he continues. "If he would get me dirt on your school, I wouldn't recommend felony charges against him for that pier stunt. I told him to spend time with you so he could get close to Sierra because I thought you were still best friends. Too bad about that, but he got what I needed anyway."

Dirt on the school. The textbook photo.

I close my eyes, as if not seeing the sheriff's smug face might make what he just told me less devastating. Zane played me. The smiles, joining the Lord Wimseys, kissing me at the dance. He pretended to like me for months, when, all along, he was only doing what the sheriff said.

"But why?" I ask, blinking hard so I don't cry. "Why go through all that trouble?"

"To hurt Lily," he says with the confidence of a person who knows no one will believe me if I repeat his words. "I was sure if the people in Cape Cherry saw the things that went on at J. Everett, they'd turn on her. And I thought if Zane was friends with you and Sierra, he could find out all of Stan Whitaker's little secrets. Lily thought she beat me in the divorce, but I was never going to let her win."

"Except you failed," I say, trying not to show him that my heart is struggling to beat. "Mayor Fox is going to win the election now that Sierra has been cleared. No one's going to care about a grainy nude."

"Maybe," he says. "But it doesn't change the fact that Zane

was always my man. Never yours." He grins wider, and I understand that my pain is his consolation prize. "Just thought you should know."

Once we're upstairs, the sheriff throws me through the back door of the station.

"If I ever catch you here again, I'll arrest you," he says before pointing to Emi's SUV. "Same goes for your friends."

I get into the car without a word and pull out my phone.

"How did it—" Emi says, but I stop her with one hand and text Zane with the other.

> You have one chance to tell me the truth. Did you come to J. Everett to spy for the sheriff?

I don't have to wait long for an answer.

> Yes, but I can explain.

Yes. My eyes drill into the word, like maybe if I glare at it hard enough, it will disappear.

I text Zane back, tears blurring the screen.

> Don't ever talk to me again.

"We need to go back to school," I say. My expression must tell Emi that something serious is happening, because she turns the car toward J. Everett without asking why.

I'm done making excuses for Zane. I spent the day coming up with ways the photo could have been stolen from his phone, only to learn he was willing to sacrifice our school to save his own skin. What else was he willing to do?

I think through everything I know. Enzo said three people put bottles on the shelf the day Xavier died: Dr. Saka, Dean Whitaker, and Zane.

Dr. Saka is a *she*, and Ms. Moss said *he*. Dean Whitaker has done everything, even steal evidence from a crime scene, to keep Sierra from looking guilty. If he was pulling Ms. Moss's strings, he would have used a different needle and wouldn't have put Sierra's yarn on the end to use as a fly guide. He also would never have shown me the video footage or canceled my in-school suspensions so I could have more time to investigate.

Which leaves Zane. His flute case is the perfect size to hide a knitting needle. He could have taken it upstairs to Ms. Moss, told her he was going outside to plant drugs on Xavier, and then stayed inside to give himself an alibi. With a single shot, his friend would be avenged, and the lead witness in his case would disappear forever.

The sheriff's words ring in my ears: *Zane was always my man.* A new thought begins to bloom in my mind like one of the greenhouse orchids. What if Zane didn't come up with the plan alone? Could Sheriff Calhoun have used him to set up Ms. Moss in order to bring down the school? Was arranging Xavier's murder the price of not going to prison?

I need more time with Ms. Moss. Maybe I can convince her to talk to Sierra's attorney. But to do that, someone needs to stop the sheriff from sending Ms. Moss to Richmond.

There's only one person I know with the connections to prevent her transfer.

"Can I see your phone?" I ask Emi.

"Why?" she asks, looking startled after the long silence.

"You have Dean Whitaker's number, right? I need to call him."

"Um, okay." She digs it out of her fanny pack while trying to keep the steering wheel steady. "Tell him I said hi."

When the dean picks up, he says, "This better be an emergency, Emi."

"Dean Whitaker, it's Dulce Castillo," I say. "And it is an emergency."

"Dulce? What's wrong?"

"I talked to Ms. Moss."

"You—what? Who let you do that?"

"It doesn't matter," I say. "I think she's being framed."

Dean Whitaker sighs. "Look, Dulce, I know you and Ms. Moss are close, but—"

"No, listen!" I cut him off, not caring that I'm snapping at a teacher. "Ms. Moss thought she was putting Xavier to sleep. She and someone else planned to frame him and get him kicked out of school. It's a long story. The point is someone went into the chem lab and exchanged the sleep stuff for nicotine so Ms. Moss would kill Xavier instead."

Dean Whitaker sucks in a sharp breath. "Do you have any idea who?"

"Yes," I say. "It was Zane Lawrence."

"No!" Emi cries out beside me. The speaker must be loud enough for her to hear both sides of the conversation.

"That's why I'm calling," I say. "How did Zane get into J. Everett?"

Dean Whitaker clears his throat. "I can't really discuss student admissions..."

"Please, Dean Whitaker. We're so close to the truth. And this might help Ms. Moss."

There's a pause, and then he says, "I guess I've told you a dozen things I shouldn't have at this point. What's one more?" He sighs again. "A few days before classes began, the sheriff called and asked me to let Zane in, no questions asked."

"The sheriff?" My heart hammers in my chest. "But he hates J. Everett."

"I know," the dean says. "I thought it was odd too. But he said the coroner's kid had gotten into some trouble at Cape Cherry High and needed a soft landing. I didn't want to antagonize Bill, so I waived the testing requirement and accepted him."

"The sheriff told me he's been having Zane spy on the school," I say.

There's silence on the other end of the line.

"That explains the news reports." Dean Whitaker lets out a long breath. "I wondered how Ricardo Best was getting all those inside scoops."

"What if the sheriff decided to bring down the school another way?" I ask. "By having Zane frame a teacher for killing Xavier?"

"That's quite an accusation, Dulce."

"He's capable of it." I don't mention my mom's autopsy report. "I know he is."

"From what Lily has told me, I wouldn't put it past him," the dean says. "But it's going to be hard to get people in Cape Cherry to believe you. Which is why I think it's time to report this to the Virginia State Police. They might be able to come over from

Chesapeake and investigate your allegations. Did Ms. Moss give you any other information?"

I almost tell him about the icehouse. But he would try to stop me from going, and I can't have that.

"No, nothing," I lie.

"I'd like to take it from here, Dulce. I'm afraid the state police won't take teenagers seriously. More shame on them, but the truth comes before our egos, right?"

"Right," I say.

"You've done an amazing job. I'll see you in school tomorrow and let you know what I find out."

I press end. "We're going to the icehouse," I tell Emi.

"Is this some kind of joke?" Her knuckles are white on the steering wheel. "Zane? Help kill Xavier?"

"He's been spying for the sheriff," I say. "To keep Mayor Fox from winning the election."

"Bastard!" Emi says, turning on Zane without question. "And he set up Ms. Moss?"

"Seems like it. When you've eliminated the impossible—"

"Hey, no cheating on Lord Wimsey with Sherlock Holmes," Emi complains.

"Point is no one else makes sense."

About a quarter mile from the entrance to school, I tell Emi to pull off the road. "I'm going to walk onto campus through the forest," I say. "Dean Whitaker is always here late, and I don't want him to see your car. He can't know I'm still investigating."

"What's in the icehouse?" Rose asks.

"I don't know," I say, collecting my backpack as soon as we stop. "Hopefully something that will prove Zane was working with Ms. Moss." I shiver. "He had us sit on the roof of the place he was scheming to poison someone."

Rose makes a scandalized noise from the back seat. "Does that mean he poisoned Emi too?"

"Double bastard!" I gasp. "He definitely knows Emi and I switch lunches."

"Maybe we should come with you," Emi says.

"No. If something goes wrong, I need you to be here so you can call for help." I sigh. "Why couldn't it have been Enzo?"

Rose chimes in softly. "Told you he couldn't have done it."

"Cat-skinning and brother-poisoning, yes," I say. "Murder, no."

Emi clears her throat, and I look at her. "What?" I ask.

"Well," she says, "since you might end up confronting a murderer and dying, I should probably tell you . . ."

"Yes?"

"I lied about the cat thing."

"What?" I burst out. "Enzo never said that?"

"I was pissed at him for leaving the Lord Wimseys," she says. "And pissed at myself for inviting him in the first place."

"Unbelievable!" I might owe Enzo an apology. "Anything else you'd like to confess?"

"Rose and I are probably going to make out in the back seat while you're gone." When she sees my *at a time like this?* face, she grins. "Kidding. I'll keep my ringer on. Don't do anything dumb, *conejita*. Love your spleen."

"Love your heart," I say with extra emphasis as the reality of the risk I'm taking sets in.

It's not far to the icehouse, but I'm so amped up I make it in no time at all. The ivy-covered hut is smaller than it seemed the night of the Poisoner's Festival and locked with a padlock. Just as I'm wondering whether hitting it with a rock like they do in movies will actually work, I see that it's hanging slightly loose.

Someone's been in here recently.

Nothing in my bag would make a good weapon, but maybe if I swing the bag itself at Zane's face . . .

It feels weird to think of escaping from the boy I was kissing at the ball only a few days ago, but didn't he tell me that night about the crimes he'd committed? Why did I believe him so easily when he said he wanted to leave that life behind?

A horrible thought occurs to me. I only have his word for it he wasn't responsible for his friend's coma. Maybe Xavier isn't the first person Zane has hurt.

I check my phone and let out a huge sigh of relief. Zane's Monday-night shift at Maldonado's has already started. I won't need a weapon after all.

I open the unlocked door and walk inside.

There's only time to register that it's dark and cool before I almost fall straight down a flight of steps. I catch myself on the wall, which feels rough, like no one ever sanded the exposed wood. I flip my phone open. It doesn't have a flashlight, but the light of the screen is enough for me to see broken bathroom tiles and rusty nails scattered across the floor to my left, as if the Everetts stored old building materials here. I angle the light back toward the stairs and walk carefully down them, one by one.

The basement is bigger than the room at the top because the walls have been carved out beyond the wooden structure, like a rabbit warren. I wrap my arm around my waist with a shiver. It's at least twenty degrees colder than outside, and my sweatshirt is stuffed unhelpfully in my backpack. No way I'm digging it out until I've made absolutely sure I'm the only one in the icehouse.

My phone is so dim I almost run into a pile of boards stacked along one of the walls. For repairs, probably. Then my eyes catch a glint of metal. It's the grommets of a blue tarp covering a small table.

"I need Enzo's gloves," I say aloud, but my words sound flat, like the dirt floor is absorbing them.

I carefully lift the tarp, trying to use the tips of my fingers to avoid exposure to whatever's underneath. When I finally rip it off, my heart speeds up.

The table is covered with chemistry supplies: a Bunsen burner, a large glass flask, plastic tubing, and a few glass canisters that look like clear cucumbers. There are also a few smaller vials lined up in a wooden holder. An iPhone, smashed into pieces, sits in a bowl.

As I lean down to get a better look at the vials, footsteps sound on the stairs above me. I whirl around, the noise of my heart drowning out the thumping of someone's shoes. Every cell in my body is longing for it to be Emi—is praying to see her platform boots step into view. But deep down, I know she's still in the car, too far away to help.

When the person comes down the final step, I begin to scream.

It's Zane, and he's pointing something long and dark at me.

31

"DULCE, STOP," ZANE SAYS HALFWAY THROUGH MY scream. He lowers whatever he's holding. "It's me."

His words don't make me feel better.

"Is that a gun?" I ask breathlessly.

Zane glances at the thing in his hands, then throws it to the ground with a *clunk*. "Of course not," he says. "It's a car jack bar. I've been trying to fix my flat tire since the final bell. I saw you running through the woods, and I guess I forgot to drop it when I ran after you. Rocco will be pissed because he's already short-staffed tonight, but I thought this might be my only chance to explain."

"Explain why you've got a table full of chemistry materials down here?" I ask. "And please don't say they're for class. I'm not an idiot."

He walks a few steps toward me, and I shift along the wall. Maybe if he comes close enough, I can dart around him.

"Why would I be hiding chemistry materials in the icehouse?" he asks, and to my surprise, I'm picking up genuine confusion.

"I don't know," I say. "Maybe to distill nicotine to kill Xavier?"

Zane stops moving. "I know you're mad about me spying for the sheriff," he says, "but you shouldn't joke about shit like that."

"I'm not joking," I say. "I talked to Ms. Moss. She didn't kill Xavier on purpose. Someone tricked her into injecting him with nicotine."

"Who?" he asks, like I didn't just accuse him.

"Were you working with Ms. Moss?"

"No!" Zane says as if he finally sees I'm serious. "A couple of months ago, I asked her to give a tell-all to Channel Z News about Xavier's blackmail, but she refused. Said she'd find her own way to handle it. The day I went to my flute audition, I asked her again, but she said no and then shooed me away. Told me her kids were sick."

"A tell-all?" I ask.

"Yeah, I thought if we both turned whistleblower, maybe they'd do a report about Xavier or at least cancel his internship. Strength in numbers, you know. I had a whole plan worked out to crush him, but she didn't bite." He eyes me with wonder, like he's seeing me for the first time. "Do you really think I had something to do with Xavier's death?"

"You're the only person that could have," I say. "Enzo was in the chem lab all morning. He saw you put a bottle back on the shelf."

Zane frowns like he's trying to remember. "I put a cleaning solvent back," he says. "Is that what you mean? I spilled some acetone during class."

"Where'd you put the bottle?" I ask. "On the right? Left?"

"Um, I think I put it . . . somewhere in the center? There was a gap, and I just put it there. I didn't think about it." Zane moves closer. "Dulce, what's going on?"

He threw the car jack to the ground. His palms are open, like an animal exposing its belly. I've seen his eyes when he's lied to me, and I've seen them when he's told me the truth, and right now they're warm and honest.

Conclusion: I'm wrong about him being the killer?

"Someone was working with Ms. Moss," I say. "They told her they wanted to get back at Xavier by sedating him with sleeping medicine so they could stage the scene to make it look like he'd brought drugs to school. But they put a bottle of nicotine in the cabinet instead. So when Ms. Moss shot him—"

"Why involve Ms. Moss?" Zane asks. "Why not poison Xavier's food, like with Emi? Then he dies in the cafeteria. End of story."

"Maybe they were afraid they'd get caught," I say. "The only reason the sheriff didn't investigate Emi's poisoning is because she pretended it was an accident. Imagine if he'd investigated. He would have figured out who had access to the fridge, tracked everyone's movements, asked people if they saw someone somewhere they wouldn't normally be."

Zane's brows are knit like he's thinking hard. "That's true," he says. "The killer would have had to prove where they were all morning. Because there's really only one way to make sure you're not suspected."

As soon as he says it, I understand the fact I've overlooked.

"Have an alibi," I say.

Zane nods and steps closer. "An alibi. Do you think I'd go through the trouble of setting up some elaborate plan and then disappear into the library when it was closed and no one would see me?" He shakes his head. "I'd make sure the whole school knew where I was when Xavier was killed. Then no one could ever prove I did it, no matter what Ms. Moss said."

The truth dawns on me in small bits. "We're looking for someone who made sure witnesses could place them inside the building."

A memory echoes in my ears: *Most people don't have perfect alibis in a murder investigation.*

"And someone who put a bottle on the shelf," I say.

Another flash: Enzo telling me the people who were in the chem lab that morning. Dr. Saka, Dean Whitaker, Zane, and Ms. Moss.

"Not to mention someone with nerves of steel," Zane says. "So much could have gone wrong. The wind could have blown the needle off course. Ms. Moss could have sneezed. Xavier might have moved at the last minute. And then the game would have been up."

A final flash: Two gold dice paperweights. Pictures of snowboarding in the Alps and motorcycling through the Mexican desert.

"A gambler," I say, my voice a dead monotone because I finally realize what a dumb, dumb *conejita* I've really been.

There's a loud thump over by the stairs.

"I'd clap, but my hands are full," says a voice, and there's no doubt about who it is.

Dean Whitaker is standing at the base of the last step, holding a giant can of gas in one hand and a flashlight in the other. I was so intent on my conversation with Zane, I didn't hear him enter.

"I figured you'd get there sooner or later," he says, kicking Zane's car jack bar into the corner so neither of us can reach it. "Though I hoped it would be later, once I was already in Florence."

He rests his elbow on the handrail of the staircase. "I was in my office when you called. As soon as I saw you in the woods, I guessed Hannah had told you about the icehouse. It's unfortunate; I would have preferred to burn it down without an audience."

"It was you," I whisper.

"I can't believe you ever thought it was anyone else," he says like he's performed an incredible magic trick. "As if one of your classmates would have the guts or know-how to pull off a poisoning."

"Did you say Florence?" Zane asks.

"Lily and I have moved the wedding up," Dean Whitaker says. "Once she accepts the results of the election next week, we're flying out for a post-campaign elopement. Sierra's not happy, but she doesn't have nearly so much sway over her mother these days."

I've been trying to stop her from marrying him.

"You framed Sierra?" I say, spitting with outrage. "So she wouldn't get in the way of your marriage?"

The dean's face, partly hidden in shadow, turns stormy. "If she hadn't been such a little bitch, I would have chosen someone else's needles. But Lily kept delaying and delaying, saying Sierra wasn't ready."

"Don't call Sierra a bitch," I say, even though I've called her a bitchwitch a thousand times in the past two years. "Why did you take the pink yarn if you wanted the sheriff to think it was her?"

"So no one would figure out the needle had been shot," he says. "Anyone who's ever seen an arrow or dart would have known immediately what had happened."

"You were going to let Sierra go to prison?" I say. "For your crime?"